For my excellent friend, Laura Myers

The
Alibi Girl

C J Skuse

ONE PLACE. MANY STORIES

HQ
An imprint of HarperCollins*Publishers* Ltd
1 London Bridge Street
London SE1 9GF

This edition 2020

1
First published in Great Britain by
HQ, an imprint of HarperCollins*Publishers* Ltd 2020

ISBN: 978-0-00-831139-1

MIX
Paper from
responsible sources
FSC www.fsc.org FSC™ C007454

This book is produced from independently certified FSC™ paper
to ensure responsible forest management.

For more information visit: www.harpercollins.co.uk/green

This book is set in 10.8/15.5 pt. Sabon

Printed and bound in Great Britain by
CPI Group (UK) Ltd, Croydon, CR0 4YY

Alibi Clock (n):
a clock which strikes one hour,
while the hands point
to a different time,
the real time being neither one
nor the other.

E. COBHAM BREWER 1810–1897. *Dictionary of Phrase and Fable*. 1898.

PRESENT DAY

Curl Up and Dye,
Spurrington-on-Sea,
North-West England

1

ELLIS

Monday, 21st October

I can't read this *Hello!* magazine again. There's only so many times I can admire Brooklyn Beckham's left armpit. It's not as though there's anything else to read either. There's a *Vogue* with dried snot on the contents page. And Charlize Theron is on the cover of *Cosmo* so I can't even touch that one. I've been afraid of her since *Snow White*. Keep thinking she'll come out of the page and bite me.

So, in the absence of reading material, I'm squinting at a cockroach scuttling across the floor with a clump of shorn hair on its back like some tiny game show host. My own hair sits lankly around my ears – it can't wait another day. I'll give it another five minutes before I go back to the flat and dye it myself over the bath with a kit.

And now the baby's grizzling. I've tried sticking my knuckle in her mouth but she's hungry. I'm not feeding her here. How can you talk to a perfect stranger quite politely one moment and then flop your boob out the next? How do women do that? And what is the stranger supposed to do? *Not* look at it? A boob is my third most private part after my feet and my noo-noo. I'd look. Not for long, but I would look.

After fifteen-and-a-half full minutes, a short Roseanne Barr-ish woman scuffs through the beaded curtain. She has Hobbit feet wedged into mint-green flip flops and tattoos up and down both forearms – Tom Hiddlething as Loki all up her right, Chris HemWhatNot as Thor all up her left.

'Hiya, I'm Steffi. Is it Mary?' Her eyes don't smile.

'Yes. Mary Brokenshire.'

Steffi's in a washed-out Gryffindor T-shirt and her hair is spare rib coloured, parted and shaved severely up the side.

'If you'd like to come this way ...'

Steffi leads me through the beads, across the glittery black floor tiles and through a grubby woodchip archway, towards the sinks but not quite *at* them. We swerve over to a side chair with a mirror in front of it and she sits me down and places her hot hands on my shoulders. She gives me an unnecessary chat about what I want done even though she already knows because I came in last week for a patch test and we went through it all then.

'Right, black it is then. Have you been offered a tea or coffee?'

'No.' I don't like tea *or* coffee. I'd prefer a juice but they don't have juice, only some value squash which I only have to look at to feel my teeth rotting at the roots. Even *I* know asking for a milk would be too childish in this environment so, for appearances sake, I say, 'I'd *love* a tea, thanks.'

Steffi disappears and returns with a cape but no tea. She waits for me to take Emily out of the papoose and transfer her to the pushchair, hoping to catch a glimpse. I get it: people love babies. I tuck her into the buggy and drape a muslin over the opening. I don't like people looking at her, or me, for too long. Just in case.

Steffi sweeps the cape around my body, rendering everything but my head invisible. I used to like wearing a cape. Or an oversized bath towel. There's nothing quite like that feeling of getting out of a hot bath, wrapping the big bath towel around you and pretending to fly up the corridor with the towel flapping along behind. Me and my cousin Foy used to do that all the time after our baths. Or was it only once?

'How are you coping with the little one?' Steffi asks.

'Fine, thanks. She's our fifth, so we're used to being tired all the time. You know what it's like, I'm sure!'

'Oh yeah,' she says, face brightening. 'We've got four and it's chaos. We love it though. Love the chaos!' We share the laugh only parents can share as she begins pasting on my colour. 'Have you got anything planned for the rest of the day?' I get the impression she's asked this question 11,000 times. There's no inflection. No real note of interest. I still answer.

'Not really. A bit of shopping. Pick the kids up. I'm still on maternity leave from my practice so it's nice not to have such a rigid timetable.'

'What sort of practice?'

'I'm a doctor. A GP.'

'Oh right. Where are they all today then? At a friend's house?'

I'm momentarily confused. 'My children? They're all at school.'

'They not on half term?'

5

'They're all at private school,' I say. 'Their half term was last week.'

'Oh,' she says, with more than a hint of lemon juice about it. 'You've got four of them at private school?'

'Yeah,' I tell her proudly, rocking the buggy. 'Apples of their daddy's eye. We're stopping at five though. I'm having my tubes tied in January, I've told him already. He'd have a football team, given half the chance.'

'Yeah, I think mine would!'

'It's our anniversary today so my mum and dad are going to have the kids tonight so we can go out for a meal.'

'Ooh, where are you going? Anywhere nice?'

What a stupid question that is. *No, we're off to a complete dive with a one-star hygiene rating and a chef who wipes his bum on the lettuce.* 'The China Garden. The one with the gold dragon hanging from the ceiling? His treat.'

'What does he do then, your bloke?'

I ignite when she says 'Your bloke'. It's lovely to have a bloke who belongs to me. 'He's a personal trainer.'

'Nice. I wish my old man would take *me* out. Do you know I don't think we've had a night out since our Livvy was born. And she's starting Reception next month.'

'Oh really?'

'Yeah. We can't afford it anyway. Rich's been laid off from the airport.'

'Oh right,' I say, with the hint of gloom she seems to expect. 'What did he—'

'—baggage handler at John Lennon. Twenty years he gave them. Went in on his days off when they were striking and everything. And he caught a terrorist.'

'Oh gosh.' Cockroach Game Show Host scuttles back along the skirting board. I pretend to have a coughing fit and Steffi asks if I'd like some water, which is when she's reminded about the tea she hasn't made me yet and scurries off to see 'where it's got to' like tea has a mind of its own.

I'm finally brought my tea and two Custard Creams – one with a corner snapped off. I remove the top of one biscuit and scrape out the cream with my bottom teeth. I put the two sides back together and munch it until it makes a neat circle of spitty biscuit between my thumbs, then I put it in my mouth 'til it dissolves. I don't realise until I swallow that Steffi has been watching me. My cheeks flame as red as my roots.

But then my phone pings in my handbag and I rifle around to find it. 'Probably Daddy, checking in on his girls.'

'Ahhh,' says Steffi, all misty-eyed.

It isn't Daddy. It's an email from eBay, letting me know about their half term sale on personalised school stationery.

'Was it him?' says Steffi, combing my colour through.

'Yeah. He's asking if I want anything brought in. Bless him.'

'He sounds like a keeper.' I hold up my iPhone screen to show her his photo. She takes it off me and squints. 'Blimey, he's gorgeous.'

I know what she's thinking – that a woman like me couldn't have possibly 'got' a guy like him. 'I'm very lucky.' She returns me the phone and I put him away safely in my bag. 'We were childhood sweethearts.'

'You started early then. I thought you looked young to have five kids.'

'I had the first one at fourteen.'

'Blimey.'

'Then the twins, then Harry. Wasn't easy with the medical degree, but we managed. Then this little surprise came along.'

'I met my Rich on a hen weekend.'

I hadn't asked and it's not interesting to me but I pretend it's *the* most interesting thing because for some reason I'm happy in her company. Two married mums together. 'I love a good knees-up.'

'Yeah it did get a bit rowdy,' she laughs. 'He did karaoke to "Once, Twice, Three Times a Lady" and pointed at me when he was singing. I knew then he was *The One*.'

I smile at the mirror. 'The One. It's a nice feeling, isn't it?'

'Oh, don't get me wrong, we have our moments. He woke up yesterday with a cold, right? And his breathing has become all like that Darth Wossit. And I said to him "Rich, I swear to God, if you breathe like that anymore, I'm gonna ram your head in the bacon slicer." He was winding me up that much.'

I don't get that. Why stay with a person whose breathing makes you want to commit actual murder on their head? So I ask her.

'So you don't love him anymore?'

'Oh, course I do,' she laughs. 'I were only joking. Just wish he worked on an oil rig or summut, so he'd leave the bloody house once in a while, you know?'

I don't get that either but, before I can ask, she hands me the same magazine I read six times in the waiting room and I'm treated to another glimpse of hairy Brooklyn and interviews with Liam Payne's mother and the *Britain's Got Talent* failure who's had twenty facelifts and still hates himself.

We used to play *Britain's Got Talent* at the pub. It would be after the kitchen had closed for the evening. Auntie Chelle would be helping Uncle Stu in the bar and the boys would be upstairs and me and Foy would sneak down for midnight feasts of still-warm chips from the fryers and leftover baguette ends dipped in salad cream. We'd take it in turns to come through from the utility room, telling a sob story to the panel of stuffed toys on the breakfast bar then screech 'Flying Without Wings' into a vinegar bottle. Miss Whiskers and Thread Bear always put us through to Bootcamp.

After half an hour, Steffi returns. 'Let's get you washed. Leave her with Jodie.'

The one called Jodie, with the shoulder tattoo of moons and stars and the white DMs, appears beside the buggy, all smiley and young. 'Yeah, I'll watch her for ya.'

'Don't let her out of your sight, will you?' I say.

'No probs. Can I have a little hold if she wakes up?'

'No, I'd rather you didn't. Thanks. She's better left to her own devices.'

Steffi leads me back across the glittery floor to the sinks. I must get some glitter. I don't know what for yet but I don't use nearly enough of it. It'll be November soon so I could get a head start on decorating for Christmas. Steffi's pressing buttons and running water before I've even sat down. As I do, a bizarre kneading sensation begins in my lower back, rising up my spine and into my shoulder blades.

'Oh my god!' I jerk forwards and I realise it's one of those massage chairs.

'Is it too hard for you?' she asks.

'Um, no, sorry. I just never tried one before.'

'Do you want me to turn it off?'

'No, it'll be fine. I think.'

'It's supposed to help you relax,' she says. 'But some people don't like the feel of it. Let me know if it gets too much.'

I lie back again and within moments I'm letting out involuntary grunts at the luscious deep kneading all over my back. I'm making noises people usually only make when they do naughties. Luckily, there are too many dryers on for anyone to hear me.

'I've recently started selling Avon on the side actually,' says Steffi out of nowhere. 'Would you be interested in a catalogue?'

'Uh—'

'And I'm organising a party at my place on Saturday night if you're free?'

I've done nothing to warrant this invitation but I'm imagining she gets the smell of money off me, knowing I have four children at private school. 'It would be difficult,' I say, between grunts. 'Saturdays are our family days normally.'

'Bring 'em all along. Our kids'll be there. They can watch Disney in the family room. The blokes usually go down the pub.'

'My Kaden doesn't drink. He's more into his coconut water and plankton shots.'

'Well he can sit in the other room watching Ant and Dec, can't he? Go on, it'll be a laugh. I can't promise any food but people usually only want Pringles and Prosecco at these things, don't they? Bring a bottle.'

'Well I can't drink at the moment because I'm breastfeeding but it sounds great. I'd love to come. Thank you.'

And while my lips are saying I'd love to, I know I won't go. I'm breaking into a sweat thinking about it. I'm like Ariel in *The Little Mermaid*. I'm ginger and I want to be with them – up where they walk and run and play all day in the sun. But I can't be part of that world. And I absolutely *cannot* be ginger. That's just how it is.

But I say no more and after divulging her address, Steffi doesn't ask me again. She vigorously rubs my head and I'm in ecstasy. By the time we're on the second shampoo I'm used to the sensations and I just want to feel the pressing of her fingers into my scalp; the rubbing and rinsing and smoothing; the kneading into my back and shoulders. I want to lie in this synthetic coconut paradise forever. I crane my neck through the archway and see Jodie rocking the buggy while scrolling her phone.

The salon's getting busy now and the radio blares out 'Despacito' which one of them has turned up because 'this was all we danced to on our holidays'. They went to Spain together, I gather, three of the staff. They spent most of the time 'paralytic' but it seems to make them very happy hearing the song again. They're obviously a close bunch. Natalya with the Princess Leia buns knows all the words and whisks her hips in time to the music. Steffi and Toni are behind me, bitch-chatting about their ex-husbands. Meg with the topknot is folding towels and chit-chatting to her client about her own disastrous holiday to 'that place where Maddie went missing'.

'It rained most days. And there were all these turds in the sea. Then we got robbed and came home.'

The taps go off and the water stops to a *drip, drip*. The chair stops massaging and I keenly feel the loss. A grey towel stinking of cooked mince wraps around my head and I'm led back across the glittery floor to get dried and styled. Jodie's disappeared to make coffee. The baby's still sleeping, no thanks to her.

Any softness in Steffi's face from the conversation about kids has skinned over. She's concentrating now – brushing me roughly as the burning air from the dryer sets about my head. She scrunches, ruffles and shakes me until I'm dry before straightening it into a jet black bob with my parting once again located.

She affords me a few more seconds of bliss as she rakes it through, shielding my eyes while caking it with Elnet. Before I know it, she's holding up the mirror. Black bob. Brown eyes. The red is dead. Nobody would know it was me.

'That alright for you, Mary?'

'That's perfect, thanks so much.'

'You're very welcome.' She removes my cape and I flick off the brake on the pushchair and wheel Emily over to the desk to pay. I'm expecting her to mention the Avon party again but she doesn't.

The radio waffles on – an advert for a conservatory firm, twenty-five percent off windows and doors, some aquatics company are giving away fish and it's Kids Eat Free at the Jungle Café – none of which I can take advantage of but I pretend like it's all very reasonable.

Then the door opens with a little jingle and three men file in, one after the other. There's no rush to their movements. The first two wipe their feet on the mat, the third wipes his nose on his sleeve. And my entire body floods with ice – I can't move. They are loud and unapologetic. All laughter and smoker's coughs.

My breath catches – I know that laugh. The short, straw-haired one with predatory eyes and a cheeky-chappy smile, like his face is at odds with itself. He carries the air of someone with power. Power over the other two. It's them. I know it is.

Think *rationally*. Think *logically*. *Breathe*. Scants is always telling me I'm paranoid. It's not them. It's too much of a coincidence, them being here, me being here. Deeper breaths. Act normal. It's three ordinary men. Three innocent customers.

Steffi holds out her chubby mitt with the gold rings, her fingers like strangled chipolatas. 'That'll be £32.00 then Mary, thank you.'

I can't concentrate on anything but the three men. Three little pigs blowing my house down. I can smell their thick layers of aftershave. Aramis, unless I'm mistaken, and something else. Lynx or Old Spice. I can't breathe.

The short, stocky one with straw-coloured hair and brown camel coat starts in with an anecdote about a crash on the motorway which meant they were late for something. Late for what, I can't figure – my brain's too busy careening around bends. And the music's too loud – screechy punk guitars now. The brown-haired one in the leather bomber jacket, skinny jeans and trainers does a selfie with the one they call Natalya – old mates? – while the third, built like a tank, is all knuckles and chins and seems happy to stand there, the limelight firmly on the other two. He's the heavy. They're all pally – Meg joins in, selfying with the brunette for Instagram. Two others join in – Jodie and Toni. Fawning like the men are rock stars. But I *know* them. I've seen them in my nightmares. And I know that laugh.

I pay Steffi and tell her to put the change in the charity box. On the counter is a box of hand-knitted animals – lions, tigers and bears – all with a Halloween Scream Egg sewn inside the head with googly eyes stuck on. I want one but I also want to leave.

'A customer makes them for the donkey sanctuary,' Steffi explains, posting the coins in the tin. I know I've got to get out but I can't decide which animal I want – a lion, a tiger or a bear. Bomber Jacket is coming towards the desk. He'll stand beside me. He'll see my face. I fumble for a knitted lion.

'Thanks,' I say, no more than a whisper. 'Bye.' I wheel the pushchair awkwardly towards the door.

Steffi calls out, 'Oh, and that Avon party I mentioned...'

I'm forced to be rude and not answer her. Unbeknown to me, The Tank has followed me to the door and opens it for me before I can get there.

I daren't look up. But at the last second, before the door closes, I thank him briefly and we lock eyes. A shadow of a frown that's either confusion or recognition.

'Mind how you go now,' he says, and his deep voice sends a freeze through me. Was it a Bristolian accent? Could have been. He only said five words but I caught a definite twang. Tears come and there's nothing I can do to stop them. All I can think about is getting back to the flat and locking every door and window.

'How are they here?' I mutter to myself, trying to catch my breath, pushing the buggy back along the road until I'm practically running, back along the high street and onto the seafront. As I pass, the doughnut man sticks his head out of his van and calls out, 'Charlotte! Charlotte! I saved you some fried doughnut holes!' But I pretend like I haven't heard him and keep running, looking behind every few steps to see if anyone's following. They're not, they're definitely not, and there's salt and sand in my eyes and my throat because it's windy, but I don't stop until I'm nearly back.

I cry *wee wee wee,* all the way home.

Through the gate and down the steps, and finally we're inside the flat. Patio doors locked tight. Main door locked and bolted. Lounge curtains drawn. The cats are all in and accounted for. I take Emily out of the pushchair and she grizzles but I hold her against me, warm and tight so she's safe. Only then does my breathing slow. I notice the answerphone flashing. *You have one new message.* I press Play.

Silence.

Crackling.

Breathing.

Click.

Dead tone.

'Wrong number. Means nothing,' I reassure Emily, though my heart pounds.

Taking her into the bedroom, I draw the blind and slump down onto the springy single bed the landlord said he'd replace soon. I hold Emily against my neck, skin to skin. Safety. My heart beats in my ears. It's the only sound.

I stare up at the walls, almost bare apart from the Frida Kahlo print the previous tenant hung there in a glass frame. I don't even know who Frida Kahlo is but the landlord said the picture was called 'Time Flies' and the guy who'd left it was an artist who died of an overdose. Frida's wearing a white dress in the picture. And there's a little aeroplane above her head. And a clock on a shelf. Her eyebrows scare me. I don't know what it means. I don't know what any of it means.

2

My name isn't Mary. It's Joanne. Well, that's the name they gave me. I can't tell anyone my *real* name. I might be free now but I still have to imprison parts of myself. And that's the big part. I don't have all the children I told the hairdresser about, either, or a successful career in medicine. Or a personal trainer husband called Kaden. I have a new neighbour with that name, and a man's sweatshirt I got from a charity shop sprayed in a free tester of Paco Rabanne that I *pretend* belongs to him, but that's all. Mary is an act. One of my many acts to keep them at bay.

But they've tracked me down, haven't they? They've found me again.

No, I tell myself, *no they haven't*. Maybe it wasn't them. Maybe Scants is right, as always, and I'm being paranoid. Or maybe he just says that because he's paid to look after me and this is what he's *supposed* to say. If it *was* them, The Pigs, this is still a big town and at the moment it's flooded with tourists, families on half term, coach loads of people on outings. I've been swallowed by all that. They could think I'm staying at a hotel or one of the B&Bs. So while I'm in the flat, I'm safe.

As a precaution, I haven't been outside in two days. I told

work Emily has a bug. She doesn't. I've just been playing with her and the cats, making the odd cake, having the odd bath, trimming up far too early for Christmas and watching DVDs – mostly Disney movies up to the sad bits, then I fast forward or switch off. I decided as soon as I was old enough that I didn't have to watch the sad bits if I didn't want to. So, in my world, Mufasa's still alive, Nemo doesn't even go missing and the Beast never turns into that disgusting prince.

I've ordered a few things off the internet – a new rug to cover most of the hideous old lino in the kitchen that the landlord won't replace, a board game for my paper boy, Alfie, that I was telling him about the other day and found quite cheap on eBay, these really cute hair slides, and some silver glitter. I don't know what the glitter's for yet – a Christmas something I expect. I know I can make use of it somehow.

I've done some research on Frida Kahlo, too. She was a bisexual feminist Mexican painter and her portraits 'allow a deeply intimate window into the female psyche'. So says the internet. She was also in an accident when she was eighteen which left her unable to have children. And she kept spider monkeys. I like the picture in my bedroom of her a lot more now. Her eyebrows don't scare me as much.

And I've had another message on the answerphone. More silence. And crackling. And breathing. Then the *Click*. Then the dead tone. Another coincidence? I have to believe that. It's a 'little nothing', that's what Scants will say. Unless it's a viable threat, I cannot pester him about it. That's the rule.

I've eaten nearly everything in the flat. Even the Findus Crispy Pancakes I keep in for emergencies. I'm like the Tiger Who Came to Tea – there's still water in the tap, but I bet any minute there'll be a cold snap and the pipes'll freeze. Emily's getting ratty. She needs fresh air. I will go out soon. Maybe I could nip across the road and get some doughnuts from the van? But it's not healthy, is it? Doughnuts for tea. I counted fifteen sugary paper bags in the recycling box this morning. *Fifteen.* Plus the one on the table I've doodled all over. I pick it up and admire the curly handwriting:

Ann Hilsom

Melanie Smith

Claire Price

Joanne Haynes

I feel greasy. I'm going to have a bath.

I settle Emily in her bassinette by the chest of drawers and she's happy enough lying there looking up at the mobile I've fixed to the side. She's so small. Sometimes I wish she was bigger so she could hug better. And then I realise what I'm thinking – the bigger she gets, the more she'll stop being my baby. The more she'll learn. I want her to stay small and unknowing and thinking the world is a charmed place where imagination is real and everyone thinks you're fascinating. Being an adult looked so much more appealing when I wasn't one.

A bath, I've found, is the nearest thing to a hug. You get fewer hugs as you get older but we had loads as kids. Auntie Chelle was always wrapping me and Foy inside her arms and squeezing the breath from us. *I can't hug you two tight enough*, she would say. It's scientifically proven that baths help depression in the same way a hug does. Something to do with balancing our bodily rhythms. As a kid I used to eat the foam. Spread it out on a sponge like a little waffle loaded with squirty cream.

Scants is funny about hugs since he got mugged in a pub in 2008. He's funny about a lot of things. I can't think about him – he'll visit when he's next in town, that's what he said: 'Don't pester me' – and he said it in his Serious Voice so I knew he meant it. *I must not call him unless it's an emergency*. It's three random men and a couple of wrong numbers. That's all. I'll leave the flat soon. Everything's normal.

I sink down in my warm bath and allow the water and essential oils to hug me all the way up my body and back down again. I picture all my worries as a kite on a string, and imagine letting go of it, watching it float up to the sky as I count backwards from ten. Gradually, the panic disappears, though I know it's only a temporary break from a world that feels so wrong all the time.

The door creaks open and The Duchess saunters in. I roll over to tickle her head.

'Hello Duchess, how do you do?'

She sits proudly on my bath towel, butting into my hand, her white fur soft as clouds beneath my fingertips. She's looking tubby today – I think I'm overfeeding her. I'd rather that than underfeeding her, though, or any of them. They're my other babies. The Duke of Yorkums and Earl Grey sleep all day on my bed while the other girls are more inclined to wander. The latest one, Queen Georgie, doesn't get on with Princess Tabitha Rosynose or Tallulah von Puss, though. She's taken up residence on the couch on the blanket. Prince Roland won't come near any of them – he prefers it at the back of the wardrobe guarding all my jumpers from Jumper Pixies who bite holes in clothes to make their little hats. But The Duchess always comes to play or say hello. Of course, I'd never tell the other cats this, but she's my favourite.

My dad used to say cats were cursed kings and queens in hiding. That's why they're all so aloof and it seems like they don't care about anything. It's not that – it's because they have royal blood. It goes against their protocol to get too involved.

I wish I could stay in the bath forever, the water lapping against the sides, The Duchess still butting my hand. I wish this was *my* bath. My bathroom.

Suddenly, an awful *buzzzzzzzzzz* resounds through the flat and my chest tightens – it's my door buzzer. It's not Scants – he always calls ahead. There's no one else it could be. Maybe it's a relative of the people in the middle flat. Or Kaden, the guy who's just moved into the top floor flat. Maybe it's a mistake. Maybe they have the wrong number altogether.

Maybe they don't.

I scramble out of the bath and yank out the plug, grabbing my towel from under The Duchess and she protest-*reeeaaaawr*s, but moves out the way. I wrap myself up and wait – it's a mistake. Or the postman? No, he's been. It can't be for me. My rhythms are all to cock. What if it's them? What if they hear the bath gurgling? What if Emily starts crying?

Buzzzzzzzz, buzzzzzzzzzzzzzzzzzzzzzzzzz it goes again.

She'll cry and then they'll know for sure where I am, where I live.

Buzzzzzzzz buzzzzzzzzzzzzzzzzzzzzzzz.

I fumble for my robe on the back of the door and slide it over my now-freezing wet body. Panic has taken over and I can't think in a straight line. I stumble into the bedroom, pull on my boots and lace them up as best I can though my brain has temporarily forgotten how to do laces.

'Bunny ear, Bunny ear, Bottom Bunny ear over Top Bunny ear, tie and pull.'

Buzzzzz buzzzzzzzzzz buzzzzzzzzzzzzzzzzzzzzz.

'Oh no, oh shitake mushrooms.' I want to cry. How do I run with a baby? And what about the cats? If I go through the patio doors and up the front steps they'll catch me. I'm soaking wet, in my dressing gown, wearing no knickers and badly tied DMs. They'll be shooting slow, fat fish in a tiny barrel.

I need to be brave, be *rational*, and take a look before doing anything stupid. Before I can change my mind, I run to the kitchen and grab the Flash bleach spray and a bread knife. I go to my door and scramble the chain off, opening it slowly onto the hallway. I'm at such a high pitch, I've broken out into a sweat and my mouth is so dry my lips stick to my teeth. My tongue feels like an invader.

I see the shadow behind the glass. One shadow. It's only one of them.

'WHAT DO YOU WANT?' I force myself to wobble-shout.

'Hi, it's Kaden from upstairs. I think the bolt's on? I can't get in.'

Relief floods through me. I deflate and the tears start pouring as I pull back the bolt and release the Chubb to find the guy from the top floor flat standing there in his leather gear with his motorbike helmet under one arm, a bag of shopping in his hand. I can't stop shaking.

'Oh god, are you alright?' he says. 'I'm so sorry. I've been away for a couple of days, and came back and my key wouldn't work... I didn't mean to get you out of the bath. I definitely didn't mean to scare you. It's Joanne, isn't it?'

NO, I'm NOT Joanne, I want to say. I have an alarming

urge to tell him my real name. I want him to help me. Tell me he'll fight the Pigs away with his strong arms. Not very Frida the Feminist Icon, but then I'm not Frida – I'm me. And not a very convincing me either. I sit on the stair, dropping the knife and spray gun to the carpet.

The front door closes. He puts the bike helmet on the shelf and there's a creak of leather as he kneels down. 'Hey. It's alright. I'm not going to hurt you.'

And I pull him into me and he wraps his arms around my back and we're hugging like two lovers. Lovers who've only previously shared Hellos and door openings for the past two weeks since he moved in. I blush every time. Because in one of my newest lies he is of course My Husband. The Father of My Five Children. The screensaver on my phone, from when I followed him to the gym at the other end of the seafront where he works, and took a photo of the picture of him behind reception – Kaden Cotterill, Certified Personal Trainer. How sad is that? Now that he's here, holding me, I can see how sad it is. Here he is real and perfect and my tears chase down his leather jacket. The back of his neck is sweaty and he smells of the sea breeze.

'I'm sorry, I really am,' he says. We pull apart, his face packed full of concern. 'Is there anything I can do?' I shake my head. 'Did you think it was someone else?' I nod. 'Do you wanna talk about it?' I shake. 'Do you wanna be on your own?' I shake again. 'Okay, well I need to go and shove some of this in the fridge,' he says, indicating the carrier bag. 'Why don't you go and put some clothes on and when I come back down we'll go for a coffee and unwind a bit, yeah? There's a nice café I've found on the seafront. They do my favourite roast.'

I sniff. 'I don't like coffee.'

'What do you like?'

'Strawberry milkshakes.'

He touches my head and his hand comes away with a chunk of white foam from the bath. He smiles and it lights up the dark, damp hallway. It's a glowing lamp in the fog. A flame in a cave. A lifeline. All I can do is smile back.

*

I sit in the coffee shop – Full of Beans – stroking Emily's head in the papoose, watching Kaden's grey T-shirted back as he orders our drinks – a Columbian Granja La Esperanza roast with hot milk for him, and a milkshake with cream and paper straw for me. I can't believe I'm here with him. I imagine we're Man and Wife. He's on paternity leave and we're out showing off our new baby. An older couple look across at us in sweet recognition. A woman in a peach overcoat stops by the table and bends down to peek at her. I instinctively pull away, covering the top of Emily's head with her blanket. I hear her grizzling.

'Sorry, she's a bit under the weather today.'

'Aww, how old?'

'Five weeks.'

'Ahhh, she's gorgeous.'

She can't even see her properly but the woman is right, Emily *is* gorgeous. All babies are. The woman thinks me and Kaden really are a couple with a baby and that's a lovely feeling. A warm, huggy feeling. Perhaps it really is Our Anniversary, like it was Mary Brokenshire's. Perhaps we Met Here.

When he returns with our drinks, I snap out of it – he's here because he's a nice man and he's concerned that he scared me. And something is clearly wrong in my life if I'm terrified of my own door buzzer. That's the truth. And the truth always stings.

He sets my milkshake down before me with a 'There you go.'

It's only when he sits down with his cup and saucer and biscotti that it occurs to me how childish my drink choice is. He's changed his motorbike gear for a T-shirt and jeans and white trainers, and the back of his neck is still slightly sheeny with sweat but he doesn't smell badly at all. I'm close enough to smell his aftershave properly now – not Paco Rabanne as I'd initially thought. It's that one in the blue man-shaped bottle. Le Male by Jean Paul Gaultier. Oh it's lovely. My cheeks heat up. Foy and I used to go mad in the fragrance department in Boots, spraying them all up our sleeves.

'Think it's going to be a nice day today,' he says, staring through the window. 'You can see the Lake District from here.'

I look out in the direction of where he points. Blurry mountains. 'Cool.'

'Have you ever visited the Lakes?'

'No. I've been to Scotland.' I can't tell him about that, so I hurry on. 'Have you?'

'Yeah, I used to go hiking in the Lakes all the time with a couple of mates from Uni. It's really stunning. It's good to inflate your lungs with a long walk every once in a while. You could take the little one to the Beatrix Potter house.'

'Emily's only five weeks old. I don't think she'd be that impressed.'

'No, maybe not,' he laughs.

'I like Beatrix Potter though.'

'Oh right.'

'I mean I did when I was a kid,' I clarify. 'Tom Kitten's my favourite story. And the one with the frog. And the patty pan one. I still don't know what a patty pan is.' I'm losing him. Men don't talk about Beatrix Potter. I need to talk about more grown up things, more manly things like motorbikes and wrestling. But I can't think of anything I want to know about motorbikes *or* wrestling. I push my drink away. 'How long have you lived in the flats?' I say, even though I already know the answer.

'Nearly two weeks,' he says. 'You?'

'Two months tomorrow,' I say. 'I don't think people live in our flats for long.'

He smirks. 'Yeah, the landlord gave me that impression as well. What do you make of him, old Sandy Balls?'

I laugh too. 'He hasn't exactly got people skills, has he?'

'Have you met the junkies in the flat between us?'

'No, they keep to themselves.' The flat between us. One flat away from us living together. One floor of separation. I wonder if his bed is directly above my bed. I wonder if he lies on top of me at night. My cheeks go warm at the thought.

'Where were you before?' he asks.

'Nottingham,' I tell him. This is true, but I was only there for a few months, less than a year. I can't tell him any more than that. And I can't tell him about Liverpool or Dumfries, or Manchester or Scarborough... certainly not Scarborough.

'Ah, fancied taking in the sea air, did ya?'

'Mmm. I prefer the flat here to the one they gave me in Nottingham.'

'Who's they?'

'The council,' I lie. 'That one was awful. I never got a full night's sleep. Drunks would spill out of the clubs below every hour through the night. And the fridge had slugs in it.'

'Nasty.'

'Yeah. The one drawback here is that it's a basement flat, not top floor, so I often get a drunk peeing in the front garden or a can thrown over the wall.'

'Better for the little one here though, I'd have thought?'

'Yeah. Much.' I kiss the top of Emily's fluffy head.

My god I can barely look at him. In anyone's storybook he is stunning. He's every Disney prince only four-dimensional and with smell-a-vision. I could look at him for the rest of my life. His eyes sparkle like the sea and he has faint freckles on his cheeks. If I get to know him better, I'll count his freckles. I'll lie next to him counting them, waiting for him to wake up in the morning. I wonder if he sleeps naked. I blush again, furiously, and it goes all down my neck too. I pretend to focus on Emily.

'Do you have any family?' he asks. 'Apart from Emily?'

I shake my head. 'No.' I think about telling Kaden the well-rehearsed lies that Scants gave me, but I don't want to lie to him. I want him to know as much of the truth as possible. So I leave out the untrue stuff. 'I live alone.'

'Oh right,' he says. Is that pity in his eyes?

'How about you?'

'No, I'm here in the short term for work. My family all live in London.' Family, he said, not girlfriend, not boyfriend, not fiancée. That's good. That means a mum and a dad. Though it could mean a wife and kids. I'm not going to think about that right now. 'I'm a PT at Sweat Dreams on Tollgate Road, at the end of the seafront?'

'Yeah, I know it.' There's a plunge of dread in my chest as I take in what he said before. 'So you're not staying here permanently?'

'No, it's a temporary contract. Six weeks' cover. My predecessor broke his leg doing an Iron Man, so I'm filling in for him until he's back at work.'

'But you'll definitely go back to London after that?'

'Yeah, as things stand, though they might keep me on longer. It depends.'

It's not enough hope to cling to, but it's small comfort. I want him to stay as long as I stay. I want to know every inch of him, even the hidden inches. Thank god he's not looking at me, I can feel yet another blush coming on. I stroke Emily's back. 'How are you coping with her on your own?'

'Fine. She's a very good baby so I must be doing something right.'

'Are you on maternity leave then?'

'No, I don't get any. I managed to find a childminder who takes them from new-born so I could still work. I'm a housekeeper at The Lalique.'

'Do you like working there?'

'No, it's not really a job to enjoy. My colleagues all hate me for some reason. There are some parts of it I like. The views from the top floor over the bay. And there's a lavender air freshener we've got in the lobby at the moment that's really nice. And the porter, Trevor, he's okay. Well, he gave me a mint once. I love meeting the children who stay there as well. I adore children.'

'Me too,' he says, and I have a sudden vision of our children buying him a Best Daddy in the World mug for Father's Day.

He'd be a good dad. I'd watched him for two hours walking around the pool at the gym, giving swimming lessons to the St Jude's kids then tidying up the floats afterwards and chatting to parents. He was so sweet with them all. I knew it wasn't an act. By the time I left I knew more about him, more clay I could add to the statue of him I sculpted every night in my mind to get me to sleep. The shape of his torso, the muscle pattern of his back, what his feet looked like in flip flops. He has a tattoo of a snarling tiger on his right shin. I imagined what Us would look like. Us on our wedding day. Us getting the keys to our new home. Us wheeling a trolley round Ikea, choosing crockery. Us at the hospital, me in labour sucking on the gas and air, him scrolling his phone for funny videos. Stroking my face. Telling me he's proud of me.

My heart thumps abnormally.

'Are you a member of the gym then?' he asks over the hissing of the coffee machine and the clanking of cutlery as a waitress clears a neighbouring table.

'No.' His face flattens. 'I was thinking about joining though.'

'You should. Or come along for a class, if you like. We've got Ladies Only Pilates, Ladies' Boxercise, Fight Klub, which is like a self-defence class but to music...'

He's staring at me – the way he said 'self-defence' was loaded with meaning. He wants to ask me more about my hallway hysteria. There's nowhere to hide. His eyes hurt me – green like ponds, flecked with tiny pennies. He touches my arm. Fingertips to forearm. Skin to skin. My thoughts are scrambled egg.

'I rescued a duck last week,' I tell him. 'On the beach. Its wing was broken.'

'Oh right,' he frowns.

'And one of the cats caught a little bird once, brought it to the door. I rescued it. Took it to the RSPCA centre in town.'

He looks at me. 'Is it her dad? The one you're afraid of?'

I bite down on my lip. I give him a nod that barely registers. He says no more about it. 'I love animals, do you?'

'Yeah, but I couldn't eat a whole one,' he winks. 'I'm gonna get a refill,' he announces. 'Won't be a minute. Do you want anything else?'

I shake my head, smile flickering where it won't stay on my face. He disappears up to the counter and I feel it this time – the ache. I resent the easy way he chats to the barista. The adoration in his eyes when he looks out towards the Lakes. I'm jealous of mountains. Of the half-eaten biscotti on his saucer. Touched by him.

When he sits back down, I know he wants to address the hallway thing so in a rush of confidence, I beat him to it.

'I can't really tell you very much about it, why I cried and panicked earlier.'

'It's alright,' he says. 'I can guess.' He offers me his new biscotti. I take it.

The smoke alarm goes off – a forgotten cheese toastie on the grill by the looks of it – and the chef spends a good minute flapping the ceiling with a tea towel.

'I'm not a weirdo,' I say. 'That's the truth. I'm just a little messed up right now. I'm a newly single parent and I'm struggling but I will be okay. Her dad – isn't a part of her life anymore. He can't be. That's all.'

'I get it, Joanne. Really I do. You don't have to say anything else.'

I deflate. I wish he'd call me by my real name. I wonder how it would sound in his mouth. But for now, I am Joanne and Joanne will have to do. 'Thank you.'

He checks his Fitbit. He's going to leave soon and I'm dreading it. 'Listen, I'm two flights up. You get scared again, or anyone visits who you don't wanna see, call me. If I'm not home, I'll be at the gym. I can put my number in your phone, if you like.'

He gestures to take it from me, but then I remember the picture of him as my wallpaper. 'I'll make you a new contact,' I say, fumbling. 'What's your number?'

I punch it in and switch it off. 'Thank you. For listening. And for the drink.' It doesn't look like I've drunk very much of my shake – I can't suck the thick cream up the flimsy paper straw but since plastic is not so fantastic anymore and I don't want to pig great spoonfuls of cream in front of my Future Husband, I reluctantly leave it.

'I better go – I've got a client in twenty minutes. Come along later and check out the facilities at the gym if you like? I can give you the grand tour. First month's free.'

'Okay, I might do.'

He stands up, gathering his wallet, phone and keys. 'See ya, Chickadee,' he says to Emily's covered head, tickling the top of her hood.

He's touched her. He's touched my baby. They have a connection now. He's growing to love her like his own, I'm sure of it.

Long after he's left, I'm still staring out at the distant

mountains he'd watched so lovingly. We'll go there someday, Kaden, Emily and me. We'll go there on holiday. Be one of those fit families that hikes in North Face coats and big boots. Emily will sit in one of those baby backpacks, peeking out over her daddy's shoulder. Our Family.

'*Helloo*, Earth to Genevieve?' A voice filters through my private imaginings. Vanda from work stands beside my table, face full of make-up, big red lips and carrying two large shopping bags. She's surrounded by children all whining for ice cream.

'Oh, hi Vanda. Hi boys. And girl.' They're not interested in saying hello – they race to the counter and start choosing Freakshakes from the menu.

'I saw you from outside. Why you not work yesterday and today?'

'I called in. I told Trevor that Emily had a bug.'

She frowns at the papoose. 'She got bug now?'

'Uh no. She's much better today thanks.'

'So you be in tomorrow, yes? I need to know or else I get cover. You don't let me know again, I give your job to someone else.'

'I'll be in at eight, I promise.'

She bats her enormous spider-lash eyes. 'You better be there or I come down on you like ton of fucking bricks, yes?'

'Yes. Thank you. I'll see you tomorrow.'

Her children are obstructing two paying customers at the till but as Vanda shrieks 'Kids move!' at them, they quickly disperse and fall into line in silence.

3

Thursday, 24th October

I leave a little tube of Smarties behind the front gate for Alfie the paper boy and drop Emily off at the childminder's on my way to work, passing by the arcades to see if Matthew's there at the bus stop, playing the grabbers outside while waiting for his school bus, but he's not. It's half term, of course. He'll be with his family.

Being outdoors with Kaden yesterday has made me feel braver, bolder, and the three men from the hairdressers seem a distant memory now. I'm expecting a normal day at The Lalique. The past fifty-odd days have been excruciatingly normal – bed-changing, vacuuming, bleaching, replacing creamers, sugars, sachets of tea. Then back along the seafront to bed and waking up again and it starts all over. The highlight of any shift is usually when I catch a child coming back to the room by themselves to get something. Then we have a chat and they tell me what they're doing for the day.

But today, there are no children about and Vanda's in an awful mood. She's always in an awful mood with me. She's like a Russian Cruella de Vil and she scares me twice as much. I'm hanging up my coat in the staff office when she storms in. No *Hellos* or *How are yous*, just: 'There's a shit in the pipe

32

Genevieve, so you lucky I don't throw you through fucking window today. Floor 2. Go help Trevor.'

'A "shit in the pipe"?' I say.

'A blockage. A stiff in Room 29. Means we're going to cordon off whole floor so the police can come and then we have to wait around and clean when they have gone. We're short-staffed as well because Fat Faith's brat has the conjunctivitis.'

'Okay.' I'm not quite sure what she means by 'a stiff' at this point but if it's Russian for poo, I better make sure my plunger's on the cart.

'Baby not got bug today?' she says as I wheel to the service elevators.

'No, she's fine today, thanks. The doctor said it could be colic.'

'She tit or bottle?'

'I'm breastfeeding her.'

'So she may be allergic to you.' It's not a question.

'She seems okay. Thanks.'

'So you express when you're not with her?'

'Yes.'

'She's young to be left with childminder. What is she, a month?'

'Five weeks. I can't afford not to work, Vanda.' The lift finally *bing!*s open.

'How much she charge, childminder?'

I'm in the lift and the doors close before I can answer. I always breathe a sigh of relief after Vanda's firing squad of questions. She interrogates where other people enquire and is always picking me up on what I'm doing right and wrong for

Emily, just because she has four children herself. She thinks she knows everything there is to know about anything, she's one of those people. Anything you have, she has double. You have a kid, she has four. You have money worries, she's broke. You have a row with your boyfriend? Her ex-husband stabbed her. Twice.

When I get to Floor 2, Trevor the porter stands guard outside Room 29.

'Alright Gen? Any sign of the police and coroner?'

'A stiff?' I say, finally realising what that means. 'You mean there's a dead person in there?'

'Yeah,' says Trevor. 'A young lass.'

'How?'

'She's in bed,' he sniffs. 'Shit herself too, by the smell of it.'

'Oh my god.'

'Oh this is nothing,' he says, leaning on the end of my trolley. 'I've been here fourteen years. Seen eleven deaths in that time. You must have seen your fair share, working in a hospital?'

My mouth is wide. I click back into Genevieve mode. 'Oh yeah. Loads. Every shift in fact. How did she die?'

'Dunno. No sign of pills or booze. Have a look, if you want.'

'What?'

'Nobody's around. Go and have a butcher's, before they get here.'

'Are you sure?'

'Be my guest,' he says, sweeping aside like the candle out of *Beauty and the Beast*, leaving the door open for me to enter. My mind is already whirring. Trevor hands me a white square of cloth. 'I'd take this in if I were you. Don't worry, it's clean.'

I don't know whether he means the handkerchief or the stiff, but in I go before I can talk myself out of it. I'm at the bathroom door when I smell her. I bundle the hanky against my nose and mouth. I'd only ever seen one dead body in my life. And it looked nothing like that. She looks asleep. Her sheets are pulled up to her chin.

'Could be natural causes,' Trevor calls out. 'I didn't look too hard. Heart condition perhaps?' Even Trevor's pungent body odour can't mask the smell from the bed. She's lying there, red hair all spread out on the pillow. Blue eyes open.

'The dead can't hurt me,' I whisper. 'The dead can't hurt me.'

Trevor's still jabbering on. 'Can you see anything? Anything obvious?'

I momentarily lift away the hanky to answer him, then shove it straight back. 'No.' But when I look closer, I see that there are red spots around one of her eyes, and the white in the other one is all red. Around her neck and under her ears are fingerprint-sized bruises.

'Do you know her name?' I call out.

'Tessa something,' says Trevor. 'She's here for the teaching conference, so him on Reception said. Maths teacher, I think.'

I spy Tessa's open handbag on the chair and I know I shouldn't but I don the rubber gloves I use for cleaning and pull out her purse. I find her driver's licence. I slide it out. Tessa Sharpe. Twenty-eight years of age. Red hair. Blue eyes. From Bristol.

Dread plunges in my chest like a descending elevator.

When I come out, Trevor's standing with his back against the wall and his arms folded. I close the door and hand him back his hanky.

'Vanda found one hanging on the back of a door once,' he sniffs. 'She's winning the Stiff Sweepstake, aren't you V?'

Vanda appears on her vertiginous heels with a toilet roll in either hand, her cart parked up against the wall, vape sticking out of her apron pocket. 'I thought he was heavy coat. He was doing sex thing.' She grimaces. 'Lot of people die in hotels. Whitney Houston. Jimi Hendrix. That guy from *Glee*. Coco Chanel. Mainly drugs.'

'I think she was murdered,' I say.

'Who, Coco Chanel?'

'No, Tessa Sharpe. I think she's been strangled.'

There's a pause, and then Trevor and Vanda look at each other and laugh the kind of laugh that prickles me all over. The kind of laugh that stops the moment I walk into the Staff Office most mornings. The kind of laugh that followed me down the corridors all through school.

'Head in the clouds again, Genevieve,' says Vanda. 'So we have a murderer in the hotel now do we? Shall we call Poirot? Or that old lady with the typewriter? Or maybe Kendal Jenner? Didn't you say you saw her working in Greggs in town? I wonder if she knows how the stiff in Room 29 died.'

'I didn't see Kendall Jenner,' I say. 'The woman just *looked* like her.'

'You said it *was* her!' says Vanda.

Trevor gives it the slow blink like he's king of all knowledge. 'Listen, back to the matter at hand – this isn't suspicious. There's no forced entry, the windows were closed, she checked in alone and she was checking out alone today after the second day of the conference. Some people know when they're gonna die and they check into a hotel to spare their loved ones. Sad but true.'

'She's been strangled,' I repeat, more vehemently. 'Her neck is bruised.'

'What are you, a chambermaid-cum-forensic pathologist now?' Trevor laughs in my face again.

'She's got bloodshot eyes as well,' I say, willing Vanda's face to soften and believe what I'm saying. They both keep looking at me. 'I'm telling you, this is murder.'

Vanda turns to her trolley and counts out four creamers to take them into Room 24 opposite. A couple in flip flops *flip flop* past the open doorway and she greets them with a pleasant 'Good morning, have nice day' as they make their way to the lifts. They don't answer and she flicks a third finger at their backs. The lift doors *bing* and they get in. She turns to me.

'And you know this because you used to work in hospital, yes?'

'Yes.'

'And you've seen strangled person before, yes?'

'Yes.'

'Was this before or after you play hockey for England team?'

'Afterwards. And I was in the youth team.'

She snarls, reeling back from me to grab two fresh hand towels from her stack.

'You must think I came in on last dinghy, darling.' She nods briefly at Trevor, then retreats back inside 24 with a stack of fresh linen. He stands there guarding Tessa Sharpe's closed door with his arms folded. They both think I'm lying. But there's a difference between lying sometimes and lying about *everything*.

Two suited men who look like police arrive on the next *bing* of the lift, flashing their IDs at Trevor before entering Tessa Sharpe's room. In a flash, Vanda reappears and instructs me to begin cleaning the rooms on the third floor while the forensics swoop in and do their thing. I want to watch them but Vanda is adamant and when Vanda is adamant I have to fall in line, like everybody else.

From a third floor window, I watch them wheel Tessa Sharpe's body out to the van parked at the back of the hotel where the deliveries come in. I can't take my eyes off the body bag. It forced me to remember the last time I saw a body bag being wheeled up the ramp of a van. I'm about to start cleaning Room 42 but before I can knock, I realise it's now or never and I run downstairs to Floor 2 and see one of the police-women enter the lift with a plastic bag full of Tessa Sharpe's belongings.

'Sorry, love, you'll need to catch the next one.'

'I wanted to know – it's murder, isn't it? The lady with the red hair.'

'Well I highly doubt she strangled herself.'

Briefly, I'm pleased I was right. But when the lift closes, panic sets in.

I think about Tessa Sharpe my entire shift. Everything I clean or wipe is tainted with the memory of that open-eyed stare, that picture on her driver's licence. Her red hair. This is a quiet, mundane seaside town. I've only been here a couple of months but the only crimes that seem to be committed are drug- or vehicle-related. The odd lawnmower stolen from a garden shed. The odd bit of shoplifting. But this is murder. And it's too much of a coincidence that she has red hair and blue eyes. And she was my age, almost exactly. *And* from Bristol.

I get my bag from the staff office and I'm on my way out again when Vanda shouts my name. Well, not *my* name.

'Genevieve?'

'Yeah?' I turn. 'I was just going.'

'You were right about Miss Dead Woman,' she says under hooded eyes. 'Fair play. I take it you saw strangled person before, when you work at hospital?'

'I knew someone who was strangled. I saw what it did to them.'

Vanda says nothing, looks to my feet and back up to my eyes and then nods and I take that as my cue to leave. She probably thinks I'm lying again. I wish I was.

The cleaning fluid smell has got into every cavity – my nostrils, my mouth, my eyes. I need fresh air more than ever. I head out through Reception and through the front door and I'm halfway across the front lawn when I hear young voices I recognise.

'Mum, it's the maid!' says a voice and the two little girls I befriended at breakfast last week come rushing across the grass towards me. 'Hi, Genevieve!'

'Hi, girls!' I say, momentarily forgetting my nausea. They're wearing T-shirts over their swimming costumes and Kiki's hair is wet at the very ends. My guess is they've spent the morning on the beach. 'You making the most of the Indian summer, are you? Been swimming?'

'Yeah,' says Lola. 'And we found a crab.'

'No, *I* found the crab,' says Kiki.

'Wow, where is it? Can I see it?'

'Mum made us put it back in the sea where it lives.'

'Well that's probably for the best. Now he can get back

to his friend Ariel, can't he?' They both giggle. 'How's your knee now, Kiki?'

'Much better,' she says, showing off the *Lion King* plaster that I put on it the other day. 'It's not bleeding anymore.'

'Lucky I carry those on me, wasn't it?'

'Yeah, Mum never has any in her bag.'

'It was a lot of blood,' says Lola, all sheepish. 'I didn't like that.'

'I was a nurse once,' I tell her proudly. 'I'm used to it.'

'We found this,' says Lola and removes a silver ring with a red heart stone in the middle of it. Costume jewellery but they're both gazing at it like it's Meghan Markle's engagement ring.

'That's beautiful,' I say, as Kiki places it in the palm of my hand. I turn it around and look at it for a bit and hand it back to her.

'It's for you,' says Lola.

'Oh, I couldn't take this,' I say, giving it back.

'We want you to have it cos your boyfriend hasn't given you a ring yet. So you can have that one until he does.'

'I don't know what to say. Can I give you both a hug?'

They fall against me and I inhale the nape of Lola's neck – salt and sun cream. 'Thank you, girls. That's very kind of you. I wonder where it came from. Maybe from a shipwreck?'

'Yeah,' says Kiki. 'Maybe it was a princess's and she fell overboard—'

'—while being kidnapped by a brutish band of pirates.'

'Yeah!' says Lola. 'And the princess is in the sea, trying to swim back to her land.'

'—but she hasn't got there yet because the swimming tired

her out so she's stopped off on some deserted island and she's been captured by a dragon.'

'And the dragon—'

'Hi, Genevieve, sorry to keep you,' comes the voice of the infiltrator – their bouncy-bobbed mother, looming behind them. 'Were you off?'

'It's fine. I've always got time to talk to my two friends.'

The girls beam and I want to hug them again so badly tears fill my eyes. I pretend it's the sea breeze.

'Thanks again for seeing to her knee the other day.'

'It's no bother at all.'

'I've issued a complaint to the hotel manager about glass bottles on that beach. I'm not sure what they can do about it really.' She turns to them. 'Girls, make sure you rinse your feet before going in that pool, alright?'

'Okay,' they sing-song in unison.

I pull a face and roll my eyes which they both understand and giggle at the woman's retreating back.

'What are you two doing now? Do you want to go to the pier with me and play the slots? I can ask your mum if it's alright?'

'We're not allowed any more money today cos we're having new school shoes.'

'We're going to find Dad and uncle Ray at the pool and then later we're going to the Jungle Café for dinner.'

'Ahh, never mind. How about tomorrow?'

'We're going home tomorrow,' says Kiki. 'So we won't see you anymore.'

I'm sadder than I want them to see.

'Auntie Sadie's going to do my hair in French plaits,' adds Lola.

'French plaits, eh?' I say. 'Well do you know what would go really well in French plaits?' She shakes her head. I hold out my fists before her. 'Pick one.'

She picks the right hand and I open it to reveal the packet of unicorn hair slides.

'Ah, cool!'

'I didn't forget you, don't worry,' I tell Kiki, offering her the remaining closed fist. She pops it open and takes out the kitten hairbands with a big shy smile. 'There you go now, you can both look pretty for your meal at the Jungle Café, can't you?'

'Thank you, Genevieve,' they sing-song again.

'You're welcome,' I say and yank softly on Kiki's soggy ponytail. 'You better go.'

It's only when the girls are out of sight that I realise I still feel sick. I smell Tessa Sharpe again, wafting out of the window of Room 29. My aloneness feels so obvious the further I walk along the seafront. I'm completely unnerved. Every few steps I'm looking over my shoulder. I cross the road to the arcades to see if Mia or James or Carlie are in there playing basketball or driving neon cars down desert highways but there's no sign of any of them. They must all be away for half term.

And the breeze is so sharp it cuts across my cheeks and stings my eyes. And the wind whips up my dye-blackened hair.

Not my hair.

My real hair is red, and I see Tessa Sharpe's red hair in my mind's eye again. Red hair and blue eyes. She didn't arrive with anybody; she wasn't intending to leave with anybody.

Whoever killed her had seen her around the hotel. I can't not think it. I can't pretend this time.

Whoever killed her thought she was me. Which means I was right. They've found me. They know exactly where I am. And when they discover that they've killed the wrong person, they'll come for me.

First day of the Easter holidays,
eighteen years ago...

4

I'm on the train, little suitcase next to me on the seat, legs swinging freely. I've got my Jelly Tots and my books and Miss Whiskers beside me, and Dad is sitting opposite, wearing his Bristol City away shirt, playing with his phone. If I close my eyes, this could be the Hogwarts Express. We could be going back on the first day of term. I'm on a huge red steam engine roaring through the misty countryside. I've bought some Chocolate Frogs and Bertie Bott's Every Flavour Beans and Miss Whiskers is a real cat, like Hermione's cat, Crookshanks, and therefore, magical. But Dad keeps talking to me and there are no parents allowed on the Hogwarts Express so I can't fully imagine it.

'You excited?' says Dad, fidgeting with his phone, turning it round and round in his hands. I nod and carry on colouring my picture. 'What are you and Foy going to get up to this Easter then?'

'Uncle Stu is going to do us an Easter egg hunt. And Isaac's going to teach me to ride his bike. And Chelle's going to do some plaits in my hair. And we'll probably play over the churchyard and in our castle.'

'The castle?'

'Our castle in the trees.'

'I thought that was Paddy's treehouse?'

'He doesn't want it anymore. He said we could have it. So now it's our castle.'

'Oh right.'

A man with a black box on his hip stops by our table and asks to see our tickets and I get mine from my strawberry purse dangling around my neck.

'Are you staying with me this time?' I ask Dad when the man has passed by.

'No, love, I've got to work.'

'I thought you didn't have a job?'

'I've got a job.'

'At the phone place?'

'No, I didn't like that one.'

'With the man on the market stall?'

'No, I didn't like that one either.'

'With those men who came to the house last night?'

'What men?' He frowns. Oops. I was supposed to be in bed. 'Oh *those* weren't men – that was the Three Little Pigs.' I chuckle. 'They're my mates. They keep asking me to build them some proper houses cos the wolf keeps blowing theirs down.'

'Liar, liar, pants in the drier.'

'It's true, Squish. They're going to pay me lots of money so we can have a brilliant Christmas this year.'

'I thought you liked working at the phone place.'

'Nah. The boss was a bit of an ogre.'

'What, a *real* ogre?'

'Yeah, a proper ogre. She'd eat whole humans for her lunch.'

'Urgh.'

'And she lived under a bridge and everything.' He checks his phone screen.

'Trolls live under bridges, Dad.' The train goes under a bridge and all goes to black, briefly. 'Like that one.' 'How come we came by train this time?'

'The car's being serviced.'

'Can I have something to eat? The lady's coming with the trolley.'

'Wait 'til we get to the station. Auntie Chelle will get you something in town.'

The train cannot roll into Taunton Station quickly enough and I'm already in the aisle with my case when it comes to a stop. My knees almost buckling with excitement, I look through every window, whizzing through the faces on the platform for signs of Auntie Chelle. And then I see her. She's in a red wrap-around dress and a blue cardigan and petrol blue boots with buckles. I can't see Foy. The disappointment comes upon me like a sicky belch. Foy said she was coming. Where is she?

And then I see her. In her blue ballet tutu and blue tights and gelled back bun. She's swinging on the bike racks behind Chelle. That's when my holiday begins properly – the moment I start running along the platform towards Auntie Chelle and she sees me coming and shrieks with delight and I crash safely in her embrace and she lifts me up and we hug so tightly and I breathe the familiar jasmine scent of her curls. The nearest thing I have to a mum is a perfumy waft that comes from Dad's second wardrobe. Chelle is a living breathing mum and it's all I can do to stop touching her.

'How's my precious girl?' she cries, stroking my cheeks with her thumbs and gazing down at me with tears in her eyes. 'Oh we've missed you, Ellis. We've all missed you *so* much.' She cuddles me against her.

'I've missed you too.'

And she sets me down and Foy skips over and hugs me as well.

'Look, I got you a surprise,' she says and then holds out her hands and I have to pick one. I pick the one that has a little cat pencil topper inside it. Then she opens her other hand to reveal a tiny fold of paper. She's drawn me a picture of us standing on top of our castle with our swords pointed up to the sky. Standing around us are some of our army – The Knights. Monday Knight, Tuesday Knight, Thursday Knight and our Chief Knight, Saturday. Our own personal bodyguard service.

'That's us,' she giggles.

'I love it!' I say. 'Did the storm blow the castle down? I was worried.'

'No, it only took the roof off so Isaac and Dad patched it up. It's really strong now. Dad found us a sheet of wavy plastic for the top. Come on, let's do this,' she says and leads me over to the bike racks while Chelle talks to Dad. I don't catch their conversation – it's usually boring brother-sister stuff. They don't hug like we do.

Me and Foy sit in the back of Chelle's car and pretend we're being chauffeur-driven by our servants. Foy is the Duchess of Fowey because that's the place she's named after, and I am Lady Kemp of Ashton Gate because I live near Ashton Gate. We are so stinking rich that we have our own castle and every animal you can think of. We are off into town to buy new saddles for the unicorns and bamboo for our pandas.

'Yes, turn here, Jeeves,' says Foy with a dismissive wave of her hand as Chelle's car turns at the traffic lights into the road at the back of the church where we usually park. Dad's come along to have a quick bite in town before his train back to Bristol.

'Dad, can you come and stay at the pub as well?' I say.

'I can't love,' he says. 'I told you, I've got work.'

'What work is that?' asks Chelle.

'Got a job with a mate doing a bit of cash in hand.'

'Sounds lucrative,' she says. And they don't talk about it anymore.

'It's for the Three Little Pigs,' I say, 'building houses for them.' Nobody laughs.

We park up in the pay and display behind the big church.

'Mum, can we go to Wimpy?' asks Foy.

'Yes, you two go on ahead and order. I'll have a Coke.'

'I'll have some chips and a Coke,' says Dad. 'I've got a quick errand to run actually so I'll meet you all in there.'

'What errand?' says Chelle.

He checks his phone, then puts it back in his pocket. 'Well there's this princess, you see, and she's been asleep for a thousand years and if I don't climb up this big tall tower and give her a kiss, she won't ever wake up. So I'll dash off and do that and I'll be back, alright Squish?'

He yanks my plait and wiggles Foy's bun and we both laugh and then he rides off like he's on his horsey, which makes us laugh even more. 'I won't be long.'

Chelle's not laughing.

Me and Foy have cheese burgers and chips and strawberry milkshakes and scoff them greedily as Chelle sits taking the ice out of her Coke and placing it in the ashtray.

'How many Easter eggs have you got?' Foy asks between red-saucy mouthfuls.

'I don't know. Dad packed them in my case to give to Chelle.'

'We've got to buy some, Ellis,' says Chelle. 'He didn't get round to it. As usual.'

'Oh right.'

'We'll nip to Woolworths on our way to the car. And I must do the bank.'

'Maybe that's what his errand was?' I suggest.

'I doubt it,' Chelle smiles, stealing a couple of Dad's untouched chips. 'Woolworths is nowhere near the betting shop, is it?'

'I don't know.'

'Anyway, never mind him. What would *you* like to do this holiday, Miss?'

This is my favourite bit of any holiday – the bit before it all begins. She leans forwards, like she's telling us both a great big secret. 'Everything,' I say, licking at the dried line of tangy ketchup around my mouth. 'I want to do everything!'

'Right, well, we're doing our Easter egg hunt on Sunday and then we'll all go for a ride out in the country to that nice tea place and have poached eggs and soldiers—'

'Yeah!' says Foy. 'They have a wicked climbing frame there, bigger than the castle. And they've got the dogs we played with last time, remember?'

I do remember, every second of it. One of the dogs had a thorn in its paw and we reported it to the lady and she gave us a free scone each.

'And then we can go asparagus picking up the farm on Monday, cos there'll be nothing open in town. And the boys will be around so I've asked if they'll take you out flying kites again, or maybe some fishing down at the stream. How about that?'

I'm so excited I could burst but I settle for kicking my heels against my chair.

'Can they take us to the cinema as well?' asks Foy.

'Yes, I'm sure they can,' says Chelle, sipping her Coke and looking at the time.

'We can go to that burger place they took us to last time,' I say. 'Where we got the free Frisbees.' The Frisbees that kept going over the beer garden wall into the stream and Isaac had to keep climbing over the wall to fish them out.

Paddy and Isaac are the two best boy cousins I could ask for. Isaac's fifteen and sporty, and always working out on the machines in the old stable behind the cellar. Paddy's twelve and he's more into art and styling his hair. Isaac'll be starting his GCSEs soon. I hope he still has time to chase us around the car park on the bikes.

'Can we have chicken pie and mash one night please, Auntie Chelle?'

'I don't see why not.'

I love it when that's the answer.

'And chocolate sponge and alien sauce?' says Foy.

'Yeah, baby! Oh that reminds me, I've got to nip in the comic shop and pick up Stuart's birthday present.'

'What is it?'

Chelle rolls her eyes. 'His dream Tardis.'

'Not a big Tardis though,' says Foy. 'A little one with a little Doctor Who inside and a Dalek and it plays the theme tune when you open the door.'

'He's had his eye on it for a while,' says Chelle.

'Can I buy him something as well?' I ask. 'Maybe a Doctor Who comic?'

'Yeah he'd love that. Do you want me to look after your pocket money?'

'Dad's looking after it for me.'

'Okay,' she smiles, looking towards the door as a family with pushchairs struggle in out of the rain. 'How is he at the moment, sweetheart?'

'He's okay.'

'How much did he get for the car in the end, do you know?'

Foy dances her little unicorn pencil topper along my arm. 'How much?'

'Yeah. He's sold it, hasn't he? That's why you came on the train.'

'He said it was having a service today.'

'Ah, right. My mistake. Finish your burger, love.'

All the ice in Dad's drink melts and his chips go cold so Chelle tips them in the trash. He sends a text to Chelle that he'll meet us at the car at 3 p.m. instead. So we do Woolworths for the eggs and Chelle banks the takings at NatWest and me and Foy steal armfuls of leaflets for our bank, which the castle doubles up as sometimes.

We're back at the car by 2.55 p.m., but Dad isn't there. By 3.15 p.m. we've played I-Spy, Yellow Car, the memory game, and Foy and me have planned all the things we're going to do in the castle when we get back – first paint the walls, then we must clean the carpet and deadhead the window box. Then play Banks. And then we have to do a supermarket run because the dinosaurs are getting low on tins of Jurassic Chum.

At 3.25 p.m. Chelle puts another hour on the car cos there's still no sign of him.

'I'm sorry, hon, I know he's your dad but he does my bloody head in sometimes. Why is he so unreliable?' she huffs. 'There's nothing consistent about him at all.'

Foy picks up Miss Whiskers and makes her growl and roar around Chelle's neck until she reacts, turning round in the driver's seat and swatting it away.

'Will you stop that, please? I'm not in the mood.'

Then we see Dad coming.

'Uh-oh,' says Foy, and Auntie Chelle slams the driver's door when she gets out. Me and Foy laugh at first but then we see her shouting at him and they both stand in front of the car, him being barked at like a stranger at the gate. Foy winds down the back window so we can hear what they're saying. Chelle's patting down his jacket and she wrenches something out of his grasp and holds it up – small pieces of paper.

'Can't fucking stay away from them, can you? You utter loser.'

We aren't laughing then. The F word makes Foy go quiet and then cry.

I hold her hand. She grips mine tightly.

'She bought Stuart a birthday present,' says Chelle. 'So you owe me a fiver.'

'I haven't got it, Chelle.'

'You spent your ten-year-old daughter's pocket money? Jesus Christ.'

Foy buzzes the window up. 'I don't like it when Mum gets stressy.'

'It's always Dad that makes her stress.'

Chelle deep-breathes and gets in the car. He follows and she starts the engine. None of us say a word until we get back to the station. Chelle leaves the engine running. Dad pokes his head through my window and fist-bumps Foy, making the sound of starburst sprinkles coming out of his hand. He kisses me on the nose.

'You be good, Squish, alright? Call me every night.'

By the time we get out of town and the car's streaming along through the green countryside towards Carew St Nicholas, I've forgotten about the row between Chelle and Dad – my mind's too full up with the possibilities that lie ahead. As we turn the corner down into the village and round the bend into the vast car park at the back of The Besom Inn, I spy Paddy and Isaac on their bikes, doing wheelies and bunny hops.

'Isaac's got a new bike!' I say. I can't wait to get out of the car.

'Yeah,' says Chelle. 'It's a Hellcat Something Something with front suspension and something-else splashbacks, apparently. He got it for his birthday. He said you could have his old one.'

'REALLY?!' I cry. 'Ah wow!' I spy it straight away, leaning up against the skittle alley wall, all shining silver and red with the word Apollo written on the downtube.

'He's pumped up the tyres for you specially,' says Foy.

I leap out of the car and run across to Apollo, wheeling it over to Isaac.

'Hey, Ellis. Like your new bike?'

'Yeah! I love it! Can I really have it?'

'Yeah, no sweat. I pumped the tyres up for you.'

'Not you again, Smellis,' says Paddy, wheeling over and

56

skidding to a halt beside me. He tickles my ribs and chases me across the car park but lets me win, like always.

After an hour of wheeling around we go inside the pub and find Uncle Stu closing up the bar for the afternoon. I give him a hug and we help ourselves to crisps and cans of Rio. The pub is a rabbit warren of low ceilings, oak beams and a warm orange glow from every doorway. There's a pervading smell of old log fire and spilled beer and somewhere a fruit machine plinks and whooshes.

Upstairs, there are four main bedrooms and two unused ones called the back bedrooms, housing old toys and various pub bric-a-brac, old tankards and unused bar stuff like beer mats and ice buckets. My hands run along the wallpaper, bumping over the little chips and dents. I want this holiday to last forever.

And once Foy's changed out of her ballet stuff, we ride, four of us into nature, along the lanes towards the playing fields, me and Foy stopping every so often to pick up dinosaur food, or petrol for the Lamborghini or the Ferrari, or new school shoes for some of our kids. We have forty in all, but we live in a castle so there's definitely room.

My ten-year-old self needs this. A break from worrying about Dad and his angry phone calls and disappearing acts in the night. I need weeks of itchy legs and Wham bars and cola cubes and board games played the wrong way and bare feet on cold evening grass playing Mad Rounders with leeks and sprouts. I need to run until my sides stitch and make up dance routines to Madonna songs with Foy.

I need to fly kites and make nests from cut grass in fields wider than oceans, in sunshine that warms our backs and stretches our shadows to look like giants. To jump on desert rock furniture and lava carpets and create assault courses from old fire guards and broken chairs and table cloths. To play for hours a day in our secret places where adults don't go – the quiet churchyard over the wall from the pub, the castle, our duvet dens – places where time is decided by the colour of the sky, not clocks and watches, and my limbs are powered by fizzy drinks and melted ice lollies.

Where every morning Chelle says 'Rise and shine, Clementine,' when she opens Foy's bedroom curtains and takes us downstairs for milky coffees and bacon sandwiches. And we help Stuart stock up the bar and he gives us five pounds to spend at the shop. And we buy felt tips and sketchpads and blue bootlaces and we take it all up to our castle in the tree where we draw our wedding dresses and watch over our land where popcorn fields sway in the wind and unicorns run wild and a T-Rex stalks the land, looking for half-open tins of Jurassic Chum.

And where everyone calls me Ellis. Or Elle. Or Ellis Clementine Kemp, when I'm naughty. Or Smellis or Elly Belly Cinderelly. But always, *always* Ellis.

If only I'd known then that everything would soon be taken from me – even my own name.

5

Friday, 25th October

Kaden is out at 6 a.m., doing little sprints up and down the seafront. I only went out to put the Smarties by the gate for Alfie but I decided to sit and watch him as it was such a peaceful, bright day. So I'm sitting on the front steps, looking across the road at the doughnut van and wondering what time he opens. I hold my glass of Strawberry Nesquik. I think about Us again. Me and him supermarket shopping, the baby sitting in the trolley seat and him making faces at her. When I'm thinking about him, I'm not thinking about Tessa Sharpe. I need him in my life. He can protect me from The Three Little Pigs. He can be my brave Saturday Knight with bulletproof shield and a lance that will pierce the hearts of my enemies.

He always seems so busy though. If he's not jogging, he's working. And if he's not at the gym he's gone off somewhere on his motorbike. I don't like to impose.

But if I *don't* impose, I'm going to keep thinking about it. About Tessa. Wondering if she knew what was happening when those big hands were around her neck. Wondering how long she panicked before the breath was squeezed out of her. Wondering if she heard Death creeping into her bedroom.

Kaden eventually appears, vest sweated through, lost in music. I call out, 'Hiya.'

He sees me as he's climbing the steps to the front door. 'Oh hey, Joanne,' he puffs, yanking out one of his earphones. His neck's all sweaty again but the big news is he's wearing shorts. And he has the most wonderful legs. Tanned, toned, soft blond hairs all over but I've never minded that. He's never looked lovelier. Beads of sweat trickle down his forehead and into the nape of his neck.

'How are you today?' he puffs.

'Yeah, I'm okay thanks,' I say, gesturing towards my Nesquik.

'Nice. How's Emily?'

'She's fine. Thanks. Asleep, for now.' I roll my eyes like Mums do when they've been up all night with their babies. 'What are you doing today?'

'Got to have a shower and then it's work at nine. You?'

'Work this afternoon,' I shrug. 'That's about it.'

I feel like I have left it open for him to ask me to spend this morning with him instead but he doesn't. One of the cats leaps up onto the wall and startles him – Tallulah von Puss. We share a laugh and he tickles her chin as she nuzzles his hand. So he's okay with cats too. He is all kinds of perfection.

'Saw a poster that looked like her a few streets away,' he says, frowning to inspect her labelless collar.

'Really?'

'Yeah. Little white patch here and everything,' he says, stroking her chest.

'Oh yeah, I saw that one,' I lie. 'That isn't her. This is Tallulah von Puss.'

'I think that one was called Pedro. Anyway, I best get going. See ya.' He jogs up the front steps to the door. I wait for him to take a second look back at me, like men sometimes do in films when they're secretly in love but they can only say it with their eyes. But he doesn't.

And Tessa Sharpe's dead face comes screaming into my mind again.

I hear the first notes of Emily's cry inside so I gulp down my Nesquik, pick up my crumby plate and go to her.

Me and her. Me changing her. Me cuddling her in the middle of the night when there's nobody else to. It's just us. It always *would* be just us, wouldn't it? And in a heartbeat I'm annoyed, my head is full of thunder and lightning. I wish, for a second, that I *was* Tessa Sharpe.

And then I feel awful, like my insides are rancid. How could I wish *I* were dead even for a second? After everything Scants has done to protect me? Because being dead means this all being over, that's why. All this running and hiding and lying. I can just be Me. Ellis Who Died. Rather than Joanne Who Barely Existed. I don't want to be the Me they tell me to be. The Me that Scants says I *have* to be. It doesn't stick.

Today I've told work I'm going to be late as I have to attend a funeral. And it's true; I *am* going to a funeral. June Busby's funeral. Whoever June Busby is. I heard them talking about it at Leonard Finch's funeral last week and I asked the vicar about it. I wonder if they'll have those mushroom vol-au-vents again after; they were delish.

I'm not disrespectful when I attend these gatherings, far from it. And I'm rarely asked for identification. I like going because funerals are family occasions and I like being around families, even if they aren't my own. People are usually so taken with peeking into the papoose to try and see Emily, they aren't bothered that I'm neither family nor friend. I could be a neighbour, a work colleague, someone the deceased met down the park while feeding the ducks. Maybe I gave her a lift to aerobics. Maybe I walked his dog for him in his final weeks. They'll never know.

I haven't brought Emily today. I wanted to go alone. I'm all in black as I walk funereally through the fog towards the big cemetery gates. I see the coffin in the hearse. Dark brown. Brass handles. Small floral arrangement on the top with a card. A large black car follows closely behind. They both stop at the doors.

The family members get out of the car. A man with a ginger beard and blond hair. Black suit. People gravitate towards him, shaking his hand, a manly embrace. A *We'll get through this* shoulder clasp. I'm handed an A5 white booklet.

Celebrating the life of June Miranda Busby.

The entrance music is listed as The Carpenters' 'Yesterday Once More'. I flick to the back page. The exit music is 'Don't Cry for Me Argentina'. Leonard Finch's exit music was 'Oklahoma!' which everyone seemed to find amusing for some reason.

There's a Welcome and Introduction by the Celebrant – Miss Gloria Andrews, whoever she is and whatever a celebrant is. Posh word for a priest, I suppose.

Then a hymn – 'Make Me a Channel of Your Peace'. Loads of verses.

Then a Eulogy and a family tribute, read by June's son Philip. Then another hymn. Then the Committal. Which is the bit when the coffin goes behind the curtains and, presumably, gets burned.

'You will come to the pub for a cuppa, won't you?' says the son, Philip, to the man standing next to me looking over the floral tributes.

'Yes of course,' says the man.

'Yes of course,' says I. And the son Philip looks at me and smiles graciously. He doesn't need to know who I am – being there is enough for him to know his mother was cherished.

I only started going to people's funerals after my dad died. I couldn't go to his – I was still in hospital and they said I wasn't well enough. I've only ever visited his grave in Scarborough once, and Scants told me not to go back again. *Never go back, it's too dangerous. Keep going forwards.* To where though? *Where am I going?*

I've tried to get out and about and meet people like Scants keeps telling me to, but it's not like it used to be as a kid. Back then you'd just say *Hey, do you want to play Tig* or *Pokémon?* and they would. Adults are full of suspicion and fear. Children themselves I find very easy to talk to. When I'm down at the pier or the beach or the arcades on my mornings or afternoons off, I can strike up conversations very quickly with kids. We have similar interests. Similar goals in life. Mainly, short term happiness. They don't think about tomorrow. I daren't.

Scants finds this too weird. *No more playing with other people's kids*, he says. *It's not friendship, it's grooming. Join a club instead, do a course, get some hobbies. Meet people your own age.*

But adults are untrustworthy and devious. Adults do bad things.

The only things I like doing besides eating and watching DVDs is going down the arcades and playing 'Guitar Hero' or bowling with Matthew or dressing up the cats. I don't go scuba diving at weekends or play lacrosse on a Wednesday night or anything like that. I'm not sociable or vivacious enough to 'join a club of likeminded people'. Who *does* that? What kind of Louisa May Alcott world does Scants live in where people just go out and, god forbid, introduce themselves to new people?

I'm not one of life's joiner-inners, I am one of life's stay-at-homers.

Except when I have to work. Or I need a doughnut.

'Hey, Charlotte!' comes the cheery greeting from inside the doughnut van as I'm walking along the front to work.

'Hi Johnny,' I say. 'How are you?'

'I saw you the other day. Had some doughnut holes for you. I called out.'

'Oh. Sorry. I can't have heard you.'

'You seemed in a rush. Where's your baby today?'

'At the childminder's. I had to go to a funeral this morning.'

'Ah no. Anyone close?'

'No, not close. Got a nice few hours to myself now to finish my novel. Thought I'd treat myself first.'

'Ahhh good idea,' he says, lowering the frying basket into the bubbling oil. 'Give me three minutes, I'll put a fresh batch on for you.' He moves his batter mixing bowl to the back bench and I slip into Charlotte Mode – my spine instantly lengthening as I flick my scarf over my shoulder.

'Thank you. I need all the sugar I can get today. Got a big rewrite underway.'

'That's not good,' he says. 'Your editor didn't like what you'd done?'

'No, I completely messed it up actually. Had to cut around 40,000 words. It's fine though, I've had worse. Every book seems to get harder to write.'

'Wow, 40,000 words? You must write pretty fast.'

'Yeah I do. I can dash that off again in a week, it's no biggy. Ooh, I'll have a Lilt as well thanks, Johnny.'

'Not a problem,' he says, grabbing a can from the fridge. 'Not seen you about much lately, Charlotte. Thought you might have found another doughnut man.' He winks but it doesn't feel MeToo-ey, just friendly. It's pretty comforting in a town where nobody knows my name and offers me nothing in the form of family.

'No, never,' I smile. 'I have a lot on at the moment, that's all. I've just come back from a book tour and a couple of my author friends had their launches this week as well so it's been a bit hectic.' I sigh like it's all been one big drama.

'I see,' he says, flicking the doughnuts over in the basket where they bob and glisten in the golden oil. A white flickering catches my eye – a Missing Cat poster on the nearest lamp-post flaps in the wind. Suki Shortcake. Missing since July. It's actually my Prince Roland. No wonder he ran off with a name like Suki Shortcake. The doughnuts finish frying and Johnny tips them out of the basket onto a tray covered with flattened kitchen roll, scattering their brown tops with sugar.

'Five for a pound or, to you, four plus one free for one hundred pence.'

'Five is good, thank you.'

He shovels my doughnuts into a paper bag and winds it

up in two knots. I hand him £2 and he places the warm bag on my palm, retrieving my change from his belt.

'They smell magnificent, as always, thank you Johnny.' I venture a hand into the bag but they're too scalding hot and my fingers burn on impact.

'How are book sales for the last one?' He leans on the counter top.

'Good thanks. Sold it to Greece and… Belgium this morning, in fact.'

Two young lads scuff towards the van, reading their options from the board.

'Ah, that's wonderful! And have you met David Schwimmer yet?'

I told him a few weeks ago that David Schwimmer had signed up to be in the movie they're making out of my book *Lovers in War*.

'Not yet. I think he's coming over in the near future so maybe I'll meet him then.'

'That's fantastic. I love Ross. Could I *be* more of a Ross fan?'

'That's Chandler,' I laugh.

'Oh yeah,' he laughs, louder. 'Which one's Ross again?'

'The dinosaur guy. Three divorces. Someone ate his sandwich.'

We both laugh when we realise neither of us can do a Ross impression.

'Thanks for the doughnuts, Johnny,' I say, picking up the cold can of Lilt which soothes my overeager fingertips.

He turns to the two lads who both want doughnuts too. 'Okay, don't be a stranger now, Charlotte. Yes, lads, what can I get you?'

I use the doughnut man, I admit that. I use him to make myself feel better. And some days it works. But today, it doesn't. The doughnuts are too hot to eat and he is too busy to flirt to the required level that makes me feel good about myself. I want to go back to the flat, cave up in my duvet on the bed and hide.

But I have to work. Afternoon shift.

There's only one more byte of information I can learn about Tessa Sharpe's death – her hands were bound with 'reusable cable ties'. I overhear General Manager Kimberley talking to the detective sergeant with the lazy eye. She says Trevor only has single-use cable ties for the TVs in the bedrooms so whoever killed Tessa Sharpe must have brought their own.

Room 29 is still out of action and the police are at the hotel all day, questioning the rest of the staff. For some reason they don't question me though and I wonder why until Trevor informs me they want to talk to staff members who were on shift between 7 p.m. and midnight on the night she died. This discounts *me* from suspicion, at least.

'Have you finished?' says Vanda as I'm craning my neck around the staff office to hear what she's saying to the investigating officer.

'No, I wondered if there were any more J-cloths? There's none on the shelves.'

'No. You have to open new box. And shut the door.'

So I do. Nobody tells me what is happening – not Sabrina, not Claire the temp, not Madge, and all Trevor says when I catch him lumbering through with boxes is, 'It's a police matter now, let them do their job.'

When was I *not* letting them do their job? I only asked if they knew who'd done it yet. Why won't he tell me?

He's mending the coffee machine in the breakfast room when I finish my shift.

'Do they have any CCTV?' I say. 'You know, of anyone not staying at the hotel who sort of wandered in?'

'Don't know yet. The detective lassie who came yesterday mentioned an ex-boyfriend so I think they're looking at him for it. They won't keep us informed cos it's nowt to do with us.'

'Of course it's to do with us. It happened in the place we work.'

'Yeah, but we're not involved.'

I bite down on my lip. 'We might be.'

'How?'

'Well, what if it's a serial killer? What if Tessa Sharpe is only the first?'

'She's not. I told you, they're investigating the boyfriend.'

'Might not have *been* the boyfriend.'

He stops what he's doing and looks at me. 'What are you saying here, Gen? You saying the murderer is still around, waiting to strike again?'

'Could be.'

'Well, who is it then, Miss Marple? Who you got pegged for it? One of the chefs? The guy who comes to clean the fryers? Me?'

'I don't know. Nobody knows. I don't feel safe here, I know that. It said in the paper this morning that she was… *raped.*'

He points at me with his screwdriver. 'A young lassie died in terrible circumstances. Everyone here feels awful about it. But you going round saying things like that will only make things worse. You'll scare people.'

'I don't mean to scare anyone, Trevor. I'm telling you how I feel.'

'Leave it alone. Let the police deal with it. The family are coming up tomorrow to talk to the police. We don't want any hysteria.'

'I'm not hysterical. I'm worried.'

'Yeah well, I'm worried 'n' all. I'm worried about keeping me bleeding job.'

He had nothing else to say. I don't know why he got so funny with me, I wasn't accusing *him*. Vanda and the rest of them had obviously poisoned him against me. They all thought I was weird. I say weird things. I eat my tea break biscuits in an odd manner – Chocolate Digestives chocolate first, then halved, then quartered; Custard Creams scraped out, put back together, bitten into a circle and rolled around my tongue; Jaffa Cakes chocolate first, cake second then suck the orange disc. I'd seen how they all looked at me. It was the way a pack of lionesses look at a deformed cub before they abandon it under a tree. I don't blame them.

On my way out through the car park, I see Lola and Kiki standing beside an estate car loaded up with suitcases and inflatables. I wave goodbye but they don't see me. I'm still wearing the ring they gave me, except it's on my fourth finger now. If anyone asks, I'm going to say it's an engagement ring. But nobody's asked yet.

I feel better once I've got Emily's warm little body snuggled against me – and we walk the long way home past the gym on Tollgate Road, where I linger outside to see if Kaden's around. He's in reception with a new member by the looks, a young woman in a leotard with long blonde hair and very thin triceps. They're sitting in the bucket seats, going through some form. He's flirting easily with her. She's smiling, tucking her hair behind her ear. My chest squeezes painfully as we walk on by.

If you get scared again, call me. If I'm not home, I'll be at the gym.

I'm not scared right now though, am I? I'm sad. Because Trevor at work hates me now, and he was my one friend. And Scants doesn't want me calling him unless it's an emergency. And Kaden was flirting with that woman. I want to go home. Back to Carew St Nicholas. Back where I was known and loved.

But that's not an option. So I go back to the flat. In the dying light I can see post in my pigeonhole. A leaflet about the new self-storage place that's opened on the ring road. End of Summer Sale at B&M. Autumn sale at Harvey's, fifty per cent off blinds. A circular from Vodafone about going contract rather than Pay-As-You-Go. And a catalogue. Addressed to Miss Joanne Haynes. A catalogue I know I haven't ordered.

A coffin catalogue.

6

Tuesday, 29th October

It's been four days since I last went into work. Kimberley, the General Manager, took the message again this morning, only this time I heard Vanda shouting in the background:

'Tell her to get fucking doctor's note so I can get some decent staff!'

But I don't care about work. My roots are coming through again. Bright orange. Little fires starting all over my head. I need to get out. I need to get food. I'm three stale pieces of wholemeal bread and a tampon away from completely bare cupboards.

I think it's a sort of emergency. And he did say to call only when it's an emergency.

So I call him.

Scants arrives around 12.30 p.m., as I'm putting Emily down for her nap. He's loaded with Bags for Life, like a pirate with a haul of treasure, only he withholds the *Ahoy there's* and timber-shivering and instead greets me at the door with:

'I'm not buying those chicken nuggets out of principle. I don't mind if they're farmed in Brazil – it's the shipping them to China for processing I don't endorse.'

'Thanks, Scants. It's really great to see you, thanks for

coming.' I want to hug him but I remind myself that Scants doesn't do hugs. He used to hug me all the time when I was a kid. Not in a weird way – the way a dad should hug a child. Even though he wasn't *my* dad, I sometimes wished he was. He didn't have any kids of his own. He once said his wife 'couldn't have them' and left it at that. Wouldn't talk about it.

'Next time why don't you do an online order?' he says, holding out his palm for the money. 'They don't always bring you sell-bys and brown bananas, you know.' He had deep grooves under both his eyes and stubble all along his jaw. For once, he wasn't wearing a suit, just a black jumper and brown cords and his work lanyard.

I grab my bag and fish out the exact right money. 'There you go.'

He takes it and heaves the bags up onto the breakfast bar. 'Oh and a message from Mr Zhang at the shop – "How's your wife's brain tumour?"' He throws me a look that could melt the ice lollies he slams in the freezer.

'How did—'

He's still eyeballing me. 'How did I know you pretend to Mr Zhang you have a brain tumour? Because I bought these things.' He holds up the three packets of blue liquorice bootlaces I had on the list I emailed him. 'And Mr Zhang said he only stocks these for Betsy, the lady with the brain tumour, and then he assumed I was your husband because "she talks about you so much."'

'Oh.'

'And she wears a beanie. And she has a baby in a papoose sometimes. Where is Emily today, by the way?'

'Asleep in her cot in my room. What did you say to him?'

'What do you *think* I said?' he spits, all pursed lips. He always gets twenty per cent more Scottish when he's appalled. 'I was struck dumb. Why did you tell him you were married to a bloke called David and you have cancer?'

'I didn't tell him *you* were my husband. I just said I had *a* husband. Called David. Who works as a roadie for Little Mix.'

'And the cancer?'

'The first time I went in there I was wearing my beanie with my hair all tucked inside it cos my roots were showing and Mr Zhang assumed.'

'He does a lot of assuming, doesn't he?' Scants leans against the cupboards, arms folded. 'Nice chap. Shame he's being played like a bloody fiddle, eh?'

Scants has a thing about the truth. He would always tell me the truth whenever I asked him about our situation as a child. Or as much of the truth as I could handle at ten years old. Maybe he was trying to make up for the fact that Dad would lie to me, all the time. Especially after he took me away from Foy.

I'm going out to see if Old Mother Hubbard needs anything, Elle. Don't open the door to strangers. Particularly if they're wearing grandmother's nighty.

Bo Peep's called. She wants me to help look for her sheep. You stay here and guard the house, Ellis. And don't answer the phone or the door.

We'll see Foy again, Ellis. I'll take you to see her as soon as the wicked emperor gives us our visitation rights.

I was a child. I'd lost everyone apart from my dad. I needed to know why. But Dad would never tell me the whole truth, however much I begged. Not being able to see Foy again. Not being able to go to our castle again. It was unimaginable. By the time I was old enough to insist he answer me properly, it was too late.

But Scants *did* tell me.

Am I going to see Foy again?

No, you're not.

What about our castle?

I'm sorry, Ellis. You can't go back to your castle. You have to stay here now.

Will those three men come and get us here?

No, I promise you, you're safe now.

I take over putting the shopping away. 'Mr Zhang said his wife had been through it as well. Grade one. They blasted it with chemo and it didn't come back. Before I knew it he was telling me which cheesecake was on special and giving me her old blonde wigs. It didn't feel right to correct him.'

Although the Cancer Beanie was unintentional, I swear it's a godsend. Nobody likes the awkwardness of taking stuff back or the agony of a queue, but if everyone thinks you've got cancer, it makes them much nicer. They either want to do something for you or they totally ignore you and want you to go away as soon as possible, so they serve you quicker. I get the best customer service with the Cancer Beanie on.

Scants tuts and huffs. 'We talked about this, you lying to everyone you meet.'

'It's not everyone. It's the odd one. Or two.'

'You still pretending to the doughnut man across the road that you're some hotshot novelist with a film deal?'

'Yeah.'

74

Scants raises his eyes to the ceiling. 'If you lie about who you are to every person, you're never going to fit in here. You're going to lose track of your lies. It's a small town, word's bound to get round.'

'I thought you wanted me to be someone else. That's what you always say: "The truth is an open door to danger."'

He has no answer to that. 'Don't lie about having cancer, that's not on. And you better tell him we're not married either.' He puts the blue bootlaces in my snack cupboard and hands me the cornflakes, tins of beans, bread, spaghetti, chocolate sponge mix, custard, and green food colouring to put in the one nearest me.

'What do I say instead then?'

'Say I'm your home help. Or your uncle. Or your pimp.' The Duke of Yorkums rubs against Scants's shin, and he nudges him out of the way.

'He's not going to believe that.'

'I don't see why not – he's bought your brain tumour, hasn't he?'

'Aww, you didn't get the kitchen roll with Woody and Buzz on?'

'No.'

'Why?'

'Because you're twenty-eight. Kettle on?'

'I'll have juice.' I tear open the KitKats. I break off the end finger, nibble the chocolate all along one edge, then all along the other side. I take the chocolate off the top, then the two ends, then separate the wafers and suck them until they dissolve.

Scants is still frowning as he's getting the teabag out of the box. I can't remember the last time I saw him smile. I think he's grown a new frown line since I saw him last, actually, slightly above the other one in between his eyebrows.

'Do you want anything to eat?' I ask him as Earl Grey jumps up onto the draining board and starts lapping at yesterday's milk in the saucer.

'No, thank you.' Scants throws me a look, pointedly, so I know he disapproves of cats on the surfaces. Scants is terrified of germs and doesn't 'do food' really, especially anything 'saucy'. I think he has some kind of phobia. He prefers meals as dry as possible, eats no vegetables and is the only person I've ever met who dreads looking at a menu. He once said he'd be happier on a permanent drip.

'When you gonna get some new lino for this floor? It looks terrible.'

'I asked the landlord when I moved in but he said it's not a priority. I ordered a rug to cover it up but it hasn't come yet.'

'It's a health hazard, that's what it is. It's not even stuck down, is it?'

I don't answer that. I don't know good lino from bad. And then we're not talking about badly cut linoleum anymore as the elephant in the room trumpets so loudly, he can no longer ignore it. 'What was it this time then?' he says as the kettle rumbles to a rolling boil. 'You said you had something in the post?'

I put on my Marigolds and remove the catalogue from the carrier bag under the sink. He takes the bag from me and opens it up. 'A catalogue?'

'Shouldn't you be wearing gloves? There could be fingerprints on it.'

He looks down at the book. 'Yeah, your postman's and about fifty other people working for Royal Mail. It's a circular.'

'Yes. But I didn't sign up for it. Look what it's selling.'

He looks around the living room. At the piles of magazines and newspapers and unopened junk mail and leaflets for money off vouchers at the garden centre and all-you-can-eat Chinese restaurants. 'You send off for a lot of catalogues.'

'Only toy catalogues and art supplies. The last thing I ordered was some glitter to make some Christmas cards. I'd have remembered ordering a coffin catalogue.'

'Well maybe you ordered it and forgot about it.'

'I did not send off for a coffin catalogue, Scants. This is serious.'

'Maybe you're on some mailing list and they sold your address to this company and that's why you're getting sent their catalogue.'

I shake my head. 'A week ago I was in a hairdresser's having my roots done and three men came in. I recognised them. Well, I recognised *one* of them. His laugh. It was them, Scants. The Three Little Pigs.'

Scants huffs. 'We've talked about this.'

'I know but I had two silent messages on my answerphone in the past week. I've got the constant feeling I'm being followed. And now these men show up.'

'Why were you in a hairdresser's anyway? We send you kits for your hair every six weeks. Have you not been getting them?'

'Yeah, but I'm sick of doing it myself. It canes my back bending over the bath. And it never looks as good. I wanted it done properly, for once.'

'Alright, keep your Garnier Nutrisse on. Chances are it wasn't them or him – the one with the laugh. It's one of your little nothings, I bet you any money.'

'I recognised his laugh. The straw-haired man. Maybe he's with a new gang?'

Scants isn't convinced. He takes his tea and, shooing Queen Georgie out of the pile of clean washing where she had been curled up asleep, sits down on the sofa. 'You're tilting at windmills again, aren't you?'

I don't know what he means but I join him on the sofa. A prolonged advertisement for Jamie Oliver's new cooking show comes on the TV, accompanied by images of stews, frying meat and a diarrhoea-coloured lamb curry. 'Join me at six for a live cook-a-long...' Scants visibly baulks and reaches for the remote.

'Kill me now,' he mutters, muting him.

I take a deep breath. This wasn't something I liked to say out loud, and Scants knew it. 'I think those three men are the same ones who killed Dad.'

'They're not,' he says plainly and starkly, sipping his too-hot tea.

'But—'

'I have told you this about ten times – the men who killed your dad are out of circulation. It's my job to monitor and review the level of risk against you at all times. That's literally my job. Two of them are in jail, posing no threat.'

'No *known* threat,' I say.

'—and the third died in hospital of sepsis following complications to remove part of his bladder which was injured in a prison fight. They're all accounted for.'

'You said there were ten in the original cartel. It could be three *other* members.'

'So who was the laughing man then, if these three were three *different* men to the ones who killed your dad?'

'I don't know, but—'

'—they're *all* accounted for, Joanne. The cartel has disbanded. There are no threats to your safety. We check every base, look under every stone. Me and the CPS, the Prison Service, all the regional organised crime units, even Border Control. We would know if anyone had slipped through the net, *believe* me.'

'Then why am I still here? Why can't I go back to my old life?'

'You're here because your alibi is working. And it's only working because you're here. Can't you just be happy?'

I shake my head. 'No. I want another identity. Joanne Haynes isn't working for me anymore. Nor is living around here. I don't fit in.'

I get the full head back groan. 'You haven't given it a chance, have you?'

'You're supposed to take it seriously when I say there's been a breach. You have a duty to protect me. I'm frightened, Scants. I'm completely on my own here.'

He scratches his eyelid. I don't think it needs scratching but he's run out of all other indicators that he's pissed off. 'In eight years, you've had four new identities: Ann Hilsom. Melanie Smith. Claire Price. Joanne Haynes—'

'I know that.'

'—and each one was because someone "looked at you funny" or you were convinced "it was The Three Little Pigs" and somehow you've persuaded the authorities you were in danger.'

'A man threw acid in my face in Liverpool.'

'No, a drunk man threw *lager* in the air when Liverpool won three-nil against Man City in the Champions League. You got in the way. This has all been checked out. Acid didn't come into it.'

'It *could* have been acid.'

'It wasn't. I can't go to them for a fifth time and apply for a court hearing and another identity because of an unsolicited catalogue and three blokes you "sort of recognised". They'd laugh me out the room.'

I move to the coffee table and sit squarely in front of him so he can't avoid looking at me. 'I knew that laugh, Scants. You said that after Scarborough if I saw or heard anything suspicious I was to call you directly.'

'This is not Scarborough. You were attacked there and that was eight years ago. Nothing has happened since.' I want to cry but I hold onto it, keep it locked in tightly in my mind box. 'The catalogue isn't anything. It's just a book.'

'For *dead people*,' I add. 'No, worse than that. For *almost* dead people.'

There's a smell – the unmistakeable smell of whisky breath. He backs off, like he's realised I've clocked it. 'Don't bullshit me, Joanne. You know I hate that.'

'I'm really not this time.'

'Did these men say anything? Give you any reason to think they knew you?'

'One held the door open for me as I left and he said "Mind how you go." And I think he had a Bristolian accent.'

Scants exhales, long and rattling. 'Look, you get a brick through your window, I can have you moved on within the hour. A forced entry, a lit firework through the letterbox, these are things I can do something about. A laugh? Junk mail? A possible accent?' He shook his head. 'Your panic button's working properly now, isn't it?'

'Yes, but even that wasn't fitted properly the first time—'

'—and you were sure the fella who came round to fix it deliberately left a wire out, yes, I've heard that one.'

I hear Emily grizzling in her cot and I go in to get her. When I come out, Scants has unmuted the TV and changed channels. *Loose Women* have a guest on, some historian. He likes old things. Art and pyramids and stuff.

I hand him the local paper that came yesterday and at first he seems nonplussed. And then he sees the front page.

TEACHER DEATH AT HOTEL: SHE WAS RAPED AND STRANGLED.

He frowns. 'Isn't this the place you work?'

'I saw her body before the police came. She was strangled, like Dad was. There were marks around her neck. Bruises. And she looked like me, Scants. Blue eyes. Red hair. Same age.'

'Did you find her?'

'No. But I saw her before they took her away. She was raped as well, Scants. You can't say I'm making this up. It's not just a coincidence. I need more protection.'

'You've been refused a protection officer because you're a Low Risk Anomaly. The chances of anyone recognising you are slim to none, you've changed a lot in eighteen years. This—' He motions towards the paper on the coffee table. 'Unrelated.'

I scuff into the kitchen to tidy up the surfaces and fold away the bags. I catch him flicking over the paper to take another look at Tessa Sharpe's happy-go-lucky face on the front page, taken from her Facebook profile. I want to believe him when he says it's unrelated. I want to believe it so much but he is unsure. I can see it in his eyes.

'I know I've lied in the past,' I say.

'You lie all the time,' he says, flipping the paper over again and picking up his mug. 'You've grown used to it. The cancer woman is the tip of the iceberg.'

'I'm not lying about this. About the funny phone calls and the coffin catalogue and the feeling of being watched. And now Tessa Sharpe. All the black hair dye in the world can't cover the fact that I *am* a redhead. I have blue eyes, same as her. They were looking for me.' I lean against the washing machine. 'I want to go home, Scants.'

He doesn't look round and his acid smile disappears. 'You *are* home.'

'This isn't home. Our castle, mine and Foy's, *that* was home.' I watch him. He's doing something slow and sly. Pouring whisky in his tea from a small canister he's taken from inside his coat. Without saying a word, he posts it back inside and sits back, eyeballing my washing on the airer.

'You should dry all this outside you know. Not healthy to dry it all in here.'

'I want to go home, Scants.'

He bangs his mug on the coffee table and heads towards the airer and without a word he begins folding my washing into an untidy pile on the sofa. 'You going to iron all this? Do you have an iron? I'm sure the budget could stretch to one if you haven't.'

'I want my real name back.'

'I can lend you an iron if you like, until you get one. And get some of that spray.'

'I was happy when I was her. I haven't forgotten it all, you know. It wasn't long enough ago. It was the only happy time. I want it back.'

Scants won't look at me. I can tell he's getting angry when he runs out of washing to fold and starts tidying away the DVD cases on the carpet in front of the TV.

I stand in front the breakfast bar, holding Emily's little warm head close to my neck for comfort. 'There was a phone-in on *This Morning* yesterday, all about closure and how sometimes you have to go back to—'

In a heartbeat, Scants swings round and points a finger right at me. 'I want no more talk about this. Nothing, do you hear me?' The room fills with whisky breath. I know it and he knows it. I don't think he even cares though. 'The truth is an open door to danger, you know that. You haven't been back to Carew, have you?'

'No. I promise, I haven't.'

'I mean it. You go back there, and we are done. They'll take away this flat, your panic alarm, they won't give you anything else, you'll be all at sea.'

'I know all this. You tell me often enough. But maybe I could—'

'Your name is Joanne Elizabeth Haynes now,' Scants thunders. 'And that's that.'

I kiss Emily's head. 'I keep forgetting.'

'That's because you keep switching roles.'

He shakes his head and looks down at Emily. 'And what about her?'

'She's my baby.'

'She's *a doll*.'

I gasp and hug Emily tighter. He's never said this to me before. I know he knew, but he's never actually said the words. He knows how much I don't want to hear them.

I smooth Emily's fluffy hair with my lips. She feels colder now. And she smells. The sweet smell of new plastic.

'Don't talk about her like that. She's my baby.'

'Since when did Amazon do mail order babies? I'm done humouring you with this. You have to immerse yourself in Joanne, forget all these other characters you play. Drown yourself in Joanne until she's unforgettable. You were born in Liverpool twenty-nine years ago next April.'

'But my birthday's on Christmas Eve Eve—'

'—you have three brothers – one moved to Brisbane as a systems analyst, one's out in Dubai and the other's in York training to be a solicitor. Your parents died in a car accident on the island of Crete ten years ago – Mr and Mrs Steven Martin Haynes.'

'They didn't—'

'—you went to art school but dropped out. Spent a gap year in India, worked with orphans in Cambodia and have moved back here because you have such fond memories of when your parents brought you all here as kids. You work as a housekeeper at The Lalique to raise enough cash to go travelling again. That's it. That is *you*.'

I sway with Emily pressed tightly against me. 'Working at The Lalique is the only truthful thing there. The *only* truthful thing.'

'Oh for fuck's sake,' he breathes out, all dramatic. 'You

accepted all this after Scarborough. "Anything to get them away from me and live a normal life," *you* said.'

He marches over and rips Emily out of my hands, throws her face down onto the sofa. She doesn't cry. At least I don't hear her.

'You horrible git.'

'You are a grown woman, so start acting like one. You think you've got problems now? Go outside and shout your *real* name and see what happens. Put your name and address on Twitter. I guarantee you'll be dead within the week.'

'Don't say that.' A tear tickles my nose. 'You said there was no threat. Sometimes I think I'd be better off dead – at least then I wouldn't be so scared all the time.'

He glances down at Emily and then at his watch. 'Fuck, I've got to get back. I've got a departmental meeting later.' He places his empty mug on the draining board, having left my lounge as neat as it was when I moved in and at no other point since.

'Will you come back again soon?'

'I don't know.' This is worrying. He usually gives me some indication of when I'll see him again, even if it's a vague 'few weeks'. As a parting shot at the door, he turns and says, 'Do me a favour, don't take the doll outside with you anymore.'

'Why?'

'You're drawing attention to yourself. Say it's gone to live with its dad.'

'*Her* dad,' I correct him. 'I can't do that. Too many people know about her.'

'Then tell everyone she's dead!'

He knows he's gone too far now. I pick up Emily from the

sofa and bury my face into the join of her cold plastic neck. Everything is breaking around me like stained glass windows. 'Why are you being so horrible?'

I refuse to look at him. I hear the door open.

'I'll keep an eye on the Tessa Sharpe case, alright? I'll do that for you. But please give me a break on the change of ID thing, hmmm? I'll call in a few days.'

I sniff. 'What do I do in the meantime?'

'Go to work. Blend in.' He glances at Emily in disdain. 'And stop lying.'

I stand up, retrieving my mints from under the shell of the little bronze tortoise on the coffee table. 'Take these for your meeting. Your breath stinks.'

7

Wednesday, 30th October

All morning, Scants's words chirrup around my head like the little birds who try to wake up Cinderella. *You have to immerse yourself in Joanne, forget all these other characters you play. Drown yourself in Joanne until she's unforgettable.*

Born in Liverpool twenty-nine years ago in April.

Three brothers – one in Brisbane. Systems analyst. One in Dubai, one York – a solicitor. Can't remember where the other one is. Parents died in Crete, ten years ago. Steven and – see, I cannot even remember my own fake mother's name.

I went to film school, no, *art* school. Dropped out. Gap year in India. Orphanage somewhere else. Came here as kids so moved back to Spurrington. I want to go travelling again so I'm saving up by working at The Lalique.

It's all complete and utter lies. And not the innocent kind of fibs I tell either. It's not like when I spin a yarn at the hairdresser's about my gorgeous husband and kids to people I won't see again or when the doughnut man asks me about my non-existent novels. That's make-believe, like me and Foy used to play. These are big fat hairy lies that stick around – my birth certificate. My passport. My job. I'm sick of it, have been since I was Melanie Smith with the job in McDonald's and

87

the sister in Burnley and the parents who'd retired abroad. I can't do it anymore. All being Joanne Haynes does is make me sad. Remind me who I'm not allowed to be:

Ellis Clementine Kemp.

Born to Daniel Kemp and Faye Ellis, childhood sweethearts. Danny was a builder, Faye a teaching assistant. Faye went through seventeen hours of labour before I was born via caesarean at 5.46 a.m. on Christmas Eve Eve. I was in Dad's arms and they'd been talking about my name – Mum's maiden name was Ellis, and something Christmassy but not too Christmassy. The smell that reminded Dad of Christmas was always the unpeeling of the first clementine. It was right as he said that that my mum stopped talking. A massive cardiac arrest, the doctors said. Major post-partum haemorrhage. Three pints of blood. A scrap of placenta left in her uterus. The coroner said it had been a 'heinous oversight for which a loving family paid dearly'. It made the papers. Dad got compensation which he used to buy our house in Smyth Road, Bristol, next to the City ground so he could watch his beloved Robins every home game.

And he brought me up alone. Girlfriends didn't stick around because Dad was unreliable. Jobs didn't stick around for long either, same reason. And Dad was sad. And when Dad was sad, he'd take risks. That's where it all started to go wrong.

How do you forget about the bricks that built you? How do you look at yourself in a mirror and be someone you know you're not? I can play pretend for a while. I can be Ann or Claire or Melanie or whoever else they want me to be, I know how to do that, but I can't just forget. That's not me. That's not Ellis Clementine Kemp.

I dragged myself in, but work was particularly diabolical today – my colleagues have found a new way to make me feel uncomfortable that they haven't tried before – instead of laughing at me or talking behind my back, they are ignoring me. Trevor responds to my questions about where my cart is and which floor they want me to start on first, but for the most part, I am a ghost. I may as well be Tessa Sharpe.

'Bye,' I call into the staff office when I clock out at 2 p.m. Nobody looks up.

It's raining hard when I step outside. I cross the road, fumbling into my bag for my capsule umbrella and some money for a bag of doughnuts, but the van's shut up shop for the day. I look across to my flat and there is a figure standing outside, hood up, green wax jacket, looking down into my patio doors. His hand is on the gate. He reaches into his pocket for his phone, checks the screen, then puts it away. He's lingering. I can't go home.

I go to the arcades. I spy Matthew at the basketball game, several strings of tickets draped around his neck.

'Oh there you are,' he says. 'Where have you been?'

'Sorry. My boyfriend took me away to Corfu for a couple of days. Little treat.'

'You don't look very brown.'

'I don't tan easily,' I say, gazing at his tickets. 'Have you won all those today?'

'Yeah,' he says proudly. 'Do you wanna go on the air hockey?' He yanks a wodge of tenners from his jeans pocket.

'Where did you get all that?'

'My dad gave it to me last night.'

'Why?'

'Guilt, I s'pose. Come on, I'll treat ya.'

He changes up two tenners for burgers, Slush Puppies and all the brass tokens we can hold in our pockets. Inside the arcades it's busy and loud and while I don't feel up to playing games, I stand alongside Matthew and watch as he does. I get the firm impression he mostly wants me there to prop up his ego. The more I tell him 'Good job' or 'Well done' or 'I'm so impressed' when he nets twenty-five air hockey pucks in a row, the more he smiles. The tickets are his thing – he wins hundreds of the things on every visit but never ever changes them for prizes at the kiosk. He must have enough for one of the larger teddies or even something electronic. But no, he only wants the tickets.

The captain of the pirate ship pops up behind a cannon and Matthew shoots him square in the face and all these bells and whistles go off like it's Mardi Gras and the machine spews hundreds of tickets out the slot.

'Wahoo! Yes!' he cries. 'Look how many I got!'

It's probably only enough to buy half a Maoam and a scented comb but I smile encouragingly. I'd like his advice, really, but I don't know where to start. And I don't want to tell him about Tessa Sharpe in case it scares him. He's got enough on his plate.

We play on all the machines until it's time for him to go home and he says 'Laters' at the door as he's checking his phone, like it's no big deal for him to leave. Probably because it isn't. But it is for me. Because it means I'm alone again. And that man might still be hanging around outside my flat.

Out of the arcades, I head down one of the side streets to the only shop I know along that row – the only place I'll be safe. Seaside Bridal. I sneak under the awning of the wool shop, closed for the afternoon, and put my umbrella on the ground, fumbling inside my bag for my little pillow. I reach under my coat and stuff it up inside my jumper. Then I make my way down to the shop, perfecting my waddle.

'Hi there,' says a blonde lady in the grey suit behind the till. 'I'm Cathy, welcome to Seaside Bridal. Can I be of any assistance?' She blinks fast and smiles falsely.

'Hi there,' I say, blowing out my stomach and patting it. 'Can you make a beached whale look pretty for her big day?'

'Ahhh congratulations!' she beams. 'When are you due?'

'Oh, not until the spring,' I say. 'Do you mind if I sit down? Getting a twinge.'

'Of course, of course,' she says, moving a stack of magazines from a grey velvet chaise longue. I sit down and from there I get a bird's eye view of the street. I can't see the man in the hood.

'My Sarah's due around the same time. Third grandchild.'

'Lovely.'

'Is it your first?'

'Yes,' I say. 'Me and Kaden have been trying for years so it's a bit special.'

I rub my bloated stomach which contains little more than two bowls of Crunchy Nut Cornflakes, a steak and onion pasty and a can of Fanta.

'Aww, well that's fantastic,' says Cathy. 'You getting all the cravings then?'

'Oh yes. All the time. I sent my Kaden out for a jar of pickled cucumbers at ten o'clock last night. I just fancied some with a slice of malt loaf.'

The woman laughs.

'Ooh!' I cry. 'It kicked!' She seems delighted for me. One younger woman offers me a glass of water. I decline, politely.

'I remember it well,' she says and sits beside me on the chaise longue. 'So, are you planning your wedding for next year then, or before the baby's born?'

'After the baby's born, ideally, so I'd need to factor that in to the tailoring.'

'No problem.'

I see the man again. Lingering. Loitering. Waiting for someone. I don't think I know him. He's jittery. Won't keep his feet still. And then he goes out of eyeshot.

Cathy is still chit-chatting about my options – accessories, fittings dates, materials, hairdressers. I can't go back to Curl Up and Dye, of course, but she doesn't recommend them anyway.

'I've seen cockroaches in there before now,' she says, all serious-face. 'And I know someone who tried the lip fillers and ended up looking like one of those fish.'

She laughs and suggests we make an arrangement to go through the racks properly next week 'when I have more time'. I can't think of anything else to keep me in the shop, so I agree and she puts my name down in a little book, then I waddle out.

I need to find somewhere else to hide. The man in the hood stands further up the road on the opposite side. He's tall. Definitely not one of the men from the hairdresser's. Maybe he's not after me. Maybe he's waiting for someone and this *is* a 'little nothing'. But why was he outside my flat? After a while he saunters back off towards the seafront. Loping walk. He's waiting for someone.

I head for the high street. I need to be around people. The farmer's market is on as it's the last Wednesday of the month.

I daren't look behind me but when I get to the corner of the street I do. The man is there, at the end. Looking around. But it's not normal looking around – it's the sort of looking around you do when you want to do something else. When you're up to something. I still can't see his face clearly.

Tessa Sharpe. Tessa Sharpe. Tessa Sharpe. It's all I can think about. He found her, he will find me. He'll do to me what he did to her.

I lose myself in the crowds, keeping my wits sharp and my umbrella firm in my grasp. I chit-chat with stallholders about their cheese, local gins, hand-woven rugs and organic vegetables. The veg man knows me as Dr Mary Brokenshire – he asks me about his wart. The plant lady thinks I'm Betsy Warre on chemo – she once gave me fifteen per cent off a pot of basil. The couple running the gin stall think I'm author Charlotte Purfleet and a connoisseur of fine wines, a by-product of attending so many book launches. They all ask after Emily and I tell them the same thing – *she's well, thanks, I'm on my way to collect her*. My dread dissipates with every new lie. Nobody bats an eye. No one here knows who I am – I am amongst my friends.

And then I spy the man in the hood, Gallaghering along outside the fish shop. He's pretending to look in the window. Nobody's that interested in mackerel. The rain has eased off but his hood is still up, his sunglasses on now. I have even less chance of recognising him. He walks my way. He's looking for me.

I can't go home, I'll be a sitting duck. And I can't go to work, they all hate me. Can't call Scants again.

I have a flash of inspiration. *I'll go to the gym*. I'll go to Kaden. He did offer.

And so I walk, fast. Using a family eating pasties as a shield, I dodge through the crowds, all the while thinking which is the quickest route. I duck down a side street towards the main road, looking behind me for signs of the man. I dart into an alley and race along it towards the main road where people walk dogs, families push pushchairs, and there are constant cars. Witnesses. Safety.

I've passed the entrance to the newsagent's when the door flies open and out strides a very angry woman with piercing green eyes, wearing pink Ugg boots over pink leggings and a faded blue tabard. She owns the place with her husband but I don't know her name – I've seen her telling kids off for reading comics for too long.

'Oi, you,' she shrieks. 'Joanna, isn't it? My Alfie brings your paper on his round.'

'Yeah, how is he? How is he getting on at school now?'

'That's none of your business,' she snarls. I've no idea why she's so angry. 'And you can take this back.' She shoves a box into my stomach, the cardboard dented at the sides. It's the Build a Burger game I ordered for him off eBay.

'This was a present,' I tell her. 'I didn't want it back. He was a bit upset one morning on his round and he told me about these two bullies at school and I wanted to cheer him up so I gave him this. That was all.'

'You been giving him sweets as well, int ya?'

'Only tubes of Smarties. He likes the purple ones.'

'Always leaving little presents for him at the gate. He don't want them.'

'He always seems to take them,' I smile.

'You laughing at me?'

94

'No, no I'm not. I just wanted to cheer him up, that was all.'

'You're bleeding grooming him, I know your game you fucking perv.' And without another word she swings back and thrusts her fist forwards at my face, hitting me with such force I lose all balance and collapse against a garden wall. 'Leave my son alone. And get your fucking paper from another place from now on, ya paedo bitch.'

'I didn't mean anything by it,' I cry, holding my nose and mouth and certain I'm going to feel blood there but nothing's coming. I can taste it at the back of my throat so I know something's broken. It throbs and aches like I've never known pain before.

Why is it so wrong, giving a child presents? I'm not a paedo, I'm not grooming him, why would I be grooming him? I don't want anything back from him. Am I a pervert *and* a liar now? My emotions bubble up and I'm in tears by the time I get to the gym, slightly concussed and fuzzy about the eyes.

All I want is to see Kaden, to be in his safe orbit. But Kaden is on his way out. I stand in the car park, checking my watch – it's 4 p.m. He's in a rush, needs to be somewhere. He's doing the long goodbye to some other PTs in Reception – that thing when you're halfway out the door but people keep talking to you.

And then he's outside. Rucksack tight to his back. He seems purposeful – needs to be somewhere. Running late. Now's not the time to counsel me. But I want to know what's so important. I want to know what he does when he's not at the flat and not at the gym. What if it's a date? That woman in the leotard he was flirting with at the gym. Ugh, please no, not her. Not anyone. I want him. I saw him first.

He's on his motorbike in seconds but he doesn't turn right out of the car park towards the seafront and our flats. He turns left and roars away.

I've never been cheated on before. It hurts all over. I feel sick to my guts.

If you get scared again, or if anyone calls who you don't wanna see, call me. If I'm not home, I'll be at the gym.

The fucking liar. And now I have no one.

Middle of the Summer holidays,
eighteen years ago...

8

One Saturday, Auntie Chelle and Uncle Stu get cover for the pub so we can all go and spend a day at the beach. Stu and Chelle always head down to Cornwall whenever they can as it's where Stuart was born and where they met. They named Isaac, Paddy and Foy after places in Cornwall too. Today we're going down to St Agnes, a place they haven't been before called Trevaunance Cove, and as a treat, me and Foy are allowed to sit in the open boot of Uncle Stu's estate on the way down, guarding all the picnic stuff. We pretend we're stowaways on a cart travelling across the desert. Kidnapped queens – Queen Charlotte and Queen Genevieve. We tie our wrists with friendship bracelets and let down our hair so it looks more dramatic.

Paddy and Isaac are in the back seat, playing games that *bing* and *crash* every now and then. They've got their earphones in.

We arrive at the cove and walk down the steep steps to the beach at the bottom, and for the first hour it's the day I hoped it would be. There's a ready tide that me and Foy run down to the shoreline to greet, tilting our buckets full of water and running back to build the moat of our enormous sandcastle. We aren't just building it, we are in it. Inside our minds. Our flowing gowns kiss the sandy walls of the hallways, our laughter echoes along the corridors. We can almost hear the tinkling of the priceless jewels that hang around our necks and the sound of the knights' horses clopping into the courtyard and bugles tooting out the national anthem heralding our arrival.

'Call us by our new names, Mum,' says Foy. 'We're not Foy and Ellis anymore, I'm Queen Genevieve and Ellis is Queen Charlotte.'

'Actually, I'll be Mary today,' I tell her. 'Because I've got lots of children.'

'Okay, we're Queen Genevieve and Queen Mary. Call us that, Mum, alright?'

'Alright then, Queen Latifah, come here and get some sun cream on your back.' Auntie Chelle's wearing a wide-brimmed straw hat and a red and navy swimming costume that makes her look like a film star. She only normally wears slouchy T-shirts and long dresses. Everyone's different at the beach. Happier. The sun can do that to people. It gets Uncle Stu out of his *Doctor Who* T-shirt and jeans and into baggy shorts, and the boys off their Nintendos. Isaac buys himself a boogie board from the surf shack along the seafront and he and Paddy take turns with it in the water.

And we eat. Every wonderful thing you can imagine. Sausage rolls and chicken nuggets and crisps and pinwheels and soft baps filled with corned beef and lettuce. Then for pudding chocolate fingers and Jammie Dodgers and me and Foy eat them in our special way, prising apart the biscuits, licking out the jam, putting them back together and eating them round and round until a small disc remains, all spitty and soft between our thumbs. It's only when I get a stomach ache that I stop. It's the happiest day. The kind of happy you don't notice you are, until you're not.

As we're finishing our castle and looking for shells to decorate it with, I see blood on my foot. It's only a little spatter but it still shouldn't be there. I must have cut myself, I think – Chelle has bought us new buckets and spades and one of the spades has a jagged edge. But there isn't a scratch anywhere. I follow the trail to see it's coming from me. Down my leg. From *there*.

A horrible thought descends and my heart quickens. I think back to the one biology lesson we had about periods. And I realise it's very definitely here, sitting in my knickers. No warning or fanfare. Just there, aged ten and eight months, ricocheting off the rubber ring around my shaking ankles. I quickly wrap myself in my beach towel and race across the beach and up towards the restaurant and adjoining toilets in the car park before anyone notices I've gone.

The toilets are dark and grimy and the tiled floor is covered in globules of wet sand and shreds of paper. I sneak into a cubicle and lock the door. The blood's patched on the gusset of my costume, inside and out. So undeniable, so red. I wind up a thick coil of clean toilet paper and wad it against myself, pulling my costume back up. My sickness comes upon me in great waves. I remember the biology lesson. *Once you've got your period, you're a woman,* the teacher announced. But this is so wrong. I'm not a woman. I'm a little girl. I'm Elly Belly Cinderelly. I'm Squish. I watch the trickle on my leg dry to a crispy streak.

Outside the cubicle, groups of screaming, sandy children slap about on the tiles, washing hands, calling for their mothers to help them pull up their costumes. A little girl peeks under the door at one point but quickly disappears. My cheeks burn with shame, my tummy aches. I don't ever want to come out.

I stare at the cold breeze blocks as another large piece of my embarrassingly female jigsaw slots into place. First there were the small fleshy lumps on my chest. Now this. 'It's not fair.'

A while later I hear my name being called. A boy's voice – Paddy.

'Ellis? Are you in there? Ellis? Excuse me, have you seen a little girl with red hair come in here? She's ten years old, blue eyes, smiley face?'

'No, sorry love.'

I hitch my feet up so he can't see them under the door.

'Ellis? Are you there?' *Bang bang bang.*

'Go away.'

'Oh thank god.' I hear him calling for Auntie Chelle. 'Mum, she's here. She's in here. Ellis, everyone's been looking for you. Dad nearly had the coastguard out. What is it? Has something happened?'

'Yes.' I have to say it. I have to spit it out of my mouth where it's burning a hole. 'I've got some blood.'

'Have you hurt yourself?'

'No.'

'Oh. *That* blood?'

I can't hold back my tears. 'I don't want it.'

'It's alright, don't worry. We'll look after you. I'll go get Mum.'

'Dad'll be cross.'

'Why would he be cross?'

'We can't afford it.'

'You can't afford to have a… period?'

I shake my head, even though he can't see me.

'Please open the door, Ellis. Nobody's angry with you, I swear.'

By the time I come out, they're all standing there. Paddy, Isaac, Uncle Stu, Auntie Chelle and Foy. And I feel like a fool. A stupid clown-sized fool like the one we saw at the circus who got covered in custard pies then tripped and fell head-first into the mound of feathers. But Auntie Chelle immediately folds me into the softest hug ever and the humiliation falls away like the shell pieces of a broken egg. Foy hugs my back so that between them I'm completely enclosed. I feel someone else stroke my hair.

'Am I going to die?'

'Course you're not,' says Uncle Stu, rubbing the top of my head. 'Isaac dived off the rocks cos he thought you were drowning.'

'Right,' says Chelle. 'Boys – I think it's time for some ice cream, don't you? And me and Ellis will go up the town and find a chemist.'

'And me! And me!' says Foy.

Chelle looks at me. 'Is that alright?' I nod. She strokes my hair away from my face. 'You've got nothing to worry about, my darling. Nothing at all.'

And that makes me cry again. They're all being too nice. She clears everyone away but Foy, who refuses to leave my side and we go back to the car and drive into St Agnes to find a pharmacy. I'm walking like a duck cos the sanitary towel Auntie Chelle's given me to wear in my knickers feels so big. Foy copies my walk which makes me laugh. Chelle parks on double yellow lines.

'Let them give me a ticket, this is more important than parking.'

Chelle buys a pack of wet wipes and two boxes of pads and all the while Foy is very quiet. Even though she holds my hand around the shop, she's looking at me like she's wondering who I am now. Chelle shows me what to do back in the car park toilets, when all the others have gone back down to the beach. It's like I have a small mattress between my legs when I walk and everything's wrong. The world is spinning a different way now. This wasn't in the plan for summer.

I don't feel like playing castles after that.

I sit on Chelle's beach towel in Foy's spare costume – I don't know where mine went. Foy sits next to me, itching to go and play on the boogie board because it's her turn. She draws pictures in the wet sand and I have to guess what they are.

'Mum?' says Foy. 'Can I start my period now too?'

Chelle laughs. 'Well you can't actually choose when it comes, baby girl, it just comes. You'll get yours when Mother Nature says it's time.'

'But I want a period, too.'

'You really don't,' I tell her. 'It makes my tummy hurt.'

Chelle hugs me close to her. 'It's really not that big a deal, honestly. The stomach ache disappears and you'll have the blood for a few days and then it'll go.'

'And that's it?'

'No, it'll come again next month. You'll have to keep track.'

'How do I do that?'

'I'll get you a diary. You do get used to it. You have to remember when it's due and get some pads in and Bob's your uncle.'

'I don't have any money for pads.'

'Your dad'll give you some, don't worry about that. I'll have a word with him.'

'He doesn't have any money either.'

'He'll have money for *that*, I'm sure,' she says on an out-breath.

Foy draws me a picture in the sand of a cat. 'That's Princess Tabitha,' she announces. 'And she's the castle cat and she makes sure none of the evil sewer rats get in and steal the cheese. Shall I go and get some shells and we can carry on decorating the outside?' I nod. When she's run off, her heels kicking up the sand behind her, I ask Chelle the question that's been nudging me since the train station.

'Can we stay with you, Auntie Chelle?'

'You *are* staying with us, sweetheart. All summer.'

'No, I mean me *and* Dad?'

'Well your dad's got to work, hon.'

'He lost his job again.'

She strokes my hair out of my eyes where the wind has blown it. She smells lemony – Verbena and fresh cotton – and her curls are soft on my nose. All the sunshine has gone from her face. 'What was it this time?'

'I dunno. He came back to the hotel one afternoon and said the manager was a witch who kept trying to poison him with bad apples.'

'Typical,' she says. Then she turns to me. 'Did you say hotel? What hotel?'

'The New Moon. It's more of a pub really but not as nice as your pub. There's too many motorbikes at night.'

'Why were you staying there? Did he have to stay overnight with work?'

'No, we live there now.'

'A pub? Since when?'

'They've got rooms. And tropical fish. The landlord lets me feed them. And their cat sleeps on my bed sometimes. He's called Jasper.'

'How long have you lived there, Ellis?'

'Since the fire.'

It's like I've jabbed her in the side with a needle. She jolts away from me. 'What fire?' It's like she's getting angry. And my answers are making her angrier so I don't answer. She cuddles me close again. 'Darling, what fire?'

'Our house. It caught on fire when I was at school.'

Then she sort of laughs. 'Your dad didn't tell me about this. So… when can you move back?'

I shrug. 'Dad says we can't.'

'And you're both living in a B&B until the insurance money comes through, that's the game, is it?'

'Don't think Dad had any insurance. I heard him shouting on the phone.'

'Of course he didn't,' she sighs as Isaac comes padding up the beach with a pair of broken goggles. She mends them without even looking and hands them back to him. 'Tell Daddy I want a word,' she tells him, and he pads off back to the sea.

Foy returns with half a bucket full of white shells and we decorate the castle. She only asks me once about the P word – 'can you feel it coming out?' For the rest of the afternoon there's a lot of quiet talking going on between Chelle and Uncle Stuart. The boys play football and me and Foy decorate the castle and play that Alanis Morrissette song over and over on Isaac's Walkman. We're planning a new routine.

In the car on the way home, it's quiet. Paddy's asleep before we hit the motorway and Isaac's in a mush with Foy because we've drained his batteries.

Me and Foy lie down in the boot, our heads together so we can read each other's thoughts. She's murmuring Alanis in my ear, purposely getting all the lyrics wrong.

'*It's like Wayne on your wedding day…*'

'Shut up,' I giggle.

'No. Shan't.'

So I join in. '*And isn't it moronic… dontcha think?*'

And she laughs as much as I hoped she would. Even though I don't know what moronic means – I've just heard Isaac use it a few times today.

'I hope you're not singing rude words back there,' Auntie Chelle calls back.

'No we're not,' we both sing and snuggle down again. And it's like nothing happened. We've had a normal, nice day at the beach. And I'm not a woman, I'm still a girl. And Auntie Chelle's not cross with Dad, she's chatting and laughing with Uncle Stu. And Foy is by my side.

'I hope you can come and live with us,' Foy whispers. 'You can stay in my room on the zed-bed and your dad can have the back bedroom. That's what Mum said.'

'Did she?'

'Yeah. Then you can go to my school. You can be my sister.'

And she tucks herself in beside me in the boot under the check blanket and I have my Miss Whiskers Cat and she has Thread Bear and we fall asleep, heads together so we can share our dreams.

9

Scants isn't answering his mobile so I try his work number. It connects on the third ring but it's an answerphone. Someone picks up halfway through the message but it's not Scants's voice – it's some woman's.

'Gina Hewer.'

'I'd like to speak to Neil Scantlebury please?'

'Who's calling?'

'This is Joanne Haynes.'

'Oh hello Joanne. I'm Neil's colleague. Sorry he's still off on sabbatical. Will be until further notice.'

'Sabbatical? Why?'

'He's been off about four months. Did he not say? Can I help you at all?'

'Never mind.'

I click off and slump against the wire fencing, my face still aching all over from being thumped by Alfie's mum. I've only just noticed how much pain I'm in. It's like a permanent ice cream headache. I step outside the phone box. Where do I go? Scants is ignoring me. My would-be husband Kaden has got another woman. And I'm being followed by between one and three bad men who all want to kill me.

What hellish direction do I go in first? Times like these (well, not exactly like these) I would dash home and sit on the bed cuddling Emily for a while to calm my nerves. But she doesn't smell right anymore. I've put her in the wardrobe now.

I want to talk to Scants.

And as if by magic, my phone starts ringing in my pocket. It's him.

'Scants? Thank god, thank god you called!'

'Why are you ringing my work phone?'

'I really need to speak to you.'

'You *always* "really need to speak to me." Do not call my work phone, alright? Use my mobile.'

'You never answer your mobile.'

'What do you want, Joanne?'

'I don't know where to start. I've been attacked, in the street. By a woman. The woman from the newsagent's.'

'Why? What happened?'

'Well her son delivers my paper and she doesn't like the fact that I've been leaving sweets out for him. And a board game I thought he'd like—'

I hear a muttered *Fuck's sake*. 'I warned you it could look like grooming.'

'I WASN'T GROOMING HIM! I was just being his friend.'

'Like you're "just being" a bestselling novelist, or "just being" a mother of five and "just being" an old school friend of Meghan Markle—'

'The girl *looked* like Meghan Markle, I said—'

'—and like you're "just being" a mother to a five-week-old baby who never eats, cries or ages. Anything else to add to the list?'

'Stop it, Scants.'

'The truth really hurts you, doesn't it? You even made the papers in Manchester claiming you were in that tram smash.'

'I was nearby.'

'Exactly. *Nearby*. Not in it. Not badly injured. *Nearby*. Seventeen streets away at the time, in fact, but don't let a little thing like fact get in the way now, will you?'

'Scants, please...'

'You befriend kids who aren't yours, you go to funerals for people you don't know, don't even *vaguely* know. You try wedding dresses on even though you've got no intention of getting married. And you go about with a doll pretending it's a new-born baby. I have told you to stop and you won't listen. I can't deal with this anymore.'

'You have to.'

'No, I don't. I don't have to, actually. You bring me more headaches and more paperwork than anyone else I have to deal with. I'm supposed to be off work at the moment. I'm gonna transfer your case officially to a colleague. Any problems you have from now on, you'll have to go through Gina.'

'No! No, I don't want anyone else. You've been on this case since I was ten. You're like a dad to me.'

'Yeah, well I'm *not* your dad. Don't make this any more difficult, alright? It's too much for me right now.'

'Why? Why is it too much? What's happening to you?'

He laughs. He laughs for longer than is comfortable. That's because it's not funny. 'My wife died. About a year ago. Thanks for finally asking.'

'You said she got better.'

'She did. Then she got worse. Then she was hospitalised. And then she died.'

'You never said anything.'

'You never asked. You're so wrapped up in your own little world, you don't notice anything else happening around you. Your paranoia, your fake baby, your kiddy friends. Your lies. That's all y'are. Lies.'

I can't hold back the tears any longer. 'You can't come off my case.'

'Oh, is that it for the sympathy, is it? Back to you now?'

'Scants, I'm sorry about your wife, I really am.'

'No you're not. You're sorry you finally pushed me over the edge. So I'll renege and go back to how things were and then in a few weeks' time, you'll call me saying you've cut yourself or you're gonna jump off the pier there and I'll jump in the car and pootle up the M5, M6, and then you'll say *What were you so worried about?*'

'Scants—'

'There are people whose folders I put to the bottom of the pile so I can deal with your crap first. I did your shopping last week as a final act to see how you were. And I think, actually, aside from the constant lying and paranoia, you're doing okay. So I refuse to feel bad about this. I'm passing you over to Gina next week she's always found your case fascinating, so she can have you.'

He's about the hang the phone up. He's about to say goodbye and leave me forever. So I have to do it. I have to say it.

'If you leave me, I'll tell your boss you're drinking again. I'll tell him you were drunk when you visited me last.'

Silence. He's still there. I can hear his breaths.

'You think he doesn't know that? You think he would blame me, after six years of nursing my wife, for hitting the bottle again?'

'I need you, Scants, please. Please tell me what to do. I don't know what to do.'

'I need you to leave me the fuck alone,' he snarls. 'How about you do *that*?'

And then the dialling tone goes dead.

*

Scants has never spoken to me like that. Never ever. He's laughed at me, called me an idiot, and he's done the whole *Don't you dare ask me about finding your family* thing many times. But he's never blown up at me like that. I don't like it.

And I don't like it when he says I'm grooming those kids – I'm *so* not! I just like kids. I like being around them cos they're not adults. And being around adults only reminds me that I'm not a kid anymore. That's why people have children, isn't it? To relive their childhoods again and again, and then again through their grandchildren. Because being an adult isn't all it's cracked up to be. And there's no going back.

I don't want to go back to the flat – Kaden will be there. Probably humping that hussy from the gym. I could go into work but they'll all be there, whispering in corners, judging me and laughing if I trip over that wrinkle in the hallway carpet.

It's getting dark. Where do I go? I feel like my nose is about to bleed but nothing else comes. I sniff and sniff so anything that was thinking about dripping out goes back up inside my head. I fish my beanie hat out of my bag and go towards a warm welcome. Towards safety – Mr Zhang's Chinese Supermarket.

'Hey Brave Lady Betsy!' The shop doors are open for a delivery of garden furniture and Mr Zhang calls out to me from his crouched position stacking shelves with bleach. He smiles so widely and it's unusual for his face to do so. Ask any customer – they do not get the same welcome from Mr Zhang as Betsy Warre. 'How are you?'

'I'm good today, thank you, Mr Zhang. A little tired, you know.'

'Ah all the chemical shit, yes?' He's staring at my nose.

'Yes,' I smile meekly. 'I tripped yesterday. I felt a bit faint after my chemo session and tripped down the steps at the hospital.'

'Oh my fuck,' he cries. 'Bloody steps. Sit down, I do your shopping?'

'No, honestly I'm fine. Just need to remember to get some tissues. Keeps bleeding. I'm really fine, Mr Zhang, thank you. I like to keep moving if I can.'

'Okay then Brave Lady, okay, you move, you move.'

'How about yourself and your wife? Are you keeping well?'

'Oh yes, very well.' He tells me about his wife's operation and how much of her cancer they cut out. He accompanies me around the whole store, carrying my basket because my 'weak chemo arms' can't possibly manage it and affords me four free cans of Whiskas and an extra kitchen roll with pink flowers on it. 'I served your husband the other day. You not feeling good then?'

'No, but I'm much better now. He's not my husband actually. He's my... dad.'

'Your dad?' He laughs. 'Oh my fuck, I thought he your husband. He young!'

'He looks young, yeah. Good genes.'

'You not look like him. You black hair, he blonde.'

'I was adopted.'

'Ahhhhh, I see. You not come out of him.'

'No, I didn't come out of him.'

He has some brand new axes on special offer behind the counter and we share a joke about axe murderers as he's ringing through my purchases. 'You tell your husband that he needs to do your shopping more often. Let you rest and get your strength.'

'I will, Mr Zhang. Thank you.'

'Bye now, Betsy, you take good care of yourself.'

*

Feeling strengthened by Mr Zhang's compassion I decide to head back to the flat, feed the cats, and then go to the police and tell them about The Three Little Pigs. It doesn't have to be Scants. Why on earth didn't I think of it before? The police don't know me in this town. Yeah, that's what I'll do. I'll explain everything.

But when I get back, something feels off kilter. I step into the main hallway and immediately my senses are heightened. The light bulb's gone. I use my phone light to guide me towards my pigeonhole – no post today. There's a smell I don't recognise. An aftershave. Not Kaden's aftershave, I'd remember it. And the junkies upstairs don't have money for aftershave. I get inside my flat and the cats all start meowing for me. Their litter trays stink. And the smell is there too. Stronger. Like someone's just left.

I switch on all the lights and check the rooms – nothing and no one. Paranoia again. I let out the cats who want to go, feeding the ones inside who don't.

'Alright, let's sort you out first,' I say, and it takes me a good hour but by the time I'm done, they're all fed and watered and clean. But I do a lot of bending over. Bending down to put the bowls by the door. Bending down in my room for The Duchess who likes to sleep in the airing cupboard. Scraping out the litter trays into bin liners. And before I know what's happening, my nose is bleeding like a tap.

'Oh my god.'

There's so much blood. It gets everywhere. It's on my bedroom carpet, in the bathroom, the sofa. My chest clenches. It won't stop. And I'm back on the beach, aged ten, crying and panicking and coiling ragged toilet roll around my little hand.

'It's only a nosebleed,' I sing-song, dashing about the flat looking for clean tea towels but realising all too soon that I *have* no clean tea towels or bath towels and so I'm wadding toilet paper again because that's all I know how to do. I want to be sick. I watch the blood bloom on the tissue again and again where it won't stop.

The bin stinks so I wrap a good thick coil of kitchen paper around my hand and stuff it against my nose, taking the bag through the patio doors and up the steps and round to the bin sheds. Of course, that's when I hear the roar of the motorbike as a headlight sweeps onto the gravel parking area. I couldn't have timed it more perfectly if I tried – it's him. Kaden. I momentarily forget how to breathe.

And he is standing here, on the gravel, inches away from me. I force myself calm by deep breathing as I drop the bag into the bin and close the lid.

'Oh, hiya,' he says, taking off his helmet. 'Popped out for some fish and chips. Fancied a pig out tonight. Been a loooooooong day.'

I make to leave but I at least acknowledge his greeting with a 'Oh, right,' and a misplaced giggle so I'm not being rude.

'What's happened to you?' he asks, squinting in the brightness of the headlight.

'Oh. I've got a nosebleed,' I say as I'm overtaken by a sudden sweat all over my back and head.

'Shit, looks pretty bad.' He dismounts the bike and comes closer. I can't smell perfume on him. It's too dark to see any love bites.

'Does it?'

'Yeah, that tissue's pretty red.'

'Oh god. It's alright, I'll be alright.' I can't breathe by this point. 'I don't actually want to talk about it cos I feel a bit woozy.'

'Alright, alright,' he says and before I know what is happening he's behind me, holding me. 'Come on, let's get you inside. Lean on me.'

And so I *do* lean on him as he coils my arm around his neck and manoeuvres me round to the front of the building, unlocks the door and helps me inside. He plonks his bike helmet on the coffee table and grabs a fresh wad of kitchen roll.

'Sit on the edge there and pinch that part of your nose for me. That's it.'

'It hurts.'

'You need to stay there for a good ten minutes or more if you can. Until it stops.'

'I can't breathe.'

'Breathe through your mouth. Relax, that's right. Look, you don't have to tell me if you don't want to but – was it him who did this? The one you're afraid of?'

'What? No, I just get nosebleeds sometimes, that's all.' He doesn't believe me but he doesn't press me on it. It's enough for him to suspect more but not confirm it.

He checks around the room. 'Where's Emily?' I don't know what to say. So I let him guess. 'Has he taken her? Your ex?'

I bow my head and give a little half nod.

'Right, I'm calling the police...'

'No, wait,' I say. He has his phone out and the numbers ready to dial. 'I said he could take her. I took her from him in the first place. He won custody. Fair and square. It's my fault.' I fake-sob into his shoulder. No love bites, I notice. Maybe he wasn't with her after all? Why did he say it's been a 'looooong day'? He left work early. He strokes my hair and I let out an involuntary whelp which I pretend is a sob.

'God, I'm so sorry, Joanne. I'm so sorry.'

'Oh I've dripped on your trousers,' I sniff, pulling back.

'It's alright,' he says, placing a gloved hand on my arm and he smiles with such a sparkle I can't concentrate on being mad at him. 'Have you got any frozen peas?'

'No. I don't really eat veg.'

'We need to get an ice pack on it, really. You got any ice? Anything cold?'

'I've got some katsu curry chicken breasts in the freezer. It's a box though.'

'I'm gonna go out and grab my fish and whack it in my oven, and then I'll see what I've got in mine.'

'Oh, I'll be alright.'

'You're *not* alright. It's bleeding through that tissue. I won't be long.'

So I sit there, on the edge of the sofa, waiting. Face throbbing, cheeks burning with shame. Mouth all dry.

And then I spot it, flashing inside his helmet on the coffee table. His phone. He's had an email. From someone called Cynthia Currie.

My heart sinks. *Kaden and Cynthia sitting in a tree, K-I-S-S-I-N-G.*

But the email seems to be about a job.

Re: December job in Liverpool of any interest?

But I can't read any more of Cynthia's message because the message flashes off.

And then I remember the morning I had the meltdown. And he took me to Full of Beans and bought me a milkshake. And I saw him punch the code in on his phone.

Three, lots of noughts, then three again. I listen for footsteps on the stairs.

I don't think anymore. I reach for it and punch in the number. His home screen flashes up. Unlocked. Accessible. Here goes everything. He has several emails, all about possible jobs. Nothing untoward. Nothing questionable. Cynthia's his boss! Oh, the relief. I click back to the Home screen and my finger hovers over Photos.

There could be another woman on there. Evidence of their romance. Them on holiday on some beach kissing under a waterfall. Rosy-cheeked bed selfies. The pain in my chest overtakes the throb in my nose. Still no footsteps on the stairs.

I need to look. Win, lose or draw, I need to know. So I click on the app.

My Albums. Cover photo is the sunset, looking out towards the Lakes.

WhatsApp. Photos of himself, posing before a mirror. Full abs. One from above. Sparkling eyes. There's one of him holding his winky so it's all strangled and red.

I can't catch my breath. 'Oh my god.'

I don't want to venture any further inside these photos but I have to know. What he does, who he talks to, what kind of messages he sends. I go into WhatsApp. Lots of messages to lots of different women. Pictures of the winky again. Pictures from them too. I click out, beginning to feel sick. He's into sexting.

I go back to Photos. They tell me the Locations he's visited in the past year. The gym. The park. A service station on the M6. Spain last summer. Lots of London.

Screenshots. Personal training invoices. I haven't got time to go through them.

Then I hear him coming down the main stairs. I click on the main Camera Roll.

And a tessellation of little images comes up. Long shots. Close ups. Zooms. All pictures of a young woman.

All pictures of me.

10

Even the doughnut man Johnny notices my good mood this morning.

'Hey, Charlotte. You're looking chipper today.' Then he frowns. 'What's happened to your face?'

'Oh I tripped over a cat on the steps. It's no biggy.' My Maybelline foundation has done its best but the bruising's come out now so the 'I just get nosebleeds' conceit won't wash with anyone.

'You ought to get that seen to. The usual, is it?'

'I'll be alright. It doesn't hurt so much today.' Nothing does. 'I was going to settle for a bottle of water, Johnny, but go on then, you've tempted me.'

'I'll put a fresh batch on for you,' he winks, lowering the basket into the fryer. There's no sign of the strange man – it's like he was never here. The sun is warm already and it feels wonderful on my aching face. 'So what's with all the smiles today then? Any particular reason?'

'Not really,' I lie. 'Well, we sold my last novel *Master of None* to Thailand and Vietnam. So that was great news.'

'Amazing! Well done you. How many countries is that now?'

'Oh I forget,' I laugh. 'Around fifty-odd. I think. Thereabouts.'

'Quite the international superstar, aren't you?' he grins, flicking the doughnuts over in the basket. 'I had a look for your books on Amazon actually.'

'Oh did you?'

'Yeah. Couldn't find them.'

I frown. 'That's strange.'

'Or Book Depository. Waterstones had never heard of you.'

'My publisher might have taken them off for the time being – they're all getting new covers.'

'Ah, I see.'

'I make most of my money abroad anyway. I'm really big in Russia. And Bahrain.' They're the first two places I can think of.

'Ah, right,' he says and I can't tell if I've convinced him or not. 'So why all the smiles today then? Got a big date tonight?'

'Oh no, nothing like that,' I smile. 'I don't get the chance. Always too busy writing. No, I'm just happy today. It's lovely and sunny. All's good.'

He flips the basket out onto the kitchen roll. 'Thought I might have competition,' he winks at me again, ripping a bag down from the string. I can tell he's only flirting harmlessly, like he does to all women who stop at his van. But as I'm walking away, flicking my scarf over my shoulder, it occurs that I must be more attractive than I think. I have TWO men lusting after me – Johnny the doughnut man *and* Kaden Cotterill, the hunk from upstairs.

Two men after me. Who'd have thought?

Today I'm officially In Love. And it feels fantastic. I had a wonderful evening with Kaden, after I'd found the pictures of me on his phone. I mean, at first I was confused and disturbed and when he came back downstairs with the peas I was crying and when he found out why he got angry because I'd been looking through his phone. Then it all came out – how he'd got this enormous crush on me and couldn't find the words. And he knew I'd had 'a tough time with Emily's dad' and he didn't think I was ready for another relationship.

And then we kissed. Well I kissed him. On the lips. For eight seconds.

I'm blushing at the memory. The *actual* memory.

He shared his fish and chips with me. And we talked. And he invited me to his Fight Klub class tonight where he's going to teach me some self-defence moves. And then we watched some '50s detective thing on TV and kissed again, this time for *twenty-two* seconds. And it was a little open-mouthed at one point, but no tongues. Then he went back upstairs, which I thought was so romantic. People on TV normally start ripping their clothes off but this felt more respectful. Like old-fashioned courting.

I barely slept. And I haven't stopped smiling since I woke up.

I am a bit worried about 'It' because he's bound to want It. A guy like Kaden, who shares naked pictures of himself online to random women, is going to want a woman who knows what she's doing. And I know nothing. Well, next to nothing. I know where everything goes. And what needs touching and licking and whatnot. Ugh. Can I really do all that? Now I'm in love, maybe I won't mind so much.

When he said those words – 'I think I'm falling in love with you' – I felt it in my knees. I'd never understood what people mean by 'weak at the knees' until then. I've been having little fantasies about him all morning, all fully clothed ones. Holding each other. Strolling round a tourist attraction or a garden centre, picking out hanging baskets. Pushing a trolley together around Lidl and crossing things off our list, in DIY stores picking MDF for our box room shelves. Living together in our own house, him mowing the lawn, me standing there holding open the bin bag. Getting married in the feathered wedding dress Foy designed for me when we were little – I found the original drawing of it folded up inside one of my Beatrix Potters.

But real, naked intimacy. Making love. *Having sex*. That would take things to the next level. A more grown-up level. It makes me shudder. We'll take it slowly. I'll ask him about it tonight at Fight Klub. Try and get a sense of when exactly he might want to put his winky in my noo-noo. Makes me giggle to think about it.

My joyful bubble bursts the second I walk into the staff office at The Lalique.

'Genevieve, your face looks like a pepperoni pizza,' laughs Claire.

'Thanks,' I say, clocking in.

Vanda pipes up then. 'A stag party threw up all over the gents' toilets last night. We have cordoned it off. You get in there now. And we're out of bleach. You'll just have to scrub and flush many times.'

I don't think Vanda has ever once said to me *Good morning* or *Goodbye*. She merely barks an order and leaves the room. I don't mind so much today. All the vomit in the world – and there was a lot of it in that toilet – couldn't stop me thinking about Kaden. I put a peg on my nose so it's not so bad.

After that I'm sent to the Floor 3 to finish off Faith's rooms because she's had to dash off to her kid's emergency dentist's appointment. But it's only the last five rooms and it's so peaceful up there, nobody about. Yes, I'm changing soiled bedsheets and bleaching toilets and wiping hairs from bath tubs with a damp cloth, but in my head, the Flower Duet from *Lakme* is playing and Kaden and I are walking around the gardens of a stately home. He's wrapping his zip up Adidas jacket around me when the breeze gets up, and asking where I want to go for lunch: the quaint tea room we passed on the way to Beatrix Potter's house or the Drive-Thru McDonald's on the motorway.

My mind is definitely not on the job. And Vanda can't wait to call me on it.

'Fuck's sake, Genevieve, why you not report the mattress burn in Room 37? Now they won't pay their bill and we'll get docked our wage.'

'Fuck's sake, Genevieve, it's two waters in Room 32, one in Room 33. And why you not put vanity kits in Room 38? How many more times?'

She sounds like the Grand High Witch when she shouts. I remember Isaac reading *The Witches* to me and Foy at bedtime once when I was staying. He'd always do the voice so brilliantly. And today I don't care. Any other day, every word would seep into my skin like acid and burn me all day long but today? It doesn't matter. Because I have Kaden now. I am bulletproof.

And as she shouts at me, getting right up in my face, I'm thinking about his body in those WhatsApp pictures. I'm wondering if he sleeps on his back or foetal like I do. Whether he snores. Maybe he sleeps naked. I chuckle to myself.

'You laughing at me, bitch?' says Vanda.

'No,' I say, bundling Room 34's sheets into the bag. 'Not at all.'

'You will not laugh at me. I kick you down them fucking stairs.'

'I'm not laughing at you, Vanda. I'm just happy today, that's all.'

'Why?' she spits. It didn't know you *could* spit saying Why.

'I'm…' She's waiting. I feel like she'll wait all day. 'I'm in love.'

And it is like a force field around me. She can't touch me. Nobody can. I'm shielded. That's what true love is. I can feel it climbing all over me.

Her eyebrow rises. 'More bullshit, I expect.'

'No, he's real and he's beautiful and he's mine. His name is Kaden.'

'What is he, your blow up doll? To match your plastic kid? Don't think we haven't always known that's a doll you carry around. Kimberley says it's your "human right" to carry around a doll and we had to go along with it. Always too shit-scared of tribunals. I used to feel sorry for you but you're pathetic. First a plastic baby, now a plastic boyfriend. He got a little inflatable pecker for you to suck too?'

'He's *real*,' I say again, brushing off the humiliation I feel knowing that they've always known about Emily, and removing my phone from my apron. I show her my screensaver. She snatches the phone and looks at the picture. And then laughs.

'What?' My heart thumps. It's like the corridor is getting longer behind them. The lift is getting further away. There's no way out.

'*You* are going out with *him*? Sabrina? Sabrina, come look…'

Sabrina's coming out of her service lifts with her cart and leaves it parked outside Room 31, scurrying over to Vanda like an obedient mouse. 'Ooh, he's nice.'

'He's her new boyfriend,' says Vanda.

I stand between them, chest clenched tight, going hotter in the face.

Sabrina laughs. 'Oh, right. He's the doll's father, is he?'

I snatch my phone out of her hand. 'No.'

'You took that from a staff picture at the gym,' says Sabrina. 'I've seen him when I take my kids for Little Swimmers.' She returns to her trolley to rearrange her mints. 'You were right, Vand. She couldn't tell the truth if her arse depended on it.'

'I knew it was too good to be true,' says Vanda. 'You sad little girl.'

My heart races. I click off my phone and fumble it back into my apron pocket only I miss and it falls to the carpet. I pick it up and run after her. 'Vanda, he *is* my boyfriend now. He lives in the flat upstairs. Last night we kissed.'

She's looking at me the way you'd look at a chicken to see whether or not it's defrosted. 'You lie again. You lie about all things. We know your name not Genevieve.'

I follow her into the service lift with her cart and she presses the button for the Ground Floor. 'I'm not a liar. I swear.'

'What's your real name then?'

'J-Joanne.'

'And when that turns out to be bullshit as well, what name will you say then?'

My face could not be more hot. My heart could not be more sore.

'If you can't have kids of your own that's one thing. But to pretend that a dolly is your baby? To have days off work because your dolly has a "bug"?' She does the speech marks around the word bug and her long red nails scratch the air. But she's not finished. And when I get back down to the staff office, Madge and Claire have heard about the argument and they start on me as well.

'The first week you started here, you told us your name was Genevieve Syson. That you knew Meghan Markle at school and you played Olympic hockey. Then Trevor looks at your papers and finds your name is *actually* Joanne Haynes. Claire heard you at the doughnut shack on the seafront, claiming to be writing a novel. Your *fifth* novel. So who the bloody hell are you?'

Claire chips in. 'My husband said he saw you in the dentist's waiting room the other week, with your stomach all blown out like you were pregnant. And he said you gave your name as Ruth.'

Madge shakes her head. 'And your hair's not really that colour. You've got red regrowth. How did you expect to get away with so many lies in such a small town?'

'I don't know,' I mumble.

'Who the hell are you then?' yells Claire.

'I don't know that either.'

Every good thought about Kaden has scurried away like frightened rabbits down deep burrows. I continue cleaning with a silent head, the lights going off in all the little rooms I have built for us to be together. It's the throwaway manner of their attack that gets me the most: they *know* I lie and they let me do it. They're watching me, wherever I go. I can't be anyone but Joanne Haynes. Whoever *she* is.

As I clock out and get my coat and bag, I pass all of them in the staff office – Vanda, Trevor, Sabrina, Claire and the concierge, Benito. I'm afforded a brief glance from Benito who nods politely before they continue with their conversation and a trail of sniggering follows me into the bar area. I catch one word: 'Pathetic.'

I don't look up as I walk through the restaurant but the noise is overwhelming. It's a cacophony of barking dogs, screaming children, clattering cutlery and people ordering food. But then I catch a face looking at me from one of the tables in the rotunda. A table for three but it's a man on his own – straw-coloured hair. A leather bomber jacket draped over the chair opposite. A wallet and keys next to a glass at the table setting beside him.

A straw-haired man looking at a menu. Alone.

Cold electricity shivers up and down my back. It's *him*. Laughing Man. He's found me. He raped and killed Tessa Sharpe and he knows now he got the wrong girl. If he sees me, I'm dead. My red roots are showing. The redness of Ellis, the one he's looking for. Right then, I have nothing to lose.

Buoyed by the myriad witnesses around me, I march towards his table and I stand there, waiting for him to look up from the menu. Chest pounding. Sweat forming on my forehead. It's so hot in here. So noisy.

'Sir?'

He doesn't hear me at first.

'SIR?'

'Uh, yes, I'll have the salmon terrine and the monkfish to follow. They'll have the whitebait and two steaks medium rare, thanks.'

'NO.'

He puts down the menu, takes a slow glance upwards. He doesn't seem to twig. Gesturing towards the two empty spaces he says, 'They're on a nicotine break.'

We lock eyes – his are craggy and lined. I know that face. I know him from TV. And then my anger tips over into something else. A feeling I don't recognise right then.

He frowns. 'Sorry, what's going on?' And I'm about to open my mouth when he sort of jumps in realisation. 'Oh, I thought you were a waitress.' He reaches into his pocket and pulls out a silver pen. He clicks it on and holds out his hand. 'My apologies. What did you want me to sign, my lovely?'

I don't understand at all. 'Stop following me,' I tell him.

'I'm sorry, what?'

'Stop following me, leave me alone or I *will* call the police.'

'What on earth?' He's looking around for someone, anyone.

A member of staff scurries over to our table in a black suit and white blouse. Kimberley Forbes, General Manager, brown ponytail sharp to a point down her back. 'Is everything alright for you, Mr Whittle?'

'I'm not quite sure,' he says, with a frown and a wry laugh. *That* laugh. 'This lady thinks I've been following her.' Tears fall down my cheeks.

Kimberley looks at me with daggers in her eyes. 'Genevieve, what's going on?'

The two men – the brunette without the bomber jacket and The Tank return on a waft of cigarettes and stand behind the straw-haired man. 'Everything alright?' says the brunette.

'Yes, this young lady thinks I've been following her.'

'You've ALL been following me,' I cry and it's only then

I realise I'm crying. Proper tears down both cheeks. 'I'm not afraid any more. You want to kill me, you do it here, where there's witnesses. I can't run anymore. I can't do it.'

And I collapse. I'm on the floor in the middle of the rotunda, surrounded by metal chair legs and crumbs and squashed chips and napkins. There's a commotion above me and someone grabs me under my arms and drags me to my feet. I'm screaming. It's a wail. It's pain in vocal form. I can still hear that laugh ringing out.

'Come on, 'adda girl, let's get you home.'

I don't realise who's talking until I'm outside, sobbing to the point of water blindness, and being walked across the front lawns of the hotel.

'Trevor, let go of me. I want them to kill me.'

'What are you talking about? Are you off your meds or something? Why on earth would you think Ken Whittle would want to kill you?'

'Ken who?'

'Ken Whittle. The comedian. On at the Winter Gardens all month. Look.'

I follow his pointed finger towards a telegraph pole on the pavement.

Ken Whittle Live! Cockney funny man back with his
sell-out one man show!
Please note: Snowflakes _will_ melt.

There's a picture above the writing of Ken Whittle giving two thumbs up and wearing a white Fedora and a few coats of fake tan.

'He wasn't wearing all that fake tan in the restaurant.'

'Yeah well he's not on stage tonight, is he?' says Trevor, hands on his hips. 'Bloody hell. What's going on with you?'

'Who were those other men?'

'His manager and bodyguard, I think. Who'd you think they were?'

'The Three Little Pigs.'

'There's no pigs here, love.' I look at Trevor and I know that face – alarm. Pure alarm. He thinks I'm crackers. I want to tell him I'm not but how can I? When everything I do or say supports the fact that I am?

'I heard that laugh,' I mumble. 'I heard it as I was lying there. They chained me up. And they killed my dad—'

And it all comes flooding back. The laugh rang out as they placed me down on the stretcher. He was a big star then, eighteen years ago. *Ken Whittle's Superstar Roadshow. Ken Whittle's Comedy Hour.* I remember them. He'd been there alright – in the corner when my dad was dying. He'd been laughing his head off.

On the TV.

'Is there anyone I can call for you, Joanne? Anyone who can come and pick you up? I don't think you should be on your own.'

'No,' I answer. And it's the truth.

Trevor disappears, leaving me for five whole minutes on my knees on the pavement, staring at the Ken Whittle poster. He returns with my coat and bag. 'Here you go, kid.' He helps me stand up and into my coat and puts the bag over my head and across my body so it's safe. He buttons me up, like Dad used to. 'You take it easy, okay?'

I walk with no direction, buffered by the wind. I stare out towards the wetlands and the pier beyond. I wish I had the courage to walk out into the sea. To drown myself, or whoever the hell this person is meant to be. I HATE Joanne Haynes. I don't want this to be my life. I'm an actress in a TV show that never ends. I need someone to pull me back. I'm not strong enough on my own anymore. I need Kaden.

11

I walk and walk until I find him – in Training Room 3. He's
tidying away the crash mats after his Fight Klub class.

'Hey,' he smiles, locking up the storage room. 'I thought
you were going to come along tonight?'

'Didn't feel like it.'

'Oh, okay. I was going to show you some self-defence
moves, wasn't I?'

'Yeah. But it's alright. You don't have to. I just wanted to
see you.'

He smiles at me kindly. It's all I need.

'Stay there,' he says, marching to the storage room he's just
locked and retrieving one large blue crash mat. He brings it
to the middle of the floor.

'Okay, on the mat.'

'Huh?'

'On the mat. I'm going to show you what to do if you're
pinned to the floor.'

I can't think of an argument so I do as he asks. I lie down
flat on the mat.

'No, I meant *stand* on the mat.'

I stand up. He stands in front of me. Sweat trickles slowly
and silently down his face, the whole way, under his chin.
Down into the pool of his neck.

'Okay,' he says, placing his hands loosely but hotly around my neck. 'So say I've come to your door and I've got my hands around you like this. What do you do?'

Kiss you, is my first thought but I snap out pretty quick and say, 'Scream?'

'Screaming's good,' he says, much to my surprise. His hands are still there on my skin. 'Anything to set a boundary is good. How do you get out of the hold?'

'Smack your arms away?'

'Go on then.' I try and smack his arms but they won't move. I yank and tug and pull but he's too strong. 'What's the matter?'

'You're too strong for me.'

'Right. And he will be too. So what you're gonna do is bring the tension into your neck to loosen the grip, bow slightly forwards and then duck straight backwards out of it. Try it.'

And I do, though I get it wrong on the first few tries but then I've got it. There's no real note of congratulation in his voice though. He says 'Good job' like he would to all his other personal training clients, I guess.

'Okay, next one – say you're walking along the street at night and you don't see or hear me coming. First thing you know, my arm is around your neck like this.'

And he does it. He comes up behind me and his arm is around my neck so my chin is in his elbow crease. I can smell his sweat now. It's all I can do to not stick my tongue in it.

'He's trying to drag you away, what are you going to do?'

'Scream again?'

'Can't scream, my arm's constricting your throat. Come on, I'm dragging you to the bushes, what you gonna do?'

I yank at his arm but it gets tighter around me. I can't breathe. I yank harder.

'Step forward on the strong leg, back out away from me, away from the choke, slip that shoulder and push me away.'

He talks me through it a few times until I do it perfectly. Another 'Good job'.

'What about if he's pushed me down?' I say. 'What do I do then?'

'On the floor?' he says.

'Yeah.' I lie down flat on the mat. 'What if I'm lying down on my back and he's on top of me? Pinning me down?'

Kaden stands there for a second, looking around. 'Okay, so if you've shouted at the guy and pushed him away and you've got out of the choke but he's somehow managed to push you down, then he's going to try and overpower you on the floor.'

'Right,' I say, breathless.

'I'm going to walk you through it, okay? If you feel uncomfortable at any point, yell "STOP" and I'll jump right off.'

'Right,' I say again.

'Okay, knees up with feet flat on the mat.' I do as he says. And then he mounts me, his thighs either side of my stomach, towering above me. But I'm not scared. Because it's him. Because he's warned me.

'So I'm going to show you what to do if you're ever attacked to the point where you're on your back and you feel like there's no way out. We're gonna show that bastard what you can do, alright?' He winks at me, like the doughnut man winks at me but with Kaden I'm absolutely powerless over my body as a result.

'Okay,' comes my breathy reply. If I squint I can imagine

135

he's wearing chain mail and holding a large jousting stick at his side – my Saturday Knight, defending me against enemies who've stormed the castle.

'Right, so everybody in this situation thinks the right thing to do is punch the guy in the nuts, but what happens then?'

'I don't know.' All rational thought has left me. What if his winky brushes up against me. What will I do?

'You're in shock because you're not expecting this, but I'm pumping with adrenaline so I'm going to be ready for it, and I'm going to hit you back, probably knock you unconscious and then you've had it, right?'

'Right.'

'So what you'll need to do is get your elbows nice and firm by your ribs to lock your position. Get your right hand over to my left wrist and grip it tight. Get the left hand on my tricep so my arm can't move. Elbows in, let your back do the work.'

I do as he says until we're tangled together in a Twister knot of arms and legs and in one swift movement I've pushed him off me with my hips and wrestled him over onto his back. I'm free. I'm the one on top of him. Straddling him. Wanting to kiss him.

'Now you can do what you need to,' he says. 'You're the one in charge. Good job, Joanne. Well done.' He wriggles free and sits up beside me. He then tells me about all the Last Resort tactics I can try. And even though he's sitting there talking about how to head-butt without causing myself too much injury, eye-gouging, stabbing with keys, jaw-breaking, temple-punching, chinning and kidney kicks, it's wonderful. So romantic in a really unromantic way.

He checks his watch. 'Do you want to go through anything again?'

'No,' I say, catching my breath. 'I want to kiss you again.'

But as I lean forward, he rears away. 'No, sorry. We can't do that again.'

It's sucked the life-force from me. It hurts all over, this rejection. His baulking away, like I'm disgusting all of a sudden. 'We did last night. Is it cos I'm all bruised today? But that'll go.'

'I know but—'

'Is it cos we're at your work? Are you ashamed to be seen with me? Has Vanda got to you?'

'Who's Vanda?'

'Russian woman, blonde hair. Absolute ogre.'

'I don't know anyone called Vanda. Joanne, we can't do that anymore. I'm sorry. I just thought you wanted to know some self-defence moves.'

'You kissed me last night. You said you thought you were falling for me?'

And I do hear myself, so desperate. And I know it's so needy and weak and there's no sign of Feminist Frida anywhere in sight, but right then I'm so confused and disorientated. It's like he's a different person today. 'Did I dream that?'

'No, you didn't dream it. We can't. I'm sorry.'

'But you're obsessed with me. All those pictures...'

He gets up off the mat.

'What's changed?'

'It's wrong, that's all. It wouldn't be right, you and me. It's unprofessional.'

'What do you mean, it wouldn't be right? I'm not even a member of the gym.'

He ushers me off the mat and picks it up, marching it back

to the store room. I say it again, following him in. 'You said you were falling in love with me.'

'I shouldn't have said that. It was a lie.'

'What?'

'Please forget I said anything.'

'How can I forget? Kaden, tell me, why is it so wrong now? What do you mean it was a lie? Is it because of Emily? She's gone now, she's with her dad.'

'It's not her.'

'Is it cos I'm ugly? Fat? I can stop eating so many doughnuts. We don't have to wait to have sex, I can do it now if you want to. Right here.'

'It's nothing to do with that.' He looks at me, and it's like the way Trevor looked at me after seeing Ken Whittle's poster on the telegraph pole. It's pity in his eyes, not love. Pity for the crazy fat cat lady. 'You're… a client. I'm sorry.'

'I TOLD YOU I'M NOT A MEMBER!' I shout. But he only looks back once as he grabs his towel and water bottle from the floor by the wall. And then he walks out.

Christmas school holidays,
eighteen years ago...

12

Saturday, December 14th – Paddy's birthday

Me and Dad have been living in Carew St Nicholas since September. Auntie Chelle and Uncle Stu 'made him an offer he couldn't refuse', and Stu had given him a job tending bar, tapping barrels and waiting tables. He still did his little disappearing acts now and again but he'd got better with money. I got new shoes for school and a new satchel and everything. We even got a new car.

I started at Foy's school, which wasn't two miles from the pub, and every single day me and Foy would walk home via the little shop. We'd buy sweets and take the shortcut through the churchyard at the back of the pub to eat them. We'd pick the flattest graves to sit on, and spit inside our Sherbet Fountains and stir the sherbet with our liquorice sticks to make a paste. Then scrape it all out of the tube. We'd sit on our Wham bars to make them all warm and soft, then tear open the wrappers and wrap the sticky gunk around our fingers and bite it all off. We'd see how long it could take us to suck our cola cubes without crunching down on them.

Our only witnesses were Mary, Charlotte, Genevieve, Betsy and Ruth.

Mary Brokenshire's grave was the oldest. She was buried

with her five children who all died before her. Charlotte Purfleet's was the newest and there were always fresh flowers there alongside the little stack of stone books – she'd liked to write stories. Genevieve Syson's had the stone angel with the outstretched wings on the top – she loved to travel. Betsy Warre's was the smallest. *Cruelly robbed so soon in life, My loving friend and cherished wife.* And Ruth Gloyne's was the saddest. She died in childbirth and was buried with her baby. A sad place for a child to sit, but it was the happiest time for me and Foy. In all our games, those were our names: Mary, Charlotte, Genevieve, Betsy or Ruth. A new name for every new game.

*

It's December 14th – Paddy's birthday, and we've just had our tea in the bar and he's blown out his thirteen candles.

He's cutting the cake and Chelle's handing around the plates. Dad clears his throat and pulls something out of his hoody pocket.

'By the way, guys,' he says, placing a large wad of money right in front of Chelle and Stu. 'For you.'

Isaac's jaw drops. Paddy goes, 'Wooooooahh!'

'What the—' says Uncle Stu.

'Danny, for God's sake,' says Chelle.

'That's some serious greenbacks, Uncle D,' says Isaac.

'Yeah man!' says Paddy. 'Can we get that Countach now, Uncle Dan?'

'Maybe next year, kiddo,' he laughs, pushing the wad closer to Stuart and Chelle whose eyes are wide. 'Take it, please.'

He's almost fizzing. 'So nice to be able to give something back for a change.'

'What is this, Daniel?' says Chelle.

'It's my way of saying thank you for letting us stay 'til we get back on our feet.'

'*Your* feet,' Chelle corrects him. 'Your being here isn't Ellis's doing, is it?'

Foy picks up the money and spreads it out in her hands. She gives half to me and I do it as well. 'Can we play Banks with this, Mum?'

'No,' Chelle snips, scraping the money out of our hands and bundling it back into a stack on the table. 'Kids – go and take your plates out and do the Viennetta please. There's homemade jelly in the fridge.'

'What flavour?' asks Isaac.

'Lemon.'

'Wicked.'

And we all do it without argument for once. It must occur to us that the atmosphere has changed and we need to leave it, but none of us says anything until we're in the corridor and even then we're just talking about what we'd spend the money on – for Paddy and Isaac it's all about cars. Lamborghini for Isaac, Porsche for Paddy. Foy wants ponies – an entire field of them. I hang back and listen at the door.

Stuart's counting the money. 'There's nearly twenty grand here.'

'Seventeen thousand, five hundred,' says Dad. 'Take it. I want you to have it.'

'Your accumulator come in, did it?' says Chelle.

'No, no that's all hard-earned cash, that is. No gee-gees,

I promise. Look.' He holds up both his hands to show his fingers aren't crossed behind his back. 'Chelley, please. I'm grateful to you both. Let me pay you back. You've taken us in, given me a job, you've got Ellis a new school, you feed us—'

'—you came down here without a penny to your name. Now three months later, you've got seventeen-and-a-half grand to give away? Where did it come from?'

'I've been saving up. You two won't take any rent.'

'We weren't taking any rent to help you get you back on your feet. Stu pays you a wage so you can save up for a new place for you and Ellis. We don't expect to be paid back, that's not what families do. Not every act of kindness comes with an invoice. We took you in to help you. You don't owe us.'

'Well I wanted to give you something. I don't get why you're being so bloody-minded, sis.'

'I'm being bloody-minded because I don't understand how three months ago my brother comes here with pockets full of dud betting slips, then pulls a few pints and suddenly he's flinging about wodges of cash like Alan Sugar.'

'Where's it from?' asks Stuart, quieter than Chelle.

Foy comes up behind me with a small bowl of Viennetta and lemon jelly. I put my finger on my mouth to quieten her. She listens in too.

'I've been doing some cash in hand. One of the jobs was big.'

'What job?'

'Building work.'

'Building what?'

'Uh, houses?' Dad laughs. 'You can believe what you want, Stu, that's the truth.'

'You're doing it again, aren't you? You're working for that monster again.'

'No, I ain't. I got out of all that.'

'What hold has he got over you, Dan?' says Chelle. She's crying. Wiping her cheeks. She starts scraping her plate onto Stuart's. 'He'll never let you go, will he?'

Foy whispers in my ear, 'Who's the monster who won't let him go?'

'I don't know.' My heart is painful.

'Are you gonna take it or not?' says Dad.

'Not,' says Chelle, yanking the pile out of Stuart's grip and handing it back to Dad. 'Now you take that back to whatever sewer you got it from.'

'I can't take it back. It's not that easy.'

'Why? Did you steal it?'

'No.'

Uncle Stu looks to the door and me and Foy back away from it.

'I only did that for a bit to clear my gambling debts, it was two months' worth, tops. It's all clear now.'

'So when you burned down your own house and the insurance wouldn't cough up, that's when you started working for him again, was it? To pay off your debts?'

'No, Chelley. It was all building work, I swear. It was a big company. Lucrative. I did a lot of work on it. And this is part of the reward.'

'Who are you lying to, us or yourself?' says Stu. He hands the money back again to Dad with a flat hand on top of the pile. 'Do the right thing, mate. Go and put a deposit down on a house for you and your daughter. For *her* sake.'

*

*Thursday, December 19th – first day of the Christmas
holidays*

The boys are supposed to be walking us back from the carol
concert but instead, Paddy meets up with his girlfriend and
her two friends, and him and Isaac go off into town on the
bus to do some Christmas shopping. Me and Foy make our
own way back to the pub through the churchyard – she sits
on Mary Brokenshire, I on Charlotte Purfleet.

Foy opens up the red tissue paper and we start tucking into
the free mince pies.

'Wonder how her children all died,' she says.

'Whose children?' I say.

'Mary's,' she says, gesturing towards the headstone behind
my back.

I glance down at it, even though I can't see much in the
fading light. 'I don't think it says for all of them. The last bit's
rubbed off. I can only read "Harold died at fifteen, David
born asleep."'

'Poor Mary.'

'Do you want to have real babies one day?' asks Foy.

'Yeah, one day,' I say, screwing up my serviette. 'Do you?'

'Yeah, deffo.'

'I hope I know how to be a mum.'

Foy chews her pie. 'My mum can show you. You'll always
have her and me.'

'Thanks.'

'These pies are lush,' she says. 'What do you want for your birthday? Mum's going to get your presents tomorrow—'

'I don't mind, listen, Foy – did you hear what Isaac said to Paddy at the service?'

'What about?' she says, scuttling over to join me on Charlotte's grave.

'He said he overheard Auntie Chelle and Uncle Stu talking last night and they think my dad's dealing drugs. That's why he gave them all that money the other night.'

She nods, open-mouthed. 'Does that mean he'll go to prison?'

'I don't know.'

'You'll live with us for definite then,' says Foy. 'If he does go to prison.'

'I don't want my dad to go to prison.'

'No, but you could still live with us if he does.'

A hardness is already forming in my throat. 'I don't know what will happen. I know he's in trouble. Isaac said he heard Dad wants to "do a deal with the police".'

'What does *that* mean?' says Foy.

'I don't know. Maybe he'll give them money so he doesn't have to go to prison?'

She frowns. Then puts her arm around me and says defiantly, 'I'll ask Isaac. Isaac will know.'

13

My new rug came this morning. The colours are different than the picture on the website. It looks horrible. Browns and oranges rather than pinks and reds. And it curls up at the edges. I don't want an argument about it. It'll cover the hideous lino at least.

My mood has dipped again. Kaden's gone – Scants has gone too, I think. I feel a sudden desperate need for a hug. A yearning for someone – a real person. Any person.

Cathy, the same lady who served me last time in Seaside Bridal, is there again today, folding white tissue paper at the counter as I walk in. She immediately looks at her colleague in the same way Vanda looks at Sabrina whenever I walk into work.

'Oh, hi again!' she says chirpily, painting on a smile I can practically hear coming. 'How are things coming along?'

'Not brilliant, actually,' I say. 'We lost the baby.'

The colleague looks at her. She looks at the colleague and the painted smile disappears. 'Oh gosh, I'm so sorry. Come and sit down. Alice – stick the kettle on, love.'

'Of course,' says Alice. She is young, younger than me, and I'm guessing probably about nineteen. She has very long brown hair with a wave in it and her shoes are ballerina slippers. She moves like she's constantly apologising for being alive but when she looks at me her face is full of sorrow.

I have their compassion, an atmosphere of sympathy swathed in cream silk and pink petals. Touching my forearm. Eager to please. Sad smiles. Friend-like, almost.

Cathy comes around the counter with her arms stretched out in front of her, like the two sides of a staple. I stand there and be hugged. This is what I wanted. But it's such a hard hug that it's not comforting at all.

'Lovey, it takes a lot of courage to come back in here after what you've been through. I'm so sorry for you. I don't know what to say, my love, except, well, I know what you're going through. Long time ago now, but the pain does ease.'

'Thank you. We're still going ahead with the wedding in February but obviously I don't need a dress the size of the one you originally fitted me for.'

'Of course, of course,' she says, with a slow blink, as though to wash her eyeballs with sincerity. 'Well why don't we have a nice cup of tea and you can scan the books again and see if anything takes your fancy, yeah? We have most collections in stock – Sassi Holford, Maggie Sottero, all the favourites. We've got some new stock in of Romantix Brides which are at the slightly less expensive end.'

'Hang the expense,' I say. 'David says he doesn't care about it anymore, not now there's no… well, not now we don't have any extra expenses to worry about after.'

I don't care that it was Kaden's name I mentioned as my groom-to-be the other day. And they haven't remembered so it doesn't matter. David's the one for me now. Whoever he is.

'Of course,' she says, giving my hand a quick squeeze. 'You have a look through those then and I'll see where your tea has got to. What was it, white with two sugars?'

'Three please.'

'Three, of course, of course. I'll see if we've got any of Prince Charles's biscuits leftover as well. Lemon, they are. Marvellous.'

The gowns in the Romantix catalogue are so cheap and nasty they make me grimace. It's all low cut or high cut, lacy and tight-fitting. And everything's under £500. The Maggie Sottero ones are incredibly elegant and all the brides are in natural surroundings, complementing the creeping vine embroidery and intricate lace flowers tailored into all the designs. There's a lingerie catalogue in the stack too. The Cathy woman comes back with my tea and two Duchy biscuits in time to see me open it.

'Ooh there's some lovely pieces in there, half price at the moment. We've got a Victoria's Secret Lace Plunge Teddy, and a very sexy Chantilly lace satin slip which was £90 but it's reduced at the moment—'

'No, I'm not interested in lingerie,' I say. 'Just a dress.'

'Of course, of course,' she says, removing the Sale catalogue from my sight and helping me open the cover of the Sassi Holford book. 'Now these, if you're looking for something ultra-classic, are to die for.' She goes red in the face. I don't draw any attention to it because that would be rude.

'Are these all in stock?'

'Most of them, yes. Except the Dominique. That's been particularly popular. As you can see it's strapless and comes with a stunning lace cape and a sash in champagne or ivory. There's a fishtail design to the skirt...'

'I want to take one home today.'

'Oh, well how about you tell me what sort of design you're after and I'll see what we can do?'

I open my bag and unfold the piece of paper with the drawing on that Foy did.

'Me and my cousin, we designed our own wedding dresses when we were kids. We always said if either of us got married, we had to find a dress that was as near as dammit to these designs.'

Cathy was looking at the picture as though it were smeared with crusty bogies, holding it loosely at the two bottom corners. 'Hmmm. Okay, so what have we got here then?' She looks at me, then looks back at the drawing. 'A long train. A veil. Long sleeves. A bit of lace is that?'

'Well it's a scribble that's meant to be lace. She's written lace next to it, see?'

'Ah yes. And feathers. Lots and lots of feathers all over the skirt. Righty ho then. I think we've got the perfect one out the back, new stock for next year, just come in. You're about a size fourteen, yes?'

'On a good day. Sometimes a sixteen. Is that a problem?'

'It's only a problem if we *make it* a problem,' she winks with a cheesy grin. 'I'll do my best for you, Ruth.'

And with that she *clip-clops* out to the back of the shop like Mary Poppins about to Step In Time on some rooftop. I drink my tea and Alice the assistant is making me another one when Cathy returns with a weighty clear dress bag draped over one arm.

'This is as close as I can get to the drawing with feathers on and in your size, my love,' she says, unzipping it from its clear bag and hanging it up on a rail fixed to the ceiling that I haven't observed before now. 'What do you think about that one?'

'It's so beautiful,' I say. The bodice is silken with long, pillow-white sleeves, the feather skirt and train flutters on a light breeze coming from the crack around the doorway. On its own it looks classic, elegant, angelic, like the little girl in the picture. Except when I put it on I won't have club feet or hands. And my hair will be black. Dyed black. Fake. As fake as my name.

'That's the one,' I say. 'Absolutely the one.'

'Aww, fantastic,' says Cathy. 'This one's from our Milo de Havilland range. He's an Italian designer and this one is brand new in. It's a little pricier than the others.'

'This is absolutely the one that I want.'

'Wonderful. Well, why don't you try it on and then we can start thinking about veils and if you would like to, you can browse around our shoe shop next door to find the perfect accompaniments.'

And I'm standing there, staring at myself in the mirror, stroking the long white sleeves and patting down my feather skirt at the sides, turning my ivory white silk shoes on their heels to look at myself from every possible angle, when I spy someone watching me from outside the window. My heart sinks – it's Vanda, on her way to work. I should be on my way to work too. She sees me, there's no hiding it. She looks daggers. And then she laughs, exaggeratedly, and walks on. I think she's going to come in the shop but she doesn't. But for once, I'm not that worried.

I could stand and look at my dress forever, and I get a few

admiring glances and comments from other brides-to-be in the shop. A young blonde called Antonia, who's about my age and is also getting married in the spring to a guy called Toby.

'Toby and Toni, they call us,' she laughs.

'My fiancé's called David,' I say. 'He's a marine biologist.' First job title that comes into my head.

'How wonderful. Well congratulations, hon!'

'You too! Good luck with it all!'

'Thanks.' Her mum, Theresa, tells me I look beautiful. And for once I believe it.

'How are you getting on?' mews the assistant, Alice, shuffling into the shoe cave noiselessly in her ballet pumps.

'I'll take it,' I say.

The dress makes me feel better. It's the same kind of 'better' as when I eat the doughnuts. I want them, ravenously, for about five minutes. Then I eat them and it's pure ecstasy – grease and sugar and dough. And then I feel satisfied. And then *horribly* guilty. When it's the doughnuts it's just fat. Yet another artery sighs and clogs.

But this is £4,000 worth of dress. There are people starving in the world, homeless cats, and I've wasted £4,000 in one morning on a dress I'll never wear.

And then I realise it doesn't matter. Because I'm going to die today anyway.

*

Trevor and Sabrina are in the staff office when I arrive at work. I don't clock in.

'Where's Vanda?' I ask them.

153

'She headed to the kitchen,' says Sabrina, clocking me up and then down. 'What you got there?'

'A wedding dress,' I say.

'What for?'

'For my wedding,' I say and I hear them laughing all the way up the corridor towards the kitchens. Vanda's checking some rota with the chef, Alexander.

She starts on me immediately. 'You are late, again. And what the hell are you doing trying on wedding dresses at 9 a.m., you freak girl.'

I hold out the dress bag. 'Not only trying them on. I bought one.'

She laughs. 'You bought one? Who are you marrying, Invisible Man?'

'Vanda?'

'What?'

'I'm leaving. Today. Now, actually.'

'Good. Weird girl. You need to sort shit out. You… crazy in head.'

And I want to say it. I want to say it so badly. And because I know I'll be dead by the end of the day, I do.

'You're a bully. You're *all* bullies. I just wanted you to know that.'

Christmas school holidays,
eighteen years ago...

14

Christmas Eve Eve

It is my birthday today – I got some Harry Potter Lego, a couple of Barbies, books, loads of Play-Doh, some scented rubbers for my pencil case, three Disney films and Auntie Chelle made me a cake with my name on it and loads of little handmade cats made from icing. Paddy and Isaac got me a new helmet for my bike and Foy got me a sparkly make-up set and a plastic sword so we can play Knights.

Just after the pub closes, we're in the treehouse drawing our wedding dresses. She draws mine and I draw hers.

'And you absolutely *have* to wear it,' says Foy.

'I will, I promise,' I say. 'Make it all feathery at the bottom, I like feathers.'

'I will,' she nods, colouring in the little ruby ring on the picture finger.

Dad appears at the bottom of the tree. 'Girls, do you want to come into town with me? Need to pick up a few things for Christmas.'

'Do we have to?' I say.

'Yeah, I need your help. Secret mission. I need my two wingmen.'

'We're girls, Dad.'

'Wing *girls* then. I'll buy you both a book…'

He leaves that suggestion hanging because he knows it's a guaranteed way of getting us to throw our pens aside and immediately climb down the ladder.

We spend most of the time in Debenhams and don't actually see most of the stuff Dad gets. When he's at the perfume counter, the jewellery counter, and chatting up the make-up lady, me and Foy are off pretending we're Queens – Queen Ruth and Queen Betsy today – and we're directing our invisible servants to buy everything we like the look of, like Elton John does.

'Yes, I'll have that bag and three hats and that brooch, no *ten* brooches and five pairs of boots, a pair in each of the castles for when I stay,' says Foy with a snooty look.

'Mmm yes, and I'll have every bottle of aftershave in the shop for all my lovers,' I add, and we both curl up in hysterics then run up the escalators to the toy department.

When Dad catches up with us he's loaded down with bulky bags. 'There you are. Come on. We need Woolworths next, then Waterstones, then a quick strawberry milkshake and then back to the pub.'

By the time we get across town to Waterstones to select our books, we're both pretty tired. But Dad keeps his promise and gives us five pounds.

We're so excited by the time we get back to the pub that we burst into the upstairs lounge to tell Chelle all about our shopping trip and the books Dad has bought us. But she has a weary look about her. And she rubs her mouth a lot.

'Okay, girls, I'll have a look at the books later.'

'He bought things for you as well, Mum,' says Foy, chewing

her straw, then realises she's starting to spill the secret. 'I can't tell you what though.'

And Chelle's face darkens again. 'Tea'll be in half an hour.'

'Shall we go back to the castle?' I suggest.

'Yeah,' says Foy. 'Let's finish our dresses.'

*

Christmas Day

I wake up far too early. I'm on the zed-bed by the window in the back bedroom and the curtains are thin and the moon big and low. It shines down all silvery onto the car park and beer garden. The window is cold to the touch and I wrap my duvet around me tighter. I can't hear Dad's snoring. I look across to the big bed but it's empty.

Then something outside catches my eye and I look out to see someone in a red robe and black boots – Santa? – scurrying around the beer garden. Climbing up the rope ladder. Rooting through the pampas bush. Climbing on the skittle alley roof. He creeps across the car park and opens the door of the skittle alley, disappearing inside.

The clock beside Dad's bed says 2.37 a.m.

I wait as he appears again, closes the skittle alley door behind him, and walks back across the car park towards the beer garden. He stops and looks up at my window. He holds his belly, cries 'Ho Ho Ho,' then runs past the window and disappears.

I may be ten years old with a vivid imagination but even I know it's Dad. 'What on earth is he doing?' I say, misting up the glass.

It's ages before he comes back in the room and by this time, I pretend to be asleep. I hear a crinkling sound at the bottom of my bed where he places my stocking – oh my God, I've got a stocking this year! – and I'm so excited I get the squiggles in my chest but I'm determined not to open my eyes and spoil it. It's so hard to drift back off, but by the time Dad is snoring again, I must do because when I next open my eyes...

It's Christmas Day!

Daylight floods the room and before I can lever myself up in bed, Foy has already run in with her stocking, shouting for us to '*Wake up! Wake up!*'

'Ten more minutes,' Dad grumbles groggily, but I grab my stocking and fling on my dressing gown and we run down the corridor towards Paddy's room. He's already awake, his normally styled hair a little bird's nest on his head and his eyes are all narrow. He grabs his stocking and his dressing gown and we run down the corridor towards Isaac's room and jump on his bed until he gets up. We all open our stockings together. All cuddled up, snuggled up together, this is my paradise.

We've nearly opened them all when Auntie Chelle comes in, all fluffy, unstyled curls, and wearing her pink marshmallow dressing gown.

'Happy Christmas, guys!' she says and kisses all of us in turn, pretending to be surprised by all the presents Santa has brought us. Uncle Stu appears moments later and does the same. But there's no sign of Dad. Until we get into the kitchen.

'Right, who's for a fry up?' says Dad, fully dressed with his chef's hat on and 'Top Chef' apron tied around him. He has everything out on the breakfast bar – bacon, eggs, pancakes, waffles, maple syrup, beef tomatoes and the thickest sausages.

'Cor, not half, Dan,' says Uncle Stu, rubbing his hands, noticing a letter propped up against the salt and pepper pot. 'Post hasn't been today, has it?'

'Dunno,' says Dad, tearing open the bacon. 'Came through the door.'

'That's odd,' says Chelle.

Stu looks puzzled too and we all stand there in various states of undress and orange juice-pouring as he laughs and then reads it out.

Dearest Keetons, one and all,
Happy Christmas Day,
To find your presents you will need,
To hunt for them, okay?
To start your quest, I must insist,
You go where birds do sing,
Up up up and away you look,
To see what gifts I bring.

'What the bloody hell?' Stu giggles, handing it to Chelle.

Auntie Chelle looks wary. 'What's all this?'

'I guess breakfast will have to wait guys,' says Dad, grinning and putting the bacon down. 'Shall we?'

And what follows is a two-hour treasure hunt around the pub, inside and out. Dad must have been hiding the presents all night. Once we have the first clue, which Paddy finds in the treehouse, we work out the next one must be somewhere in the Inglenook in the main bar, so back we go, all seven of us in our slippers and dressing gowns, across the car park, all breathing excited clouds of white air.

'What have you done all this for?' says Chelle, a begrudged smile on her face.

Dad cuddles her in. 'It's not me, sis. It's Father Christmas, all this.'

Chelle isn't sure at first but by Clue 3, she's into the swing of things and us kids are so excited it's hard not to be infected. Chelle finds presents for her – a rose gold watch with diamonds around the face, a soft pink jumper and the biggest size perfume bottle, in the scent that she loves but never treats herself to. Stuart finds a bottle of his aftershave and a Bristol City season ticket and a George Foreman grill cos he's always on about those as well. Paddy gets a phone. Isaac gets a PlayStation. And me and Foy get books, dolls, cooking equipment for the castle, felt tips, sparkly nail varnish and a complete set of Beatrix Potters for me and a complete set of Roald Dahls for her.

The last clue, Clue Number 25, has us stumped until Isaac points out that *Long run* could mean skittle alley, so the four of us race across the car park and right down to the other end of the alley where we find a shiny red box covered with fairy lights. Paddy is first to reach it and he just stands there.

Isaac joins him. 'Go on then,' he says breathlessly. 'See what it is.' Paddy tears open the box, while Isaac yanks free the tissue and they pull out a plain white envelope.

'Open it then, Pads,' says Stu as we catch up with them.

So Paddy does. He tears into it. Then he frowns. 'It's tickets.'

'It's seven tickets to Florida,' adds Isaac, eyes glinting in the fairy lights.

Chelle's hands go to her mouth and her eyes fill with tears. 'Oh my God.'

'Oh my shit,' says Uncle Stu.

But the four of us kids scream. We dance back down the skittle alley and into the beer garden and we don't care about anything else – we're going to Disney World. All of us. Together. It's more happiness than any kid can bear. And for a split second, I catch Dad's face and his eyes are shining and I think he must be so happy too.

It only occurs to me much later on that it's not happy tears.

Not once that morning as me and my cousins are dancing around the beer garden or as we're planning what Disney characters we're going to meet or as we're putting on each other's glitter cheeks and getting into our new party dresses, do we consider the consequences of such gifts. Do I consider why Chelle has to keep leaving the table during lunch.

Do I consider why Dad has treated us all to such an unforgettable Christmas.

15

There are several things one must get in place before one kills oneself. I found a list online. *First things first – consider those you will be leaving behind.*

And seeing as Emily is just a doll, I realise she doesn't need taking care of or leaving on anyone's doorstep. I wrap her in her blanket and put her in her car seat inside the wardrobe. And I close the door.

But the cats are different. I have to do the right thing by them.

The local RSPCA centre sends out a man in a van and he arrives around quarter past twelve. He's wearing a navy uniform and a white shirt and I watch him get two cat boxes out of the back of the van. The name on his badge says Sean Lowland. I'd seen him down at the centre when I took in an injured duck last month, but I think he's more out and about. He seems young but as it turns out he's the exact same age as me.

'Yeah, I've been working there for three years now. I love it. I love animals.'

'I love animals too,' I say, handing him a mug of tea.

'I think I've seen you before,' he says. 'Down at the centre. Didn't you bring something in a few weeks back?'

'Yeah,' I say. 'A duck. He had a broken wing. I think he'd been hit by a car.'

He brightens. 'Yeah, I thought so.'

'Was it alright?' His lips go tight. 'Oh.'

'They always do their best,' he says. 'But broken wings are a bit tricky. I'm sorry.'

'That's alright,' I say. 'I didn't know the duck personally or anything.'

He smiles. I don't know what's funny but it makes me smile too. He's got curly brown hair and kind eyes. 'So how many cats have you got then?'

'Three. They're not exactly mine. I found them all, on the streets. Half-starved they were, all of them.'

'Oh right,' he smiles. 'So you saved them?'

'Yeah, I saved them. The white one I found in a tree. The other two were huddled up under a wheelie bin by the pier a few weeks ago. They looked awfully scraggy so I took them in, fed them up, brushed them, got them flea treatment.'

'Well really it's best to give us a call straight away,' says Sean. 'There are a few worried families around here.'

'Are there?'

'Oh yeah, there's posters up all over. A few people have come into the centre asking if we've had them in.'

'Were they children?'

'Um, yeah, one of them was. It's alright, I'm sure they'll just be pleased they were being looked after so well.'

He seems so friendly and nice. So I tell him. 'There might be more.'

'More what?' He slurps his tea.

'Cats.'

'Oh. Where?'

'Here.'

'Okay. How many?'

'One or two.'

'Two?'

'Three.'

'Oh right.'

'Well, four. But that's it. There are seven of them in all.'

Sean seems dumbstruck.

'Princess Tabitha has put weight *on* since she's been with me. They were definitely under-feeding her. And Prince Rupert had conjunctivitis. I got him treatment for that, *me*.'

'Why not bring them in for us to look after? Why put yourself through the trouble and expense of looking after someone else's cats?'

'I just wanted… something to look after myself. I wanted them.'

He drains his tea and stands up. 'Yeah, I know what you mean. Right, well if you could show me where they all are I can get them loaded into the van. I think I've got enough boxes. Might have to put the two smallest in the one box. The centre's not far.'

'Are you going to call the police?'

'Eh?' He turns to me.

'Because I stole them.'

He frowns. 'I should. But you're giving them back now. And they're all looking good. So no real harm done.' He smiles at me. I smile back. He's only being friendly.

The next twenty minutes are spent rounding up all the cats and I can't help it but every time one goes into a box, I cry as

I'm closing the cage door. I post a treat through the wire and tell them it's been an honour to look after them, all quiet so Sean can't hear me and think I'm even more of a freak than he already does.

We find them all except The Duchess, she's nowhere to be seen, and I realise I haven't seen her for a couple of days. She's not in any of her usual places – under my bed, on the back of the sofa, or curled up on the towel stack in front of the bathroom radiator. I don't know why but it's fun looking for them all with Sean. Even though he most probably thinks I'm this weird girl who steals cats and lives like a pig and has a doll in a car seat in her wardrobe, I like being with him. It's a nice way to spend a morning. It makes saying goodbye to the cats a lot easier.

Sean's taking the last of them – Tallulah von Puss – out to the van and I watch him closing the doors and making his way back up the front steps.

'All done,' he says. 'Do you want to give me your contact details in case any of the families want to get in touch with you and thank you?'

'Uh, no, I don't think so,' I say.

'Oh, okay.' He lingers in the hallway. 'Well if you find The Duchess give me a bell.' He fumbles in his jacket pocket for a business card and hands it over to me.

'Sean Lowland, RSPCA Inspector,' I read. And there's a number.

'That's my mobile so I can come and get her when she turns up.'

'Okay. Thank you.'

'Sorry, I don't think I caught your name,' he says.

Something about his eyes. Something in them beckons me to tell the truth. And so I do. 'My name is Ellis. Ellis Clementine Kemp.'

His face lights up. 'Wow, what a great name.'

'Thank you,' I blush.

'Okay, I better go now. Thanks again for looking after the cats so well. I hope The Duchess turns up soon.'

'Me too.' The blush deepens, red hot. I hope he can't see it. 'Thank you.'

He blushes too for that matter. I'm expecting it to be awkward and it is for a short moment but then we're both smiling. He hands me a couple of leaflets. One says 'Thanks for being a Friend to Pets' and has a detachable sticker on it of a dog giving a thumbs up. Another is all about Adopting a Pet.

'You should think about adopting The Duchess properly, if nobody claims her. I've recently adopted a dog myself, actually.'

'Oh really?'

'Yes, a Jack Russell called Arthur. He's a proper scamp. Comes out in the van with me sometimes. He's not with me today though. He's having his you-know-whats off, poor little man.'

'Ahh.'

'No, it's good for him. It'll calm him down a bit and keep him healthy for as long as possible. I'm going to take him to socialisation classes when he's better. Well, best be off. Thanks again, Ellis.'

I like hearing my name in his mouth. And I realise then that I don't want him to go. Because when he goes, I'll have to take Step 2 on the checklist:

Prepare your method of suicide.

I don't want to do it now. I want to talk to Sean. I want to know more about him.

But he's down the steps before I can say anything else. He turns to me when he's back at the van and says, 'I'll be in the Smuggler's tonight on Cook Street, if you fancy a drink? Around seven-ish?'

'Okay,' I call back.

What does *that* mean? Does he want me to meet him? Even after knowing that I'm a weird woman who steals cats and pretends she has a new-born baby? He's gone before I can say anything else. How could a guy like Sean possibly be interested in a girl like me?

If he does want me, it won't last long. Relationships are based on trust and I'll have to tell him about all the lies I've told and then he'll run for the hills. Or he'll kiss me like Kaden did and he'll find out what a terrible kisser I am and then he'll back away from me, giving me the same look. Or he'll use the same excuse: *It's unprofessional. You're a client.* When what he really means is *You're a pathetic, lying freak and you disgust me.* I deserve to be on my own.

*

The stupid thing about the suicide website is that it gives you all these warnings about hurting yourself. *Talk to somebody first. Get it out of your head. Before you take the final step, have a final meal. And during your final meal, you can make your preparations: the How, the Why and the Where.*

But I don't know anybody. And I'm not hungry.

I think about Sean and how it could be. But I am sick of

thinking of how things *could* be. Unicorns don't exist. And neither does me and him together. Me and anyone. Grow up. There's nothing else to do. It's all too hard.

And so to the How – I have a choice of gunshot (no gun), hanging (no rope, and I can't find my dressing gown cord), a plastic bag over my head (too sweaty), drugs (might be sick, and I hate being sick), carbon monoxide poisoning (no car), jumping off a high building (The Lalique's only four floors high and if I'm going to do it, I want to be sure I'm not going to wake up in some hospital afterwards), jumping under a train (no, poor driver) and drowning.

I look out at the churning sea. Well, I have plenty of water, that's for sure.

How do you drown yourself? I go to Google again.

There's two ways, apparently. You can drink yourself to death or you can load your pockets with heavy stones and throw yourself in an 'expanse of water'. I could do it in my bath. Some people fall asleep in the bath. But I'm not tired. I could take sleeping tablets. Haven't got any though. I'll go out and get some.

It's early evening in town and the streets are full of loud people, ogres and trolls shouting and staring at me as I make my way through the streets, trying to go unnoticed. I pass the Smuggler's Arms on Cook Street around 7.15 p.m. and I look in the window to see Sean sitting at a small round table by the fire, looking at a paper. I want to go in and sit with him. He invited me. He wanted me to come. Or was he just being nice? He was just being nice. I shouldn't disturb him.

And so I go home. By the time I get back to the flat, I am ready. I go into the bathroom and run myself a hot bath, using the last of the bath foam and a bath bomb I bought ages ago at Mr Zhang's shop. 'Moon and Stars' it's called. I was saving it for a special occasion. I place it under the running tap and it immediately spews a rich royal blue into the water and all these tiny gold stars flood out and float up to the surface. I reach into the pharmacy bag and pull out the boxes of sleeping pills. Then the Morrison's bag, and two more boxes. Then the Tesco Metro bag, for the last two boxes. I didn't know they won't let you buy more than two boxes at a time in any shop.

I call Scants. He doesn't pick up but I don't expect him to. I leave a message. 'No bullshit and to the point,' just how he likes things. I'm fuzzy enough to want this now. I hang the wedding dress on the bedroom door, smoothing out the feather skirt so I can admire it. It is the most beautiful dress in the world. I walk into the bathroom and disrobe, leaving my clothes where they land. I set my phone to Spotify, to the playlist of all the songs we used to listen to as kids: Alanis Morrissette, Madonna, Kylie – I place it on the stand on the window sill.

I sink down beneath the warm water, allowing it to cover every part of me but my head. It warms me through, thaws my fingertips and toes. The little gold stars float and bob around me, over me, wrapping around me until I whisk off inside my head to another place. Home. The pub. Me and Foy making up a dance routine in the beer garden. Auntie Chelle clapping and whistling when we're finished.

I have my treasure bag, one of my mum's old handbags that I found in Dad's wardrobe. It's full of the stuff I can't be without: a bottle of pearlescent Tinkerbell nail varnish, a syringe from my Fisher Price medical kit, my fake diamond princess necklace, a tree decoration, shells, crayons, penny chews, obsolete coinage and a tiny Jeep I got from a Kinder egg. Me and Foy are in our dress-up bride's dresses. We've absconded from our double wedding to the evil princes and we're on the run.

'Oh shitake mushrooms!' I say. 'Look at the time! We need to go to the shopping mall before it shuts and get the Jurassic Chum.'

'Okay, let's go.'

We scamper down the ladder and race across the lawn to our bikes – if we don't go now then the Mall will shut and all the animals will go hungry. The Mall, or skittle alley as it is widely known, is still open when we get there, thanks to our Lamborghini Countach and Ferrari Testarossa, so we sprint straight to Feathers and Fins, the pet shop, to get what we need: polar bear steaks, bamboo for the pandas, seed for the dodos, tins of Jurassic Chum and bananas for the gorillas.

We didn't play The Castle Game all the time. We also played The Den Game. The 20 Children Game. The Treehouse Game. The Marshmallow Factory Game (same as The Den Game except we work in a marshmallow factory) and *The Honey, I Shrunk the Kids* Game where we pretended we were tiny. But The Castle Game is what I remember.

We park up the supercars and scamper back up the ladder to our castle and get the sketch books out. We're building extensions – having the blue whale enclosure made bigger and we're adding a racing track so we can race the velociraptors.

The castle is warm and stinks of fresh paint. We've put two flower pots in the window – a pansy and a crocus bulb that'll come up in spring. The knights are all practising their jousting and taekwondo in the arena – both Thursday and Sunday Knight are top of the leader board. The sound of Foy's felt tip pen colouring in blue soothes my worried mind. She doesn't look out the window as much as I do, but I feel like I have to drink every second of this place up before it's over again for another holiday. The sweeping grassland. The unicorns prancing and flicking their rainbow tails and manes. My lions sunning themselves beneath the oak tree. The T Rex gobbling his Jurassic Chum inside his pen. If I'm quiet, I can hear the magic cows with the strawberry milk tearing and chomping the grass. Foy smooths over the feather skirt of her dress. I smooth over mine. We are the fairest in all the land.

I hold my breath and sink underneath the water. It closes over my head. I open my eyes, see the blur of the dingy light-bulb on the ceiling. If I can calm myself. If I can float away like the stars and lose myself in sleep. But I'm running out of air. My body wants to stay down but my brain is screaming at me to *slide up, come up, get up, breathe, fill your lungs, breathe*. So I don't move and I breathe in.

I'm bolt upright and coughing my lungs out – the only witness to my attempt, if you can call it that, is the patch of mould in the corner. I want to try again, but I also don't. It's too shallow anyway. And I'm too aware of my own need to survive. I need to disengage. Perhaps I'll take one pack of the pills for now. See if that does anything. Let me try again. Relax. Relax. I pop them out of their packets, one at a time, and line them up along the bath.

I feel myself slip slowly beneath the water until my cold face is warm again. And I stay there. I'm safe. No one can hurt me.

Not the strange man outside, or whoever killed Tessa Sharpe. The stars collect above my face. The water stills.

But as I open my eyes, a shadow passes over me...

24 HOURS LATER

La Galerie de Lorraine de Courcy,
Dijon, France

16

FOY

Modern art makes me angry. All that unmade bed and upended urinal crap. My brother Paddy loves it and every chance he gets he drives into Dijon to this overpriced, pretentious gallery to look at the new installations. Today, I'm on full meltdown alert and he suggested I go with him to 'get me out of the house'.

'It'll do you good, sis.'

'Why on earth would I want to go there? You know I hate modern art.'

'It's not about the art. It's about getting you out of your own head for a few hours. Come on, it's free.'

I knew it wouldn't help. Nothing seems to. But a break from brick dust and piss-useless builders and rotten wood and over-expensive paint was on the cards and so I went. And as expected, I hated it. I knew from the second I was met by the snooty anorexic on the desk who handed me a map. The place stank like a crematorium.

The first room was four walls of pictures of red. Nothing else on them. Same colour red. Just red.

'I don't get it,' I say. 'Why is that even worth doing?'

'It provokes a reaction, doesn't it?' Paddy laughs. 'Anger. Maybe that's it.'

'I'm already angry,' I spit. He sits there looking at it for ages, from all angles, taking it all in. In the next room, five chairs. One has a giant white egg on it.

'Why is that art?' I say. 'An egg on a chair?'

He wheels round to face me. 'Doesn't that say something to you? The pristine white egg and the battered old chair with one of its rungs missing?'

'It says to me someone's put an egg on a chair.'

'It's not *put* on the chair though, is it? It's hanging *above* the chair. See the wire?'

'Oh yeah.'

'So what does *that* say to you?'

'Someone has *hung* an egg over a chair.'

He rolls his eyes and wheels on into the adjoining room. A couple of old men smile down at him in that patronising way people do when they see a wheelchair user. I stare them both out and Paddy grabs my arm and drags me away. We pass an assortment of impossibly thin people in strange angular clothing, walking achingly slowly, pointing things out to their pointy-nosed companions in stunned silence.

I want to shout IT'S ALL FUCKING CRAP. GET A LIFE. But I don't. Because I *wouldn't*. And because of Paddy. He likes it here. I'm here for him.

But there's this anxious gnawing in my chest I can't ignore. It taints everything.

His face lights up as we stand before the next piece. 'How about this one then?'

'Jars hanging from a tree,' I say, arms folded.

'And?'

'*Empty* jars hanging from a tree.'

'Look at the tree trunk.'

'Empty jars hanging from a tree which has a glass trunk but wooden branches. Well excuse me if I don't roll over and shit Mars bars.'

He sighs. 'Do you want to go to the gift shop while I finish up in here?'

'It's ridiculous, Paddy. Doesn't it anger you? You spent years at fine art college only for this bollocks to get its own gallery?'

'I think it's amazing.'

'A vacuum cleaner stuck to the wall? A deflated balloon? A squirt of paint and an empty skip? *That's* amazing?'

'Yes. You're not looking at it all properly. You're not unpicking it.'

'Oh I think I am. It's crap. I'm sorry, I know this is your thing but…' I stop beside a stick leaning against a wall. 'This is art?'

He laughs and wheels over to me. 'It's the representation of a life in crisis.'

'No, it's a stick leant against a wall.'

The next exhibit is a sheet of blue silk going back and forth on the floor, pulled by a tiny train on a track. 'What is *that* saying?'

'What does it say to you?'

'The sea. Pulled along by a tiny train.'

'Well there you go.'

'What do you mean, *there you go*? Why? And what about this?' I stand next to a large glass box and inside it is a huge pile of clothes and in the middle of the heap is a marble statue, poking out, only its arse visible.

'Reminds me of you in TK Maxx.'

He bites down on a smile but I see it before he swallows it. 'It's a work of art consumed by modern accessories.'

'Next.'

'You just need things explained to you.'

'No I need to see some proper art. By someone who can fucking draw, maybe?'

'Think of it like a puzzle. You have to put the pieces together. Doesn't any of this speak to you at all?'

In the next space, mutant butterflies, large papier-mâché clouds raining condoms and a collage of rancid fruit covered in maggots.

'Stunning. That really takes some thought and talent, doesn't it?'

It's when we come upon the last exhibit that my ire bubbles and brews in my guts. All four walls are adorned with the tiniest pictures, no larger than postcards, and which you can only see when you get right up close. The artist is there, with a scraggy plaited beard and more holes in his ears than actual skin. He's talking with his hands and gesturing to the pieces to two stick women in multi-coloured twat tights.

The pictures, the artist explains, were drawn by his dog. A spaniel called Desiree.

'Did he say his fucking spaniel drew these?'

It's at this point that I walk out, heading towards the café.

'Wondered how long it would take,' I hear him chuckle behind.

Even the café is poncey, the chairs all look like balloon animals but made from steel and the walls look like there's been a food fight recently. I order two pain escargots and coffees, that's all fucking cold by the time I pay. I find a crumby table by a window at the back of the room and wait. I feel like crying.

Outside in the pristine garden, a metal sculpture catches the light and momentarily blinds me. Irritated, I get up to move but then I look at the sculpture – it's a head, being pressed into the ground by a giant hand. And the expression on the face is all gnarled and distorted. Rage, being kept down. I get that. I *am* that.

A poem reels in my mind, one Mum used to read me sometimes before bed: 'Wynken, Blynken and Nod' by Eugene Field.

'*Wynken, Blynken, and Nod one night sailed off in a wooden shoe, Sailed on a river of crystal light, Into a sea of dew. "Where are you going, and what do you wish?" The old moon asked the three. "We have come to fish for the herring fish That live in this beautiful sea…'*

I repeat it until I see Paddy again.

I watch him wheel in, momentarily stopping to chat to an elderly woman who bends down next to him like he's a little boy who's banged his knee. She keeps him for a good five minutes. I try my deep breathing exercises the quack taught me. When he eventually arrives at our table, I'm already on the defensive.

'What was that about?'

'She asked if I was in Helmand with her son. That's how he lost *his* legs.'

'Nosy cow.'

'Jesus Christ, will you calm down?'

'I can't help it. Patronising old bag.'

'She was making conversation, that's all. I met her in the gallery and we were chatting about one of the installations.'

'Which one, the bale of hay? The broken cheese grater? The pants full of piss stains? She was patronising you, I heard.'

'No, she wasn't.' He sips his coffee, eyeballing me.

'*What?*'

'Talk to me.'

'It's a bad day, that's all. We all have them. I am entitled.'

'I know,' he replies, calmly. 'But you're having more than most at the moment.'

'Oh, sorry, am I not allowed to have a bad day today? Is it my turn tomorrow?'

'Foy, for god's sake.'

I take a deep breath and lean on the table, hand on my mouth. It's all in my throat. It's all in my eyes. 'Sorry.'

I know I'm being selfish. Life's chewed Paddy up and spat him out, minus two legs, and he just smiles and carries on. Why can't I be grateful? I have two brothers alive and healthy, two beautiful nieces and a nephew, I live in one of the most stunning regions in France. We have money, not much but enough. And it's a sunny day. Why can't I focus on all that rather than the gnawing pain inside me every minute?

Because I'm me, and he's him. And that's how it is.

'You don't have to apologise,' he says. 'Talk to me.' I shake my head. 'If you can't talk to me... what about Isaac?'

'What's there to say? You both know.'

'I don't know what it's like to lose a husband,' he says.

'It's a bit like losing two babies, really. Or a bit like losing Mum and Dad only a pinch more painful. Okay?'

He blows out his cheeks and sips his drink. 'So what are you feeling today?'

'Oh, we're gonna do this here, are we? A public counselling session in an art gallery café? Don't tell that artist with the beard. He'll probably want to film it for his next installation. *A Study in Desperation. Starring Foy Vallette and Paddy Keeton.*'

'It shouldn't have happened. He should be here.'

'Yeah, he should. But he's not. And do you know what Isaac said to me yesterday? "It's been eighteen months, Foy." Like there's a time limit. Eighteen months, right, that's it. You can stop grieving now. You can stop missing him. You can stop feeling that pain every time you take a shower because his razor and shower gel are still there on the shelf, waiting for him. You can remove his coat from the banister now. You can take his shoes to the brocante because he's not going to wear them anymore, is he? It's so obvious.' And now I'm crying. 'It's pathetic.'

'It's not pathetic,' he says. I push my crumby plate away. 'Have you thought anymore about planting a tree for him in the garden?'

I shake my head. 'Not yet.'

'We can scatter him near the trees we planted for Mum and Dad?'

I shake my head again. 'I'm not ready, Paddy. I know it's stupid but while he's in the urn it's like he's still there, in the house.'

He puts his hand on top of mine. 'He's not though, is he?' He cries with me. 'He's not there anymore, sis. I'm not going to mention it again. But I want you to know that when you're ready, we'll do it, all of us. We'll all be there with you.'

I nod. It's the only thing I can do.

I feel a little better after letting off steam, and afterwards we go round the rest of the gallery and I don't make any more comments, though I'm filled up with them and I know Paddy is waiting for me to say something about the gun firing turds and the stack of broken pencils. But I don't feel the need now. I just want to go home.

*

When we get back, Isaac's still up the ladder fixing the light in the salon.

'Oh my god are you still doing that?' I say, tripping over a mound of dust sheets that he's left by the door.

'Yeah, bloody rose keeps coming down. How did you two get on?'

I look around for signs of Paddy but I can hear his voice echoing off the kitchen units, talking to Lysette and Isaac's husband, Joe. 'Crap,' I mouth. 'But he enjoyed it.'

'Oh, there's a guy keeps phoning for you. Left his number in the hallway.'

'Who's that? If it's that sodding stonemason again, I'll tell him to take a running jump off the chip on his shoulder.'

But the note, which I can barely read, says *Kaden Cotterill. Call urgently*. And a number. 'Who's Kaden Cotterill?' I call out but Isaac doesn't answer. Joe comes out of the kitchen with two mugs of coffee.

'Hey, Fizzle. Do you want a brew?'

'Hey, Joe, no thanks. Who's Kaden Cotterill when he's at home?'

'No idea.' Joe disappears into the salon. I pick up the phone and begin dialling the scribbled number. I catch a glimpse of myself in the mirror – I've had chunks of plaster in my curls since Wednesday and there's still a smidge of lemon paint on my neck. We haven't painted since Monday.

The phone picks up on the third ring.

'Yeah, hello, this is Foy Vallette. I have a message to call this number?'

'Miss Vallette, hi, it's Kaden Cotterill here.'

'It's *Mrs* Vallette and I don't know a Kaden Cotterill, who are you?'

'I work at Middletons, Mrs Vallette.'

It takes me a while – my head has been so jam-packed with Luc's death and the house refurb there hasn't been room for much else. But this is important. This is so important, I made myself forget it was happening in case it didn't.

'Oh yes,' I say, a rush a breath invading my body. I grab for the banister and sit down on the bottom stair. 'Sorry, I wasn't expecting to hear from anyone. Someone was going to email me at the end of the job, weren't they?'

'That was the original plan, yes.'

'Have you found her? Have you found Ellis?'

'Yeah. I did find her.'

Another deep breath. 'Wow. Gosh, fucking hell. Okay. Where is she?'

'Initially I located her to the Nottingham area and then about a month ago she moved on quickly to Spurrington-on-Sea It's in the North West, near Blackpool. She was quite difficult to track down.'

'Well yeah, she's been in witness protection nearly twenty

years, she should have been nigh-on impossible to track down. So what's happened?'

'Um, well I wanted to talk to you about that and fill you in properly. I located her to a small apartment complex on the seafront. She had been placed in the basement flat and I was able to grab the empty place on the top floor so I could keep a close eye on her. Get you all the information you requested.'

I feel like I'm swallowing rocks. 'Why do I get the sense there's something wrong? Has she moved on again? Tell me that – is she happy and settled?'

'No, I can't say for sure that she is.'

This is not the news I wanted. But I've handled bad news before. I can handle it again. We can do something about this now we've found her. While she's alive, there's hope.

'What do you mean?'

'She was mostly frightened. Vulnerable. And now she's gone.'

'Gone where?' I notice a bit of the newly laid plaster is bubbling on the staircase wall. I pluck at it with my one remaining nail. The plaster comes off in palm-sized chunks, falling to the floor as dust. Bloody builders.

'I got back to my flat a few minutes ago and there's a guy here. Think he's her social worker. He questioned me about her. He said she's disappeared.'

'Wha—?'

'Yeah. I don't know any more than that I'm afraid. He did say there was some blood on the carpet.'

'Oh my god.'

'The way the flat's been left, the questions he was asking me, suggests she left in a hurry. Or she was taken...'

I can't breathe.

'One option is that she may have rumbled me. Known I was following her.'

'How?'

'The other night, I got back from work and she fainted. And I brought her inside and she had a nosebleed. I went up to my flat and got some peas to put on it and when I came down, she'd gone through my phone. And she'd found pictures that I'd taken of her. The ones I was going to send to you next week with my report.'

'Oh shit.'

'I tried to pass it off initially as a crush. I said I was low-key obsessed with her.'

'So you pretended to be her stalker?'

'Not a stalky kind of stalker. More a quietly lovelorn one. Kind of thing.'

'And it freaked her out?'

'No, she was quite enamoured with the idea. And we kissed. I know it was unprofessional but I had to throw her off the scent. It was a mistake, I realise that. But then the night before last, I was teaching her some self-defence cos she was worried about being attacked and I told her I didn't want to start anything. She took it badly.'

'Why was she worried about being attacked?'

'I assumed she had a violent ex who was looking for her and her baby.'

'She's got a baby?'

'That's another weird thing. I've been inside her apartment and the baby's there. But it's *not* a baby. It's a doll.'

'What?'

'She'd been pretending it was a baby. It's one of those reborn things you can order online. She was pretending.'

'Oh my god, what's happened to her?' I say it more to myself than him.

'I've got photos, interactions, everything you asked for…'

'But you haven't got *her*, have you?' I say, with thinly veiled fury. 'Some bloody private detective you are. Mr Magoo would have done a better job.'

'I'm not her bodyguard. You asked Middletons to get photos, a sense of her daily movements, a picture of her life. That's all you wanted.'

'I asked you to keep an eye on her and get me a full picture of her life. I wanted to know she was happy and settled.'

'Well, you can make your own mind up about that. But in my view, no, she's not happy. Or settled. Woman's a freak.'

'Don't you dare call her that.'

'I'm sorry, I shouldn't have said that. I apologise.'

'Oh whoopee fucking shit,' I cry. 'What am I meant to do with an apology, Mr Cotterill? Maybe *that* can be my cousin instead? Maybe that will do, eh?'

'I don't know what else to say.'

'You *knew* she was vulnerable. You *knew* she was in hiding and afraid. Why didn't you… why weren't you… ugh, Jesus Christ.'

'I don't *think* she's been kidnapped. The flat's not exactly hidden away. It's right on the seafront. Somebody would have seen or heard something.'

'Why didn't *you* see or hear something? That's what I'm paying you for, you bloody idiot.' The hardness in my throat

gives way to tears. I wipe my cheeks roughly with my palm.
'I'm coming over. I can't sit around here doing nothing.'

'Alright, well, I'm gonna head back to London then.'

'What? You're going back to London *now*?'

'There's nobody here to watch anymore, Mrs Vallette. If Ellis is not here, then I don't need to be here either. This is a job.'

'Do you still want paying?'

'Excuse me?'

'Do. You. Still. Want. Paying?' I spit.

'You've already paid me.'

'Via cheque, and it's post-dated.'

'You can't do that.'

'You fucking watch me. Now you sit tight and I will be there as soon as I can. Send me your location. And you better hope she turns up alive in the meantime or I swear on all that's holy, there'll be blood on *your* carpet.'

Third day of the Christmas
holidays,
eighteen years ago...

17

I'm in the castle treehouse with Ellis, my little legs swinging out over the rope ladder in the doorway. Ellis is stirring the Stone Soup for dinner.

'Did you feed the mongooses?' she asks me.

'Yeah.'

'What is a mongoose?'

'A bird I think,' I say. 'We better go and get some more penguin steaks for the polar bears later, before the shops shut.'

I sneak another Jelly Tot from the packet we're saving for after tea. Ellis sneaks one too.

'Is your dad alright?' I ask her.

She stops stirring the soup. 'Yeah. Why?'

'I saw him crying this morning. My dad was crying too. Last time I saw them crying was at Grandad's funeral.'

'My dad cries all the time,' says Ellis. 'He cried at that RSPCA advert on telly the other day. And when that woman won the speedboat on *Family Fortunes*.'

'My dad doesn't at all,' I say. 'I told Mum but she just said he'd been peeling onions. He hadn't though cos we've got fish pie for tea and there's no onions in that.'

'Let's not worry about it,' says Ellis. 'I'm dishing the soup now. Sit at the table.'

And I do. And we pretend-slurp together. Then we wash up

together, I dry the plates and put them in the box cupboard. Then we eat the rest of the Jelly Tots.

'I'm thirsty,' says Ellis.

'Shall I go and get us some more cans?' I pick up both our Rios from the shelf and shake them – both empty.

'We won't be allowed anymore. Chelle said we could only have one a day.'

'She won't know. The pub's shut now, they'll have gone upstairs for the afternoon. I'll get us a couple more.'

I race across the beer garden and through the back door and bomb through the kitchen and along the passageway into the bar, but though I'm expecting to see the place in near darkness, except for the daylight coming in through the diamond-shaped leaded windows, the lights in the main bar are all still on. The jukebox is playing. Voices. I duck down behind the beer pumps.

'It'll be alright, sis.' Uncle Dan and Mum.

'It won't be alright. It won't be alright at all. Will it? You have no idea where you're going. And what about Ellis?'

The music stops and clicks over to another song. A harmonica. It gets louder. 'Come on. Dance with me.'

'No,' Mum sniffs. 'I'm doing this.' She's cleaning ashtrays at the tables. I don't know where Dad is. Maybe he went upstairs already.

'Come on, come here,' Uncle Dan says. 'Please. Dance with me.'

I hear the longest sniff. Mum's crying. The song is called 'He Ain't Heavy, He's My Brother'. I have no idea what that means but it seems to upset Mum no end. I peek out and see them, holding each other, moving in a circle in the middle of the bar. He's stroking her hair. She's just holding onto him. He's holding onto her.

'There has to be another way. You have to talk to the police again.'

'It's me or them, Chelle. That's what they said.'

'I don't want to lose you. Either of you. I can't.'

'Let's just dance, sis. Come on.'

I peek out again, and they're dancing. He's in his red Bristol City shirt, she's in her blue flower dress. They're both crying with their eyes closed. What on earth is going on? I can't ask, Mum will shout at me for sneaking around. She did that time I snuck in to borrow her perfume to make our marvellous medicine, and her and Dad were in bed. I hear the jukebox click to silence. Another click. And the same harmonica sounds.

'Let's play it again, come on,' Uncle Dan sniffs.

'Song's not long enough,' says Mum, and when I look they've stopped dancing. They're still and hugging.

I carefully grab the two cans of Rio from the bottom shelf, and move two back ones forward so Mum doesn't know they're missing, and duck down underneath the counter, racing back out to the beer garden. I tuck one can in each pocket of my hoody and climb the ladder. Ellis is drawing when I get up there.

'Here you go,' I say, placing the cans on our welcome mat. 'Ooh, I need a wee.'

'Okay.'

I race back inside and up the stairs, two at a time (nearly) like Isaac does. Dad's playing PlayStation in Paddy's room. I sprint up the corridor to Isaac's room and I don't even knock.

He's sitting beside the front window under the net curtain

looking quite bridal, taking sneaky drags from a cigarette. When I burst in, he jumps about a foot in the air, flinging the cigarette outside and wafting the air in front of his face.

'Fuck, I thought you were Dad,' he gasps, making out he was about to have a heart attack. 'Bloody knock, Foy! I've told you before.'

'Mum and Uncle Dan are crying and hugging in the bar,' I blurt, all breathless.

'What?'

I repeat: 'Mum and Uncle Dan are crying and hugging in the bar.'

'So?'

'And they put a song on the jukebox twice. And sort of danced to it except the dancing wasn't very good and they were sort of crying and turning in a circle.'

'So?'

'So why are they doing that? The last time I saw Uncle Dan cry it was at Grandad's funeral but that was ages ago. They wouldn't still be upset about that, would they?'

'Nah, course not,' he says, going back underneath his white veil and lighting up another cigarette. 'Keep an eye on the door for me.'

'So what's going on?' I ask him, imploringly, as he smokes his cigarette and seems to have no cares in the universe.

'I dunno, do I? Ask Pads.'

'He's playing PlayStation with Dad.'

'Where's Ellis?' asks Isaac.

'In the castle. Should I go and get her?'

'No.' He stubs out his cigarette on the windowsill, closes the window and picks up a small white bottle which he squirts into his mouth. Then he wipes his hands on a wet wipe and grabs a pack of Juicy Fruit from his desk. 'Listen, you're not allowed to tell Ellis this, alright? Uncle Dan doesn't want her worrying about it.'

'Worrying about what?'

'I heard him and Mum and Dad talking the other night and he's in a shit ton of trouble. Like proper police trouble.'

'Oh my god. Why?'

'Dunno, I only caught some of the conversation. But the police were going to send him to jail. Serious, serious jail. For, like, years.'

'Oh my god.'

'I didn't hear all of it. They had the telly turned up too loud. But he might have to go away for a bit.'

'To jail?'

'Maybe. Maybe somewhere else. You know like when they used to send prisoners away to other countries instead of prison? Like Australia and that?'

'Is he going to Australia then?'

'Don't say anything to Ellis, alright?' He puts the cigarette packet back inside a small wooden box which our grandma brought him back from Egypt to 'keep his key rings in' and peels back the corner of the carpet behind his desk. Then he crouches down and lifts two of the floorboards, posting the box underneath. In seconds, the carpet's back in place, the room smells of spiced apple and cinnamon room spray and the cigarettes, lighter and breath spray have all magically disappeared.

'What will happen to Ellis when he goes away?'

'She'll have to go into care or something.'

'No, no way,' I say to him.

'Shh, keep your voice down.'

'I don't care, she's not going to an orphanage. She's not an orphan, she's *ours*.'

Orphanage. The word made me think of when we'd been to see *Annie* or *Oliver!* at the theatre. The thought of Ellis being in one and wearing rags and scrubbing floors and being looked after by some horrible old hag who beat her made me feel sick. I would have to do something.

'She's staying here with us,' I tell him, in no uncertain terms.

'It might not work out like that, Foy,' he says, all big-brotherly and irritating.

'It *will* work out like that because I'll *make* it work out like that. They're not taking her away. I'm telling Mum.'

'No, you're not, Foy. Don't; she'll know we were snooping. You know how she hates that.'

'Me and Ellis will run away then.'

'Don't be soft, you ain't going nowhere.'

'Well they're not taking her. I won't let them.'

When I get back out to the treehouse, it's empty. Ellis has tidied away the dinner things and there's no sign of her or our cans of Rio at all. I turn in wild circles, praying for some sign of her. For a horrible minute, I think she's gone already, vanished in a puff of smoke like the genie in that film we watched at the weekend. I think she might have fallen out of the treehouse and banged her head so I check out the back window. What if a strange man has taken her away? Or a witch has turned her into a mouse? What if they've sent her to the orphanage or to Australia already? I shouldn't have left her on her own. I can't stop the tears.

Then, from the top of the castle, I spy a movement from the corner of my eye – she's wheeling around the top of the car park on her bike. She waves out to me and my whole chest deflates. I swallow hard a couple of times and wipe my eye and I scamper down the ladder and across the car park, where she stops wheeling and stands still on the bike while I grab mine and cycle over to her.

'You were ages,' she says, handing me a can of Rio from her cardigan pocket.

'Sorry. Needed a poo as well. What are you doing?'

'Getting the polar bear steaks. The shop was shutting soon.' She points to the skittle alley. And in a heartbeat, I am back in our world and we are in our Lamborghini and Ferrari, and racing each other home to the castle in time for tea.

*

The last time I see Ellis is at the airport. We've come back from the surprise Christmas Florida trip that Uncle Dan's treated us all to. My guard is down and I'm tired and groggy after a delayed flight, a sleeping pill that has made me feel sick, and a horrible dinner on the plane. We've had a brilliant holiday – I don't think we spent more than a few hours out of the pool or the parks the whole time, and I've eaten so many pancakes with maple syrup that all of my clothes feel tighter. But it's over now and we're all a bit quiet. It's January 15th. A Wednesday.

'Shall we go to baggage claim and you guys go to the toilets?' says Mum, as she, Ellis and Uncle Dan veer off. 'We'll see you at the car. Car park E, bay 114.'

'Okay,' says Dad.

'I'll stay with Ellis,' I say, but Mum says no, go with your dad. And I let go of her hand. It's a small moment, a tiny moment compared to the last two weeks we've spent together, but it's the one I think about the most.

'Why can't I stay with Ellis?' I'm asking my dad this question all the way through arrivals, out of the airport terminal and all the way down the rank to the shuttle bus, waiting to take us on board. A man loads our luggage. I hang onto my Minnie Mouse toy. Mum got me one the same as Ellis won in the hotel raffle. 'Why, Dad?'

He keeps fobbing me off. And I know something's wrong. I don't know what, but I know he's lying cos he won't look at me.

We're almost back at the car when he turns to me, sitting beside him, and to Paddy and Isaac, sitting together behind him and he says, 'Uncle Dan and Ellis aren't going to be coming back with us.'

'Why not?' I say, stroking Minnie Mouse's ears.

'They're going to their new home,' he says, looking out the window.

'But they live with us,' says Paddy, frowning. I look at Isaac but he's looking out the window too. There's a little movement in his jaw, like he's chewing.

'They got a new place. Uncle Dan got a call while we were in Epcot the other day. That's where he disappeared to. Remember we were queuing up for churros? That was what the call was about. But they had to go now.'

'So where is their new house?' asks Paddy. Isaac looks like he's going to be sick.

'I'm not sure, mate,' says Dad, stroking my hair the way he does when I've fallen over. But I haven't fallen over. He can't look at me.

I look behind at my brothers. They can't look at me either. 'Why today?'

'It had to be today, Foy,' says Dad. But he seems so sad.

'But I didn't say goodbye.'

'I know, it's not the best timing.' He licks his lips. His eyes fill with water.

'But Ellis will come at half term. And I can call her tonight, yeah?'

Dad looks at the boys. The boys look at each other. I never saw Isaac cry before.

'I can call her tonight, can't I? Dad?'

'Maybe, love. We'll see, yeah?' And he strokes my hair again but I take his hand off my head because I don't like him doing that today. I don't know why he's doing it. And he turns to the window and I can see his eyes in his reflection and he's crying as well. All three of them are now. And I've had enough of this, all the crying and the vague answers and the not telling me what's going on.

'Dad, why is everyone crying?'

His eyes close in the reflection. I look back at Isaac and he's not saying anything. Paddy's got his head down. I look back at Dad and I remember what Isaac said to me.

'Did the police come and get Uncle Dan and take him to jail? What about Ellis?'

'Ellis will be fine, love. She's got her dad.'

I don't remember much else about that day, only what Isaac and Paddy have told me since. I have a total meltdown in the car park and my dad virtually has to drag me back to the car and pin me in my seat. It's only when Mum comes back, on her own with her suitcase, that I even begin to calm down. She sits with me in the back seat and strokes my head the whole way home. Paddy sits next to us, Isaac in the front and nobody says anything but *Pass the mints* or *Anyone need a wee? Service station in nine miles*, all the way back to the pub. I'm told properly when Mum tucks me in that night. I don't remember exactly what she says. There's only one bit I recall for sure:

'We're not going to see Ellis again, Foy.'

'Not ever?'

'No, darling.'

And she stays with me in my bed because neither of us can stop crying.

18

Sunday, 3rd November

There was a fly in my Petit Filous. I should have taken that as a sign that today would go tits up and take on water. Next up: disgruntled lorry drivers chose to blockade the ferry port, so all the planes are over-booked. I manage by the skin of my back teeth and a shit-load of grovelling to get booked on a flight to Manchester, for which money I could have gone to New York and back again.

And the flight itself is interminable. I have a portly gentleman on one side of me with a suspicious rash all over his neck, who coughs from take-off to landing, and on the other side of me a screaming toddler who keeps kicking me in the thigh. My anguish isn't over when we land. Once we hit the tarmac I'm faced with an hour-long security check and a 45-minute wait at Rent-a-Deathtrap while the guy on the desk – Jeff – locates the booking for my hire car.

'I only booked it yesterday afternoon,' I say. 'It should be at the top of the pile.'

'There's no record of it, Miss.'

'Mrs,' I said. 'It's *Mrs* Vallette. If you found the booking you would know that.'

I'm getting hotter and hotter because I have two jumpers and a coat, plus scarf and hat on, to save room in my luggage, and a sheen of sweat is beading on my brow. I'm this side of huffy when the magical Arnold From the Back Room appears, scratching his groin, biscuit crumbs on his tie and says, 'Oh yeah, Mrs Vallette, that one came in last night, Jeff. The keys are here.'

I'm all huffed up with nowhere to go then. I have to calm myself and my heartburn down, take the keys from Jeff and then escort myself to bay 204 and a just-washed Peugeot 308 that smells like feet.

I'm bombing along the M6, now, which is the only thing that's been kind to me the whole journey. It's good to hear Radio 2 again. By the time I reach Spurrington, the sky is full of bruised clouds like there's a storm rolling in, but the still-open cafés and arcades light the puddles along the road and give off a somewhat comforting glow. It's around 5 p.m. I find a car park along a side street that the hotel – The Lakes View Pub and Rooms – has directed me to on its website, but when I get inside, I discover there's no reception – only a short blonde woman behind the bar looking pissed off.

'Alright?' she says.

'Yes, I booked a room for three nights. Mrs Foy Vallette?'

There's a board of keys hanging up behind the cash register. She turns to it and unhooks one, then turns back to the computer and taps some keys.

'You go across the road to the red door and it's second floor up first left.' She hands me the key for Room 10.

'Oh right,' I say, somewhat at odds. She offers no other information.

'I haven't had any staff turn up today,' she says. 'Three of 'em, all with hangovers. I mean, what do I do?'

'Erm, what time do you serve breakfast?'

'If you want it, it's from seven to nine over here.' She gestures vaguely to the bar area behind us. 'There'll be no one to bleedin' serve it to you, mind.' She then turns on her heel and disappears through a swinging door.

I decide that I like her. I respect her inability to bullshit. She's in a mood and she doesn't care who knows it. I know where I stand with people like that. It's bullshitters who get the brunt of my ire. It's then that the Cotterill bloke crosses my mind and the rage I felt at the airport in the car hire queue resurfaces.

I leave the bar and cross the road to the red door and make my way up a stygian staircase to Room 10. The whole stairwell stinks deeply of damp, old cigarettes, and spiced Apple PlugIns. I haven't had a cigarette for ten years but every now and again the smell of them makes me yearn. I soon forget my craving when I notice a turd in the middle of the stairs. At least I *think* it's a turd – the bulb's gone so I can't see a damn thing in the weak glow afforded by the exit signs.

My room is an adequate size – a double bed, a single bed and two faux leather bucket seats overlooking the bay. It's just as well the view is good – nothing in the room is. 'Christ's sake.'

I dump my bag on the coffee table and take in the facilities. I can see the dip in the centre of the bed from here. There's no TV, no kettle, no shower. Mould around the bath, a slightly sloping floor and creaky floorboards. There are Venetian blinds at the two bay windows but many of the slats are missing. The carpet has a few cigarette burns. Oh, and the main light bulb has gone as well.

I get out my phone to find the map Cotterill sent me to Ellis's flat. Two minutes along the seafront. Turn left out of the hotel, along the promenade, past the arcades and it's in the bank of private apartments after the road with the Chinese supermarket. And I feel it in my chest then – the ache. I'm not thinking about the expensive and uncomfortable flight, or how bad the traffic was getting into the town, or where I'm going to get a bite to eat before everything shuts. I'm just thinking about Ellis. How close I am to where she is. Where she *was*.

She's always been ten years old in my mind. Ten years old, red hair, sun freckles, wearing a pink and yellow sundress and clutching a little Minnie Mouse. She hasn't aged, she hasn't changed. Startling blue eyes, little bounce in her walk, little turned-in feet. I unzip my suitcase and get Thread Bear out of the top. Even if she's forgotten me, she'll remember him. She'll remember us sitting him and Miss Whiskers on the breakfast bar in the kitchen, playing *Pop Idol* auditions or whatever it was. Sitting in the treehouse. We called it our castle. Seems so funny now.

I put Thread Bear in my handbag, lock the room and venture back outside and along the seafront in the direction of the flats. I keep walking and eventually my app tells me I'm on Ellis's road – Marine Road West – and so I look for the apartment numbers. 74a, 76a, 78a then *bam*, there it is – 82a. Basement flat. There's a light on in the lounge window. And there's a man in there. Walking around.

Cotterill.

I walk up the front steps to the main door and press the buzzer for 82a several times. My heart pounds painfully for no apparent reason and I have to keep reminding myself that it's not Ellis I'm going to see but him. The man who I've been paying to keep an eye on her. The man who's lost her. The man who called her a freak on the phone. And my guts start to simmer again.

The front door opens and two incredibly scrawny men lumber out, one with a huge tear in the back of his jeans and the other with a limp and scabs up and down one arm. They barely notice me and carry on padding down the steps. Another man appears in the doorway. Tall, blond, stubbly beard, eyes as grey and heavy as the sky.

'Yes?' he says, with more than a note of suspicion.

'Oh so you decided to stay then?' I say. 'So nice of you.'

'I'm sorry? Are you a friend of Joanne's?' He has a Scottish accent. Cotterill didn't sound Scottish on the phone. In fact he *wasn't* Scottish.

'Why are you Scottish? You weren't Scottish on the phone. Are you in character? I'm Foy Vallette.'

He looks confused. 'I'm sorry but I think—' And then he stops and looks at me silently. '*You're* Foy?'

'Yes. And you're Kaden?'

'No, I'm Neil. Scantlebury. You're *the* Foy?'

'How many Foys do you know?'

'Claire Foy. The actress.'

'Well I'm clearly not her, am I?'

'You're Ellis's Foy?'

My heart misses a beat and the next one thumps hard. 'Yes.'

'You need to go.'

'I've come all the way from France. I'm going nowhere until I see my cousin. Where is she?'

'No, you need to leave.'

'Please, please, I need to see her.'

'I'm sure you do but that is information I can't give you right now.'

'Why not?'

'You don't need to know.'

'I *do*, I *do* need to know, let me in.'

'How do I know you are who you say you are?'

'What? You said you knew me, you said "Ellis's Foy". I'm her cousin. I want to know if she's alright, please.'

'Prove it.'

'How?' He folds his arms. He's not going to let me cross the threshold until I do. 'I don't know her now, I knew her then.'

He's still not letting me through.

I hold up my passport on the photo page. He cranes his neck to look at it closer but he's still not budging. I pack it away. 'She has red hair and blue eyes. She has a scar on her inner right thigh – no, left – from where she was hiding in a patch of barbed wire when we were playing 123-In when we were six. She has two chickenpox scars on her right wrist. She loves animals. And Disney movies. And riding bikes. And imagining. She lives inside her head. And any time I was afraid she would hold my hand until I stopped. That's the girl I knew.'

He scratches the beginnings of a blond beard on his jawline, standing to one side to let me in.

Even though I have no idea who this man is, he seems to know about me which means he must know Ellis. Her boyfriend? Cotterill's report, which I read on the plane on the way over, said she didn't *have* a significant other. Some bloody private detective. Couldn't find his arse with both hands.

The door opens into a lounge area-cum-kitchenette and off that appears to be a small single bedroom with a bathroom next door. The patio doors in the lounge open out onto a tiny courtyard with steps leading to the seafront. The place stinks of damp and rotting food and there are cat hairs everywhere. Is this his place? No. By the way he folds the blanket on the sofa he's as disgusted by animal hairs as I am. But I can't immediately sense Ellis in this room.

'How do you know me?' I ask as he rounds the breakfast bar and sticks the kettle under the tap. He's good-looking in a stern, doom-laden sort of way and his back is broad, his hair a dirty blond colour. Same as my dad's. Except he doesn't wear glasses. Or smile very much. 'Where's Cotterill?'

'Tea?' he offers.

'Yeah. Thanks. Where's Kaden Cotterill? Who are you? Where's Ellis?' I pull my jumper cuffs down over my fists. It's freezing in here.

'Which first, tea or questions?' He turns to me, eyebrows up.

'Questions. Where's Kaden Cotterill?'

'Gone. Back to London. I arrived as he was leaving.'

'I knew he wouldn't hang around. Bastard.' I sit down on the edge of a two-seater sofa, the arms of which are covered in cat scratches and hairs. 'I'm so bloody cancelling that cheque. What a shyster.'

'So you were employing him to follow Ellis? He told me.'

'Yeah. And now she's gone.'

The kettle boils and clicks and he pours water into two

mugs. 'I took a statement from him in case the police need it.'

'You're not the police?'

'I work with the police but no, I'm not a copper. I'm not supposed to be here, I'm on leave, but I've been working with Ellis a long time. Since she… left her old life.'

He won't look at me. He stirs the mugs. Pours the milk. Takes the bags straight out. It can't have brewed. 'You make it sound like she had a choice.'

'She talked about you all the time.'

'She did?' I say, a well of emotion rising in my throat. 'I think about her a lot too. You work in Witness Protection then?'

He frowns. 'I shouldn't be talking to you about this.' He brings the mugs over and sets them down on the coffee table before me.

'Then why are you?' I pick up the mug meant for me. 'My mum told us everything, after Ellis and Uncle Dan had gone into hiding. Well she told us what she knew. Which wasn't much. Are you a social worker?'

'No, I work for the UKPPS – UK Protected Persons Service. We look after people who are at risk from criminal entanglement.'

'Uncle Dan grassed on some drug dealers, yeah?'

'I… can't go into this.'

'Yeah you can.'

He sips his tea and settles it down again. 'His testimony got six of them put away for life. He sang like a bloody canary for us. He was afraid. It was a £700k supply line, spanning the whole country. Major dice. When police raided one of the addresses, they found an industrial pill press making more than 200 ecstasy tabs a minute.'

'Oh my god.'

'They had twelve-year-olds in the supply chain. It was frightening. That's when your uncle drew the line. His testimony stopped it in its tracks. He pissed off quite a few big bads though. That's why we had to hide them.'

'So, do you think something's happened to Ellis? The big bads?'

'No, I don't,' he says flatly. 'I think she's playing silly buggers *again* and any moment she's going to walk through that door, *that's* what I think.'

I look towards the door he's pointing at. It remains closed. 'What?'

'This is what she does, Foy. She lies. She plays games. She runs off, pretends something's happened to her, gets everybody worried and worked up and then, Hey Presto, back she comes, like butter wouldn't melt.'

'Now hang on a minute...'

'No, *you* hang on. You haven't seen her since you were, what, ten years old? She's not the Ellis Kemp you remember. She's changed a lot in eighteen years.'

I spy a Lego model of a castle on a high shelf. A Roald Dahl book with creases in the spine – *The Witches*. A note on a small blackboard written in pink chalk – *Buy cheese, eggs, blue bootlaces*. Ornaments – The Snowman. George and his pot of marvellous medicine. Scented erasers. DVDs of Disney movies we used to watch together. A tiny Christmas tree with a small pile of presents around it labelled neatly – her handwriting's the same. The Minnie Mouse cuddly she got from Disney World – the white bits all grey and shabby and her dress all flat where she'd been well-cuddled. The unicorn pencil topper I gave her is there too. I walk over to the window-sill to pick it up. Definitely the same one, though its mane has fallen out and the face is rubbed off.

'Actually,' I tell him, 'I don't think she's changed much at all.'

19

Sunday, 3rd November (afternoon)

I switch on my phone and call home to let them know I've arrived safely. Isaac answers. Hearing his voice settles my anxiety somewhat. Even if he is mad with me.

'Where the fuck—'

'I'm in England.'

'You're *what*?'

'I'm in England. I knew you and Paddy would try and talk me out of it.'

'Out of what?' I overhear him telling Paddy and the words *fucking England?* 'One minute you were on the phone, the next we call you for dinner and Joe finds a note taped to your bedroom door. The fuck, Foy?'

'Okay. A few months after Luc died, I employed a private detective. To find Ellis.'

'Oh god, not this again.'

'Yes, this again. They found her.'

'They *found* her? Oh my god. Is she—'

'She's alive, at least. Somewhere. But she disappeared suddenly.'

Isaac sighs, like he's deflating of all his air. 'Sis, you should have said.'

'I knew what you'd both say – *you're chasing rainbows again, Foy. She's a different person now, Foy. She won't remember us.* Well, I needed to find out for myself.'

'You can't cope with this right now, not on top of everything else. Shall we come over, me and Pads?'

'No, you've got enough on your plates. And the roofer's coming later today and you need to be there to make sure he puts those slates back on right. I'm okay. There's a miserable detective guy here who's supposedly on the case.'

'I'm worried about you.'

'Yeah, I'm worried about me too but I'll be fine.'

'Alright, but you call us if you change your mind and we'll be there. Call us if there's any news too. Love you.'

'Love you too.' I ache when the screen fades to black.

In the lounge, Neil sits before the TV, his brown lace-ups propped up on the coffee table. He's watching a programme about Hampton Court.

'What did you mean when you said she'd done this before?' I ask him.

He sips his tea, not taking his eyes from the screen. 'When she was living in Manchester. She ran off. Left a note saying she'd had enough. By the time I got there, having done eighty-plus on the motorway thinking she was going to throw herself off a bridge, she opens the door to me, as good as new. Twice she did that. I got firm with her in the end and she didn't do it again.'

'What do you mean, "got firm"?'

'I said if she tried it again, I'd stop dealing with her case and pass her onto one of my team. That was all it took. That was before the tram smash.'

'She was in a *tram smash*?'

'She *said* she was in a tram smash. She was actually nowhere near at the time it crashed. Next thing I know, she's on TV news talking about her injuries.' He goes back to learning the intricacies of King Henry's velvet piss pot. 'She lies about everything.'

I sit down tentatively on the single armchair, brushing the cat hairs off the arm, which is a losing game because there are so many. 'Like what?'

'You name it,' he says. 'She changes her name daily, depending on who she's talking to. She has seven cats, none of which actually belong to her. I'm only giving you the very tip of the iceberg though. She's... messed up.' He looks at me. I can take that from him. He knows her. It's not like when Cotterill called her a freak on the phone – he's only known her a month.

'Where have you come from, Edinburgh?'

'No, I'm still based in Bristol. Well I was. I've been staying at my parents' place in Dumfries for the last couple of days. Bit of a break.'

'So how did you know she was missing?'

He turns his attention back to the TV. The historian's reading out Henry's weekly food ration. It's a long list. I don't think Neil's going to answer me, but all of a sudden, he does. 'She left me a voicemail. I put off listening to it because it's usually the same thing. Asking me to visit. Paranoid she's being followed. All *Peter and the Wolf* stuff.'

'But the wolf eventually got Peter.'

'That's why I listened to the message. Always that possibility, isn't there? I found some broken glass when I came in.'

'Where?'

'Some in the bedroom, some in here. She's done a *Gone Girl*. Planting clues.'

My chest clenches. She could walk in that door any second. And then she'll see me. And we can be together again, like it was. Well, not *exactly* like it was. I lose myself in a trance for whole moments. When I come to, Neil's sad grey eyes are staring at me.

And then it strikes me – he can fill in the gaps in my understanding. He can tell me things about Ellis I've always wondered. I reach for the tea he's made me but it's so milky, my stomach turns over. I leave it alone.

Some historian's poring through a dusty old book in white gloves.

'I had nightmares for years about Ellis,' I tell him. I don't know if he's listening. He's watching the book-fingering. 'We weren't allowed to ask questions after those first few days but we talked about her, me, Paddy and Isaac. They're my brothers.'

He affords me an eyebrow raise, but nothing more.

'I pretended she'd shrunk, like in *Honey, I Shrunk the Kids*. And I had to find her. I'd have nightmares about losing her. Or Dad mowing the lawn over her.'

Neil frowns. 'Bit daft.'

'Yeah, it was daft. But that's the only possibility I could handle, rather than accept the fact she'd fallen off the edge of the earth. I had this stupid ritual I made Dad do every time he was about to cut the grass. He had to shout that the lawnmower's coming, so Ellis had time to run to safety. I'd scream if he didn't. My poor dad. Later I got to thinking she'd been taken by a big bird. I'd climb trees and search nests for her. Maybe she'd been turned into a bird herself. But she never ever flew back to me.'

'Must have been hard,' he mumbles, but doesn't look over, which allows me to cry. I have such a headache and it starts banging. The crying seems to make it worse.

'When I was about thirteen, fourteen, I read an article at school in an art lesson – we were doing papier-mâché and tearing up all this newspaper – and this girl, about my age, had been knocked down and killed on her way home from a party. I thought she was Ellis. I tried to convince myself that she'd died. But there was always that little voice that thought *Maybe not*. What happened to them, that day at Heathrow Airport?'

Neil cracks his knuckles. 'It's all classified stuff, really.'

'Oh come on, it was eighteen years ago. It doesn't matter now.'

'Still classified.'

'TELL ME.'

'They went to Scotland, to a safe house. After a time, they went to Liverpool. Settled there pretty well for a couple of years.'

'Then?'

'A few members of the cartel tracked them down. The more money in the business, the bigger their reach. So we had to move them – to Scarborough. They were fairly happy there until Ellis was eighteen.'

His face had changed. Darkened. I said nothing but I waited whole minutes for him to say anything else. The history program went to an ad break. Then he said it.

'Three men broke into their house. They didn't get away that time.'

'What did they do?'

He swigs his tea. 'You sure you want to know?'

'I *have* to know.'

'They beat your uncle badly. All morning. Tied him to a radiator. Finished him off by strangling him. Ellis was there.'

He says it so matter-of-factly. There is no warmth in the room at all.

'Ellis saw it?'

'She got home from college later that day and found him tied up in the living room. They'd waited for her, tied her to the rad at the other end of the room and beat her up too. They didn't strangle her though. They just made her watch.'

'Did they... touch her?' I ask, wiping my cheeks again.

'No. Thankfully. There was one guy in the cartel who used to intimidate female witnesses that way, but he wasn't there. He was in prison at the time thank god. Nasty bastard. He used to carry a rape kit round with him. So no, she wasn't touched. But she was badly hurt. That's the reason she can't have kids. Had to give her a hysterectomy.'

'Oh my god.'

'I hadn't checked on them for a few days. Dan wasn't answering calls. So I went round. And I found them in the living room. She still had a pulse, barely. He was cold. I don't know why she forgave me for that day but she did. I got home that night, opened a bottle of JB and downed the lot. I didn't want to stop.' He rubs his eyes.

'You saved her life?' I can't stop the tears then. They keep coming. Next thing I know, he's handing me two sheets of kitchen roll.

'After she came out of hospital, she was moved to

Manchester for a time then back to Liverpool. Did a spell in Nottingham before she came here, two months ago.'

'Always with new names?'

'New names, new identities. New jobs. Passports. Ann Hilsom. Melanie Smith. Claire Price. And now Joanne Haynes.'

'She can't have known if she was coming or going.'

'It's all part of it, I'm afraid. I visit her sometimes. See how she's doing. Bring her shopping when she can't go out. I don't have to do that anymore, but I do.'

'Why can't she go out?'

'She gets paranoid. I come up and see how she's faring. But since she's been recategorised as low-risk, it's not been as often and she's struggled with that.'

'Probably looked on you as another dad.'

He didn't answer that. 'The cartel Dan grassed on are no longer operational. But she thought three of them were following her a few weeks ago.'

'And were they?'

He stares into space. 'No. She was making it up.'

'But she *was* being followed. By Kaden Cotterill, for one. For *me*.'

He shakes his head but doesn't say anything else. Christ, he's so miserable. Talk about dour Scot. I'd have thought the least he could afford me was a reassuring smile. It's all so gloomy in here. Damp in the corners, brown cat-scratchy sofa, brown chair, small TV with a crappy aerial. Avocado bathroom suite. Everything is so ugly and sad and cold. I want to burn the place to the ground. He seems to want to watch TV.

'You didn't take her warnings seriously, did you?'

'No, I didn't,' he almost-shouts. 'There are no new threats.

You have no idea what I've had to put up with over the years with her. I've gone down every single rabbit hole she's dug me. She keeps making up these stories about silent phone calls and coffin catalogues and men following her. It's all attention-seeking bollocks.'

'Okay, okay,' I say, for once the calm one in the room. 'Jesus, I only asked.'

'This is what she does,' he says, springing to his feet and pacing the floor. 'This is who she is now, she's an Alibi Clock. She tells one time, she strikes another and neither one's the right fucking time. This last year she's been a nightmare to monitor.'

'What did her message say? The voicemail?'

'I can't remember now.'

'You do. It's on your mind, isn't it? What did she say? TELL ME!'

He gestures towards the plug in the wall by the patio doors, and his phone sitting on a small table linked by a white wire. 'She said she'd had enough. She said she wanted to die. And then she said she was sorry. And hung up.'

He's more worried than he's letting on, I know he is. I sip my tea because I'm thirsty and too-milky tea is better than none, but it tastes funny. 'Urgh, what's this?'

'Tea.'

'Is the milk off?'

'No. I put a wee nip in it. For your nerves.'

'My nerves are fine, thanks.' I put the mug down. He seems jittery. And then I get it because I've seen this before in my own dad. He's drunk. I spy the bottle of Bells Whisky on the breakfast bar, tucked behind a dying pot of parsley.

'How much have you had?'

'Oh, Christ, don't you start.'

'If you shout at me again I will punch you in the face,' I warn him. 'I do NOT do alcoholics. Alright?'

He holds up his hands in mock surrender.

'On the phone Cotterill mentioned something about blood on the carpet?'

'Yeah, I saw that,' says Neil, 'but he said she had a nosebleed the other night. I don't think it's significant. The bath's half full though. I don't understand that.'

He doesn't seem worried, merely perplexed. I head for the bathroom, pulling the light cord. The lino is wet in places and the bath is half-filled with bright blue water with tiny gold stars floating on top, rippled by a breeze from a crack in the window. Along the bath and on the floor lie several blister packs of tablets. All empty. In the bin are the empty boxes for the pills – Rock-a-bye Night-Time Sleep Aids, 50mg tablets – all from different stores.

'Don't touch anything,' he calls out. 'Just in case.'

'In case of what?'

'In case there's more to it than the current situation suggests.'

I pull the light and head out again. I go into her bedroom. The décor matches the lounge – dark and drab with dirty yellow wallpaper and a shabby single bed, with creased sheets and a thin duvet. In a child's car seat on the floor of the open wardrobe, a new-born baby lies sleeping, wrapped in a knitted pink and yellow blanket like a piece of woollen Battenberg. I bend down and touch the doll's face. It's so lifelike. I remove it from the car seat. It's got the heaviness of a baby but it smells of plastic. There's a tiny wheel on the back – Cry, Wind, Urinate, Sleep. I click it over to Sleep and throw it down on the bed. I touch the covers where she sleeps. The bed feels damp.

I come back into the lounge. 'The bed's all damp.'

'The whole *flat's* damp,' he says. 'It wants condemning.'

'No, it's *really* damp.'

I come back to the coffee table and pick up my whisky tea. I try it again. No, still disgusting. I move to the kitchenette and pour it down the sink.

'Why would she leave the bath half-empty? Why would the bed be damp?'

'Wet towels left on it? I don't know.'

'Why would she have taken so many sleeping tablets?'

'Maybe she didn't. There's a load of blue stuff at the bottom of the bath.'

'But why put sleeping tablets in the bath? What does that mean?'

'To make us *think* she's overdosed,' he says. 'You're going up a blind alley.'

'Has she taken any of her clothes?'

'Don't know. Her phone's on the windowsill in there.' He tilts his head to the bathroom. 'It was playing music as I came in.'

'How did you get in?'

'I have a spare key. I'm the only one who does. There's no sign of broken entry, if that's where this line of questioning is going.'

'There's a crack in the bathroom window though.'

'That's probably been there a while. Landlord's not known for his punctiliousness.'

'What the hell does it all mean?' I ask, walking around the lounge, picking things up, putting things down. I note the names on one of the presents around the little Christmas tree – Prince Roland. Then another – Princess Tabitha, written in silver glitter. 'They're presents for her cats,' says Neil.

'What cats?'

'They're around here somewhere. Out catching mice, I suppose,' he says, rubbing his eye and scuffing into the bathroom. He closes the door and I hear a distant tinkling of water. I notice there are seven presents. For seven cats.

When he comes back, he's taken his coat off and hung it on the bathroom door. He then absentmindedly scratches his balls, before realising how rude that must seem.

'Sorry. I'm a bit out of practice.'

'At what? Manners?'

'Christ, it's freezing in here. Where's the thermostat?'

'Have you only just noticed?'

'I've only just taken my coat off.'

'Listen to me, Neil – there are seven presents around the tree, all named for different cats but I haven't seen one cat.'

'They're not even *her* cats. She steals them. She went through a phase of doing a bit of amateur animal rescue, stealing cats she thought were being abused. She spends all her money on the things.' He swigs his tea and empties the mug.

It was another upsetting puzzle piece in the Ellis tessellation – stealer of cats.

'Yeah but my point is where *are* they all?'

Neil looks around the flat. Opens a cupboard. Goes out into the hall. Comes back in. 'Where's the boiler? We pay her heating bills, there's got to be a separate boiler somewhere here. Aren't you cold?'

'I'm freezing but I have two jumpers on. Anyway, focus. The cats.'

'Why do you keep banging on about the cats? They're not relevant. Could never stand the things anyway. She let them roam all about the place. Unhygienic.' He reaches across me to the cupboard above the sink. Still no sign of the boiler.

'When did you last visit her?'

'Few weeks ago.'

'And were the cats here then?'

'Yeah, I think there were a couple about. I don't know what conclusion you're trying to draw from this.'

'No, neither do I actually,' I mumble.

He leaves the kitchen and crosses the lounge into the bedroom and I hear the click of what must be the boiler coming on. In moments, something ignites and the radiator nearest the patio doors begins to gurgle into life. I stand next to it.

'Foy?'

'What?'

He doesn't call again, so I rush to join him in Ellis's bedroom. He's bending down with the airing cupboard door open. He looks up at me and I move closer to see what he's found. Inside the cupboard, inside a little nest of towels and bedsheets, lies a perfect fluffy white cat, purring proudly, suckling six tiny wriggling pink kittens.

20

By the time the white RSPCA van draws up outside the next morning, I am spoiling for a fight. Powered by a twitchy night's sleep in a freezing cold flat, three vile instant coffees, and the troubling thought that something more sinister may have happened to Ellis than Neil was ready to admit, I know that somehow Sean Lowland, the name on the card we find in Ellis's fruit bowl, can provide the information we need.

'She looks great,' says Sean, carefully moving a fluffy grey kitten into the oversized cat box he's brought for them all. He'd lined it with soft sheepskin and has put a little warm bean bag underneath it. 'We were looking for her for ages the other day. And this is where she was all along. They seem to be feeding really well.'

'How do you know Ellis?' I ask him, as Neil carefully picks up the last two kittens and snuggles them in next to The Duchess in the box on the bedroom floor.

Sean hand-feeds the cat a couple of high calorie treats and closes the little door. 'I've seen her before down the centre. She brought in an injured duck. That was about a month ago. And the other day she called us to report some cats. She wanted to find their real homes. I think she'd been looking

225

after them.' He carries the box into the lounge and places it down carefully on the coffee table.

'Why did she want to rehome them?' says Neil, arms folded.

'She didn't say. Just that they were cats she'd found and taken care of. She said most of them were half-starved when she found them.'

'Yeah, she did the same thing in Scarborough for a time,' Neil says with a sigh, for mine or Sean's attention I couldn't tell.

'She'd looked after them all really well. I think she said one had conjunctivitis and she got treatment for it and everything. She said she wanted something to look after. I understand that. I'm a sucker for animals as well. We have that in common.'

'But she didn't say why she was giving them up now?'

'No, she didn't. I assumed she was going away. When will she be back, any idea?'

'Later.' Neil throws me a look I can't read but the contrast between them is quite startling. Sean's happy, cherubic face, brown curls and big brown eyes in stark contrast to Neil's sour expression, steel grey stare and pallor. 'How did she seem to you?'

'I dunno. Maybe a bit flat? A bit depressed? I guessed it was cos she didn't want the cats to go. I might have crossed a boundary. I sort of asked her out.'

'Why?' I ask.

Sean shrugs. 'I liked her. We had a few things in common. I go down the Smuggler's some nights and I wondered if she wanted to meet for a drink. She said okay but she didn't come. I waited for a couple of hours, just in case. She might have thought I was being too forward, I don't know.'

'What did you two have in common?'

'Well we both like animals and we're both quite quiet. I dunno, I liked her.'

'When was this?' asks Neil.

'Erm, night before last?'

'Time?'

'Hang on, am I missing something here? She is alright, isn't she?'

'She hasn't come home,' I tell him. 'She's probably staying at a friend's house. We think. We're a bit worried about her.' I can tell I've said the wrong thing because Neil bats his steely greys at me.

Sean looks from me to Neil and back again. 'Oh god, really?'

I take a deep breath and let it out slowly. 'Yeah. We are quite worried.'

Suddenly the buzzer goes, a horrible resounding noise and I'm sure each of us jumps out of our skin. I race Neil to the door and yank it open. It's a delivery man. UPS. I sign for a box with her name on it – Joanne Haynes. Neil says that's the name she was using. I bring the box inside and tear it open with a rusty bread knife from a kitchen drawer. It contains boxes of hair dye, six in all. Black hair dye. And four boxes of coloured contact lenses. Brown. I set the whole lot down on the breakfast bar and try to calm my breathing. I really thought it was going to be her.

We all stand there in the living room. I for one have no idea what to say next. Sean clearly can't tell us anything.

'You've got me worried now,' he says with a nervous laugh.

Neil shakes his head. 'She'll be fine. She's just taking some time out I expect.'

Sean's eyes betray him – he's scared. 'Will you let me know when she comes back? I expect she'll want to know about The Duchess, won't she?'

'Yeah, I've got your card.'

'I'll take her and her kittens back to my place until they get old enough to rehome. Keep an eye on them, you know. I've got just the spot in front of the radiator.'

I want to say I'm sorry for shouting at him but no words will come out. I don't know if he's naturally super-duper nice or if he's *too* nice. Half of me wants to punch him, the other half wants to hug him. I keep thinking about the empty blister packs of sleeping pills in the bathroom, stacked up in the bin. How Sean said she was 'depressed'. He used that actual word.

Neil holds the door open for him as he manoeuvres out to the hallway with the cat box. 'Thanks for coming and getting her.'

I watch from the patio doors as Sean loads the cat box into the passenger seat of his van. Neil joins me at the window. It is raining. He's in the van talking to the box on the passenger seat.

'Match made in heaven, those two,' says Neil, joining me at the window.

'What do you think of him?'

'Seems clean. I'll check him out though. He's sweet on her.'

'He called her Ellis,' I say. 'She told him her real name.'

'Mmm. I don't think that's significant.'

'Why don't you think anything is significant? Maybe she didn't tell him her real name because he knew it already. He could be in the cartel.'

Neil looks at me. 'Sean's the same age as you and Ellis.

I doubt he was involved in making ecstasy tablets and bars of cocaine when he was still in short trousers.'

'He could be the son of one of them? You said there were twelve-year-olds in the supply chain.'

Neil shakes his head. 'Doesn't strike me as that sort. I think he's clean.'

'Well what then?' I say, my anger finally spilling out. 'She's been missing two days. Are you still thinking she's just buggered off, and is biding her time?'

'No,' he says, biting his lip and sitting down on the edge of the sofa.

'So what *are* you thinking?'

'I'm thinking I want to see some seafront CCTV from the other night, see if we can spot her. There's a few cameras outside the arcades. Maybe start there.'

'Start there to find out what? Which way she went? Tell me,' I say, almost too quiet for him to hear.

'There's only one reason she could have for getting rid of those cats the day she disappeared. She knew she wasn't going to be around to look after them anymore. She wouldn't have left them otherwise.'

'So she *has* run off?'

'Maybe. We could rule it out at least.'

'Don't say it, don't even suggest it.' But we're both looking towards the windows, towards the sea. I need him to be the rock face today. The sour-faced Scottish cliff face he was when I first walked in. But there are cracks in the cliff face now. And his eyes bear the same expression as Sean's – fear.

21

We wait all morning and afternoon for Ellis, clinging to the last hope that she will walk back through the door at any moment. But she doesn't. Nobody comes. We take it in turns to go out and buy coffee and snacks from a café on the seafront, though I learn that Neil is the fussiest of eaters. Can't have a bacon sandwich if it's been buttered, can't have a toastie if he can taste cheap cheese or there's dressing on the garnish, coffee's too strong, too weak, not hot enough. Must be a nightmare to cook for.

'You can blame my mam for that,' he says. 'She was the same. No, she was worse. Wouldn't stay in hotels cos she was convinced all chefs wank in the mash.'

This is the only time I laugh all day. I laugh until there are tears in my eyes.

We're side by side on the sofa. I feel grotty and overtired and the four walls of the flat feel as though they're closing in, getting smaller, strangling me. I'm on the verge of another meltdown when Neil turns off the TV and makes a suggestion.

'Why don't you go back to your hotel and have a wash and a kip?'

'Are you calling me dirty?' I say, through hooded eyes.

'Not at all. But I'm wrecked and I managed some kip last night. You didn't.'

'You expect me to sleep when my cousin's body could be pulled out of that sea any minute, do you?'

'You almost fell asleep standing up just now,' he says. 'Go on.'

'Fuck off.'

Now, any normal person would vacate the space at this point. That's what Paddy and Isaac always do when I'm gearing up for another mood tornado. They retreat to their air raid shelters until the all-clear. But Neil stays.

'Go back to your hotel and freshen up,' he says again, slowly. 'You're in no fit state to get through this day the way y'are.'

'Don't tell me what to do.'

'You know I'm right.'

'You're not right. You're a twat.'

'Thank you. Anything else?'

'Yes. She called you. She said she'd had enough and you ignored it.' He shakes his head and stands up. 'You've as good as killed her.'

'Don't you dare say that to me,' he snaps, glaring down at me. 'I've blamed myself for what happened to her and Dan ever since. The fact that between then and now she hasn't said one damn word of truth is *not* my fault.'

I stand up too, almost to his level, and I look him in the eye. 'She's dead, isn't she?' I say. He doesn't answer me. 'I'll believe it if you say it.'

He shakes his head. 'I can't tell you what you need to know, Foy.' And then he unexpectedly reaches for my hand. 'I'm sorry.'

I shout at *him* and call him a twat and *he* apologises? This is too much. I crash into him, pulling him into a hug. At first I don't feel his arms around me. But then I do and it's so comforting in that moment. That's what I need right then: safety. Not shouting or angry accusations. Just to be enclosed.

His voice is softer when he speaks. 'Do you want to go back to your hotel and take a break from this? I'll wait here. If she turns up, I'll call you.'

I shake my head. 'It's a bloody horrible hotel. There's mould around the bath.'

He exhales sharply as he pulls away from me and the granite expression returns to his face. 'Have you complained?'

I shake my head. 'No point. The landlady didn't seem fussed either way.'

'Well you're not staying there.'

'There is nowhere else. I got it last minute.'

'You can stay at my hotel. I'll take the chair. I don't sleep a lot anyway.'

'No, that's not right.'

'Don't argue. Go get your stuff, check out of the fleapit and go to The Lalique.' He pulls a key card out of his pocket inside a small cardboard wallet. 'Room 48.'

'Did you just order me about?' I frown.

'Yes. Now fuck off.'

'What are you going to do?'

He stares through the window. 'I'm gonna do what I said I'd do. Ask around. Watch some CCTV. And I'm going to inform the coastguard.'

*

232

By ten o'clock that night, Neil and I stand on the jetty looking out at the disappearing light of the orange rescue boat as it bobs and bounces rhythmically on the choppy waves in Spurrington Bay. They've been at it for ten hours and they're coming back in now. New weather system alert. Nothing more they can do tonight.

Neil went to the Smuggler's Arms to learn that Sean's story checked out. The landlord said he was in there most of the evening, but not with Ellis. Another barman who had been taking out an empty barrel to the yard saw a woman matching Ellis's description walk past in the direction of the seafront. So we went to the arcades to watch the CCTV. By the time the twelve-year-old gorm in charge finally found the right tape for the evening she vanished, I was ready to ram his head through one of the fruit machines, but the sight of Ellis on the black and white screen stopped me in my tracks.

'There she is, that's her! Isn't it?'

He can't deny it. 'It's her alright.' Walking past the doughnut van on the Esplanade at 9.39 p.m. Alone. Eyes wide. Dark hair. The same girl I remember, only eighteen years older and much more scared. I watch her on the screen, stop and look out into the black night, before retreating out of shot. Stop, look over the wall, then disappear. Stop, look, go. I rewind it six times.

There's no other movement but flying litter and sea spray rising in quick spurts above the sea wall – until 10.27 p.m. From the other side of the road, a figure in black runs to the same spot with a large black shape – maybe a bin bag – and heaves it over into the angry tide. Their face is covered by their hood. Then they disappear.

'Who is that?' I say, afraid of the sound of my own voice. 'Was that her?'

'Can't tell,' says Scants, rewinding the footage.

'Is that a rubbish bag? Is it heavy?'

'Fairly heavy. They're dragging it there, look.' He plays the footage from around the same time on the second machine. We still can't tell who it is.

'Man or woman, do you think?'

'I don't know, Foy.'

'But who's it more likely to be?'

'It's strange that they should stop at the exact same spot on the sea wall that Ellis did earlier to look out. But I don't know for sure.'

That's the only CCTV Neil can check – the two cameras further along the road nearer Ellis's flat are out of action, as of three nights ago. Conveniently vandalised.

The gorm comes in to tell us he's locking up soon, ergo we need to leave, but we watch both tapes once more to triple-check every angle. All we know is we don't know anything. We don't know who threw the bag and we don't know what's in it.

After Neil informs the coastguard, two officers from the local constabulary come to the flat and we tell them everything we know. About Kaden Cotterill and Ellis's paranoia about being followed. Neil explains how he originally thought she was acting up, how she's done this before to make him feel guilty, but never for this long. He explains about the silent calls, the coffin catalogue and the message she left him.

I hear her voice, for the first time in eighteen years.

'Scants? It's me, Ellis. I've had enough. For real this time. I don't want to be here anymore. Not like this. I want to go. I'm sorry. Thank you for everything you've done.'

And then the click. It doesn't sound like her. It's not the Ellis

I remember. But what do I remember? A ten-year-old girl with a laugh like jingle bells and a smile like the sun coming up over the horizon. With each passing moment she's not here, I feel more distant from her. More distant from that ten-year-old who'd been fixed in my mind like a mosquito in amber all these years. When all the time she was growing, transforming, mutating into this... liar. This girl full of stories, this depressed cat-stealer with occasional brain tumours. And it makes me sadder than I ever thought possible. I had employed someone to find her, a specialist, because I wanted her back. I wanted that little ten-year-old girl back where she belongs, with us. Her family. But I didn't know her anymore. I had thought she could slot into one of the many gaps that had been left by other people, and make me somewhat complete again.

It never once occurred to me that she was incomplete herself.

I stand on the seafront until first light, watching. Occasionally crying. But looking out into the water, catching shadows, drifting shapes on the water, clods of white foam on the jutting rocks. Thinking I see her face in the inky black water. But I don't. It's only when I smell coffee that I turn around.

'Here you go,' says Neil, and passes me a disposable cup, warm to the touch, and a bag containing one Danish pastry.

'Thanks. What's the latest? Did you speak to the police?'

'They're gonna keep me posted,' he says, sipping his cup and exhaling gladly. 'We've got to wait. See what happens.'

See when her body turns up, he means. I don't want that thought in my mind. I don't want to see what the tide's left on that shoreline when it finally retreats. I gulp my searing hot coffee and let it burn my throat, gives me something else to focus on.

'You said you were on leave from work,' I say. 'Why is that?'

'My wife died. I was her carer.'

There it is, that infuriating collision of sadness and understanding I know so well. 'How long ago?'

'Nearly a year now.'

I nod. 'Cancer?'

'Leukaemia.'

I nod again. 'I'll see your wife. And I'll raise you one husband.'

He turns to me. 'You're young to be losing your husband.'

'Yeah. We got married when I was 22. I lost him at 26.'

'Cancer?'

'Heart.'

Neil nods. 'Jesus. OK, I'll see your husband. And I'll raise you both parents.'

'You said you visited your parents in Dumfries?'

'I visited their graves in Dumfries. And their house. I go back there sometimes. I haven't got round to sorting out all the stuff yet.'

'Same.'

Sunlight begins to break through a crack in the clouds and lights his face marmalade yellow. 'Shit, you're young to be losing your parents too.'

'Well you're not exactly old. What are you, thirty-seven?'

'Thirty-nine.'

The temperature feels icy all of a sudden so I zip up my coat. 'Thirty-nine? So you were, what, twenty-one when you started working with Ellis?'

'She was my first case, yeah. It's been a long time.' He sips and doesn't elaborate.

'I lost my mum when I was sixteen,' I tell him. 'She had lung cancer. Doctors said it could have been passive smoking from working in the bar all those years. And my dad went to pieces after that. Started drinking.'

I glance at him but he sips his coffee and looks out to sea.

'One night he drove my brother Paddy home from a twenty-first birthday party in town and they crashed. They crashed into the only tree on that stretch of road. Paddy survived but they had to remove both his legs below the knee. Dad was crushed by the steering column. He wouldn't have felt anything.'

Neil posts his hands inside his pockets. 'Bloody hell.'

'Yeah, it was. I went through a stage where I hated Ellis. I thought she'd caused it all. I hated Uncle Dan more. Mum was so unhappy. It was the not knowing. "The abyss," she called it. Like they'd fallen into it and we were all supposed to forget they ever existed. That's what did for her, I know it was. And my dad, he was the knock-on effect. Paddy suffered. Me and my other brother Isaac helped him as best we could. Then one day, when Mum and Dad's estate had been settled and we got our inheritance, we decided to get out, peel ourselves away from all the memories.'

'Understandable.'

'None of us wanted to talk about the past. So we moved to France. Bought a place big enough for the three of us, and got out of Carew. We've been doing it up. It's been chaos at times but good chaos. Isaac got a boyfriend, who became a husband, and he moved in. Thank god he's good with electrics cos it would have cost us a fortune in French electricians. And Paddy got a girlfriend who became a wife, Lysette, and she moved in as well. That's what I wanted – people around me. Family again. We'd lost so much.'

'Where does your husband come into it?' he asks. I smell the whisky on his breath from his lidded coffee.

'Luc. I met him in a French market one day. We got talking. I fall in love quite easily and he was easy to fall in love with. Soft, sensitive. It was a bit of a whirlwind but I was looking for a whirlwind. And one day we were in Paris, the ultimate cliché, but he proposed outside the Musée d'Orsay. An old guy was having a stroke under a tree nearby which sort of broke the mood. But for a while, it was all magical again.'

He looks at me. He knows what's coming.

'We were all so happy. For a good three years. In my mind I thought that maybe the curse had ended. But it had waited for my guard to go down, that was all. Then I had a miscarriage at thirteen weeks. And then another one at twenty-two weeks. We tried again but nothing happened. I was too tense, I think. And one morning I woke up to find him cold next to me as well. No warning. Undiagnosed heart condition.'

Neil puffs out his cheeks. 'Christ almighty.'

'Full house,' I say to him, as a tear rolls down my cheek. 'God, I don't think I've stopped crying since I arrived.'

'You needed to,' he says.

'I'm so afraid every day, Neil. I'm afraid for Isaac, for his little boy, his husband. I'm afraid for Paddy and his wife and their two girls. And I'm afraid for me. I'll be left alone without them all one day. It was Luc's death that made me want to find Ellis. I need to find the family I still have and cling onto them, because I don't know how long they'll be around.'

Neil looks at me but doesn't speak. He lets me carry on.

'I'd Google her relentlessly, going through every single social media account and searching for her face. Her blue eyes. Her shock of red hair. I wrote to Avon and Somerset Police, begging them to help me find her. I wrote to the Home Office six times. Kept coming up against brick walls. Then a friend of mine, Pamela, a fellow expat I met at a book group, mentioned one night that she was having her husband followed by a private detective. And she told me about Middletons, this company in London who track people down, spy on adulterers, do background checks on employees, all sorts of things.'

'This is where Cotterill comes into it?' asks Neil.

'Yes. Pamela said they were very efficient. Her husband was a careful man but they still got a ton of evidence on him. So I thought *Why not*? Middletons have been on the case for fifteen months now. Never thought they'd find her. I've missed her.'

Neil places his cup down on the sea wall and puts his arm around me. I cry against him. It's more tiredness than anything but I'm so grateful for it because I don't really get hugs anymore. Me and the boys went through a period of hugging all the time but after a while they don't think you need it. Maybe I come across like I don't – I'm pretty spiky. But even the spikiest porcupines need hugs if you are brave enough to get close. And Neil does seem brave. Great ribbons of grief pour out of me as he stands there, holding me, as strong as a castle. I'm crying for all of them – Mum, Dad, Luc, the two babies I lost. And for Ellis. Wherever she is.

'She was always talking about you,' he whispers, even though he doesn't need to whisper. There's no one else around.

I don't want to pull out of his hug. Even though he's a perfect stranger, it's the best hug I've ever had.

'She would tell me about you two guys as kids. Your tree-house. The unicorns. The T-Rex. Riding your bikes. You were her everything. Every summer.'

'It wasn't only summer,' I sniff. 'It was every Easter, every Christmas, half terms. I didn't know life without her. She was half my world.'

'She still is,' he says as he pulls back to look at me and wipes the tear from my cheek. I smell the whisky on his breath again, even stronger.

'You need to stop drinking,' I tell him.

'I know, I know,' he says, pulling right away from me, picking up his cup and sinking the dregs, probably afraid I'm going to toss it over the wall any second.

'Seriously. I know how this ends if you don't.'

'Pretty difficult,' he says. 'I don't actually feel like there's any reason to stop.'

'Then find one,' I say. 'Your wife wouldn't want you to drink.'

'Should have stayed and kept an eye on me then, shouldn't she?'

There's a storm brewing up out in the bay and it's my turn to hug him then because his eyes are full of water though the tears won't drop. It's like he's willing them to stay put in his eyes. He holds onto me so tightly. It feels so right to be next to him like this. To press his cold, stubbly cheek against mine. I pull back and stare into his sad grey eyes, wiping over the tear tracks on his cheeks.

'I've been free falling without her. I don't give a shit anymore, about anything. I never used to be this angry, believe it or not. I feel angry about everything now.'

'Two tornadoes together,' I say.

'Huh?'

I grab my coffee off the wall. 'Come on. You need a shave and I need a sleep.'

22

I don't often allow myself to think back to Carew. There are too many memories I've locked away, but when I hear a snippet of them from Neil, the box opens and it all comes spewing out again. Dad's Easter egg hunts. Uncle Dan's Christmas present hunt. Fishing in the woods. Our treehouse 'castle'. Every memory before I was ten contains Ellis. Every single memory afterwards, she was on my mind. But when Neil said that – *I never used to be this angry, believe it or not. I feel angry about everything now* – it rang the loudest bell. We were the same, me and him. He dulls his pain with whisky, I open the gasket now and again and blow my top. But neither method of therapy is working.

Back at The Lalique, Neil's bed is soft and crispy clean. He draws the curtains and settles on the armchair beside the glass table, resting his feet on his bag and covering himself with the spare blanket. I have the whole double bed to myself, something I used to crave when Luc was around but which now I detest. We had thought initially they were twin beds pushed together but they weren't separable so he took the chair. I feel awful. I can't get to sleep anyway. Every time I close my eyes I hear the storm whipping up in the bay and imagine Ellis out there, clinging to a rock.

And I am back there, in Carew St Nicholas. I'm eight. The bells of St Nicholas are sounding. Sunday morning. The morning after Easter. I'm racing across the beer garden after Ellis but she's too fast for me.

'Ellis, it's alright, it's alright.'

She races to the treehouse, scampers up the rope ladder and scuttles across the carpet tiles to the corner where she tucks herself into a ball.

'It's alright, Ellis,' I say, peeking in the doorway. 'Mum won't mind.'

'It's one of her best plates.' She's crying hard. Her pink cheeks glisten with tears. 'I just wanted to do something nice to say thank you for having me so I started to do the washing up but it slipped out of my hand.'

'She won't care. She probably won't even notice it's missing. She's got loads.'

'She'll send me home and take away all my Easter eggs.'

'Has she sent you away before?'

'No.'

'When we scrawled on the toilet wall with charcoal?'

'No.'

'When Dad caught us peeing on his runner beans?'

'No.'

'When we ate all Isaac's birthday cake?'

'No.'

'Well then. She won't care about it, I promise. Where are the broken bits?'

'In my laundry bag.'

'Okay, go and get them and we'll hide them.'

'Hide them where?'

'I know just the place.'

Isaac and Paddy have gone into town on the bus so we sneak into Isaac's bedroom and peel back the carpet where he keeps his stash of pictures of naked men. He doesn't think I know about his hidey, but I caught him putting the carpet back one day and he shouted at me for not knocking. There's always a reward for not knocking.

'There you go,' I say, wrapping the broken shards of plate up in an old pillowcase which I hate cos it makes me cheeks itch. 'She'll never find it in here.'

'What if Isaac finds it?'

'I'll stuff it right to the back. And if he does, I'll tell Mum about his dirty boy books and his cigarettes that he stole from the bar, won't I?'

'Are you sure?'

'Yes. Forget about it. Let's go and play.'

We kept all sorts of stuff down the hidey that year – treasure maps, broken plates, DVDs we aren't allowed to rent but which the boys let us watch when Mum and Dad were down in the bar, like *The Terminator* and *American Pie*. If the pub's still there, so are all our secrets, hidden in the floor.

I must get to sleep at some point because when I wake up it's gone 10.30 a.m. I got a few hours in at least. That's enough. I look across at Neil in the chair, his blanket rucked up around his feet. He lies all crunched up for warmth, uncovered. I get up and tuck him back in. I shower and dry my hair and he still doesn't stir.

I lean down to him and listen to his short breaths – he still stinks of whisky. I whisper, 'Neil? I'm going to nip out for a bit, why don't you take the bed?'

Across the bay, another storm brews and gunmetal grey clouds gather to form an enormous dark mass on the horizon. It's raining hard against the windows – I can't even open one because the wind's too strong. The wetlands are circled by litter and great big clumps of sea foam. It's on the rocks too. No signs of life though. Or death.

I scribble Neil a message on the phone pad and head out.

In the corridors, an assortment of activity is going on – women in black and white uniforms with the Lalique logo on the left hand pocket scurry about with vacuum cleaners and piles of bedsheets. Men in business suits saunter along to the lifts with small suitcases on wheels. Two kids run to be first to press the button, their families trailing along behind. I remember that: when all that mattered in life was to get there first and press the button. That button was everything.

A grey-haired janitor man in navy shorts and Aertex shirt appears with a stepladder under his arm and a bunch of keys on his belt and sets it up beneath a vent outside one of the rooms. Air conditioning's on the blink, if I hear correctly.

He says 'Good morning' as I pass him, and I make a mental note to seek him out later. First I want to start with the house-keepers, the people Ellis works alongside. There's a short blonde pock-marked one with a ferocious ponytail that tapers to a point, a painfully thin black-haired one who moves at the speed of light, and a brunette with holes in her trainers who seems to find everything funny.

I attempt her first. 'Hello.'

'Morning,' she says, a fake smile shuffling into the place of a real one.

'Can I ask you some questions about your colleague, Ellis?'

'Who?'

'Ellis Kemp. She works here?'

'Don't know her. Vanda will if she's new though. Are you police?'

'No, nothing like that. She might have used a different name. Maybe Mary?'

'Don't know a Mary, soz.'

'Which one's Vanda?'

'She's on the second floor. Blonde hair, short. Quite serious-looking.'

The ferocious ponytail.

'Yeah, I've seen her. Okay, thanks.'

I head up in the escalator to the second floor and locate the room with the housekeeping cart outside, but the woman who comes out with a bundle of laundry is black with yellow hair accessories and a slight limp.

'Hello,' I say, 'could you tell me where Vanda is please?'

'She's on Floor 4, I think. What's up?'

'I'm trying to find some information about a colleague of yours, Ellis Kemp?'

The woman frowns, like the brunette had done. 'Don't know her, sorry.'

'She's been working here for the past couple of months? Quite quiet, I believe? Red hair? Blue eyes?'

She frowns harder. 'No one like that here, sorry.'

Another dead end. 'Oh, okay, thanks.' I'm at the escalator when I remember the black hair dye from Ellis's flat. The contact lenses. I turn back to the woman's cart – she's inside the bedroom, laying out a fresh bedsheet.

'She might have had black hair and brown eyes the last few months.'

'Sounds like Genevieve. Yeah I know her. Right weirdo.'

'Genevieve?' I remember the only other time I've heard that name. I haven't thought about that name for years. 'Genevieve Syson?'

'Yeah, that's her. Is she in trouble or owt?'

'No, I'm a relative, wanting to get in touch. I'm sorry to bother you.'

'Vanda worked with her more than me,' she calls out. 'She's on Floor 4, probably sneaking a vape through the end window.'

So I head for Floor 4 remembering vaguely that Genevieve Syson's headstone was the one with the angel. My chest fills with poison, imagining Ellis's name on a block of stone. No, she is still alive, I *know* she is.

I find Ferocious Ponytail Woman exactly where the limping housekeeper told me she would be – vaping through the end window, sitting on the sill. When I approach she stops vaping and sneaks the instrument into the front of her apron.

'Hello, is it Vanda?' I ask.

'Who wants to know?'

'My name's Foy, I'm looking for my cousin who works here and I've been told you would be the best person to ask about her.'

'Who is your cousin?' she asks.

'Well, you know her as Genevieve—'

'Huh,' she huffs, getting her vape out again. 'Waste of space. We keep her job open, let other good girls go, and you know how she thanks me? Pisses in my face.'

'I'm sorry?'

'She pisses in my face!' she shouts. 'She never work. The manager keeps giving her chances cos she afraid of a tribunal for sacking mental ill person. And when she *is* here, she lie. She lie about who she is, where she goes.' She points her finger at me. 'You talk to her one day she's Genevieve, a nurse who knows strangling techniques, next she Joanne with dead parents. People say she has other names too. Nobody know who she really is. She go to hairdresser where my sister works and say her name Mary.'

'Mary Brokenshire?'

'Yes, fucking Mary Brokengirl. I mean, where does she get these names? Does she steal passports? She disgusts me.'

'She's got a lot of issues.'

'Huh,' she huffs again. 'Tell me about issues when you've got three kids under ten, your husband walk out on you, you cannot pay rent. *Then* I listen.'

'She needs help, Vanda.' I hold her stare. 'I need to find her before she... before something happens to her.'

'What, she missing?' She makes a short, sharp throat-slit motion with her hand and continues puffing out the window.

'She is missing, yes. For the past four days. I need to build up a picture of that last day. Did she come to work? Did you speak to her?'

'Oh yes, I spoke to her,' she says. 'She come in to show me her wedding dress.'

'Wedding dress? Why did she have a wedding dress?'

'I see her in window of bride shop on my way to work. And I laugh, *ha ha ha*, because I know she only go in there to try on dresses. She has no boyfriend. Just a dolly and herds of cats. So I laugh at her through window. And then she marches in here with the dress saying she bought it. She freak girl.'

'She bought it?'

'Yeah, or stole it. Then she tell me she leaving and that I a bully. *Idi v pizdu*, she says – go fuck yourself.'

'Ellis said that?'

Vanda nods slowly and surely. I don't believe it for a second.

'She crazy girl.' She swans off then, back to her cart, her job. 'I need to work. I can't afford to take time off to go missing or breastfeed dollies. You ask Trevor if you want know more. He's done jail time – he knows a weirdo when he sees one.'

She then passes me by, lifting two folded bedsheets from her cart and knocking on the door of Room 43. We are done.

I spend ten minutes searching for Trevor the janitor, eventually hearing his infernal whistle coming out of the ground floor lifts. The key bunch jingles at his waist as he lugs his way across reception towards the seating area outside the restaurant, overlooking the beach. It's windy and cold but he's only wearing short navy sleeves and shorts. He has tattoos on both calves – I can't make out what they are because his legs are too hairy and the tattoos too crap. He's mending a wobbly chair leg.

'Trevor?'

'Yep, be there in a tick.'

'I'm looking for my cousin, and your colleague Vanda said you might be able to help me piece some clues together about her whereabouts?'

'Who's your cousin, lovie?'

'You know her as Genevieve Syson?'

He stops fiddling with the chair leg and stands up. 'Is she dead?'

This blows me away. As does the sudden pong of his intense body odour, even in the howling wind. 'Why would you say that?'

'Well she hasn't been in for a few days, nobody knows where she is. And the last time I saw her she was in a hell of a state.'

'Was she?' I sit down on a nearby seat.

'Oh yeah. Accused one of our VIP guests of stalking her. Ken Whittle, that comedian on at the Winter Gardens. She point-blank accused him in the middle of the restaurant. Kiddies about and all.'

'Why did she do that?'

He made a twisting motion by the side of his head. 'She's nuts, in't she?'

'NO SHE'S FUCKING NOT!'

'Hey, calm down, sweetheart. I was only jesting. What would you call it then?'

I breathed through my nose as 'Wynken, Blynken and Nod' began to dance around my head in the wrong order. 'She's sad. She needs help.'

'I'll say. She's paranoid too. A woman was murdered in this hotel last week. Genevieve was obsessed with it. Thought there'd be another one. Maybe one of us.'

'Why?'

He shrugs theatrically. 'Vanda said Genevieve weren't her real name, either – the name in her file's Joanne. Did you know her as Joanne?'

'No, I knew her as Ellis.'

'Ellis?' he almost-shrieks. 'Bloody hell, who was she then?'

'She was Ellis. She *is* Ellis.'

'Well, she's a very troubled young girl if you ask me. The young woman who died here – Genevieve *knew* looking at her she'd been strangled. Said she used to work in a hospital and had seen someone strangled before. That was all bullshit, I reckon. But how could she know about them injuries unless she'd seen them before?'

'She *has* seen someone strangled before. Her dad.'

'Eh?'

'She watched her own dad being strangled to death by three men when she was eighteen. The same three men who did that kicked the crap out of her and left her to die. *That's* how she knew. And *that's* the truth. When the truth is too hard to bear, you make shit up. And that's what she did. Perhaps if any of you had been more approachable or given her a chance, she wouldn't have had to tell so many lies.'

'She thought Ken Whittle wanted to kill her 'n'all. Kept saying he was one of the Little Pigs, whatever that means. She's not in her right mind, darlin', stand on me.'

I thought about this, and I came to the conclusion that The Three Little Pigs were the three men who broke into their house and killed Uncle Dan and attacked her. Had to be. But Ken Whittle being one of them? That's insane.

'That girl is broken,' says Trevor with some finality. 'She needs locking up.' He gets to his feet with some awkwardness, rubbing his knee which is white with dryness.

'She needs looking *after*,' I tell him. 'She's been missing for four days.'

'Blimey,' he says. 'Probably gone over the sea wall. That's where people usually end up when they go missing in this town.'

That smarts, like being pricked by a pin. 'Vanda said you'd done time, Trevor. What was that for?'

His face darkens. 'That's none of your business. Vanda's no right telling you.'

'Well she did tell me, and my cousin is missing in mysterious circumstances so you either tell me, quietly, what you went in for, or I will follow you, shouting it from the rooftops until you do.'

He glares at me, more with embarrassment than anything. 'Burglary. Alright?'

'Where?'

'What do you mean "where"? How is this information you need?'

'I just need it. Now tell me. Where?'

'When I lived in Dublin, alright? I did a couple of burglaries with some mates. And I did my time.'

'What mates?'

'I ain't listening to this,' he says, with a flap of his hand, and starts to walk away, back through the patio doors and into the restaurant.

I get in front of him and stare him hard down. 'If you burgled someone in Scarborough eighteen years ago, you tell me now.'

His voice lowers and he grabs my arm. 'I ain't never been to Scarborough, what are you talking about? I'm trying to wipe the slate clean, here, you're not being fair. Why are you asking me about this?'

'Did you ever hurt anyone when you did these burglaries?'

'No, I didn't.' He again tries to leave.

Again, I step in front of him. 'I will check on this and if you're lying to me, I will make sure you pay for it, I swear.'

'Get out of my way.'

'I will follow you, I will hound you and even if you kill me, I will haunt you until I find out where she is. Stand on *me*.'

But Trevor pushes me firmly aside and stamps back across reception, keys jangling as he walks.

23

Still Tuesday, 5th November, (late morning)

There's only one bridal boutique in town, a tiny place called Seaside Bridal in a back street. It's a depressing little place with the most hideous gowns showcased in the poky bay window and an overpowering smell of PlugIn as you enter. The woman in charge is clearly an idiot. I know it before she opens her mouth.

'Oh, hello there, my dear, come on in. Did you want to browse or are you looking for anything in particular that I can help you with today?' She's so simperingly polite that I fight the urge to vomit right there on the coconut doormat.

'Uh, yeah, you might be able to help actually, well, not with a dress.'

'Oh.' She starts looking around like this is some big joke and she's on camera.

'I'm looking for my cousin, Ellis Kemp, and I believe she came in here the other day. Well, I *think* she came in here anyway. She's gone missing.'

Both hands fly to her mouth. 'Oh my gosh. You mean she got cold feet?'

'No, um, there is no wedding as such. She just came in to buy a dress. She might have been using an alias. Maybe Mary? Or Genevieve?'

The woman frowns. No recollections at all. 'What did she look like?'

'Black hair with probably ginger roots. Brown eyes.'

'Ah, you mean Ruth?'

I'm washed all over with recognition again. 'Ruth Gloyne?' *And her unborn babe Henry. Died 1830-something.* We used to sit on her grave, eating blue bootlaces.

'Yes, yes, that's the one. Oh, do you know I thought there was something odd about her at the time. She seems a very troubled young lady.'

My chest fills with poison. I am so sick of hearing that.

'Are you okay? Do you want to sit down? Alice – tea.' At the click of her fingers, a short mousey woman with an apologetic walk disappears out the back and I hear a kettle clicking on. I'd initially taken her to be one of the vile polystyrene statues of Greek goddesses that are dotted about the place with their faces picked off.

I post myself on a grey velvet chaise longue near the till. 'She is very troubled.'

'Well she has recently lost a baby, so perhaps it's understandable that's she's a little out of sorts,' says the woman – Cathy, she announces. A miscarriage now – another bloody lie. I feel bile rising in my throat.

'I'm trying to piece together her last movements.'

'You're a policewoman?'

'No, I'm her cousin. Nobody else seems to care about her very much.'

The Alice girl returns with a steaming cup and saucer, with a Jammy Dodger on the side. I take it gratefully and she returns to her position, hands clasped in front of her, between the rails. I went off Jammie Dodgers years ago. Too sweet.

Cathy bites her lip. 'She probably just needed some time. You know, to process the loss of the baby.' She does seem genuinely worried, which somewhat cools my ire, but I can't let her believe this latest tall tale. That's a bridge too far for me.

'She wasn't pregnant,' I say, with a sigh.

This makes Cathy start. 'She wasn't?'

I shake my head. 'She's a compulsive liar. There was no pregnancy, no wedding. I don't understand why but, basically, she's lonely. And I need to find her and help her. I need to tell her that I'm here.'

Cathy doesn't know how to take this – she's clearly not used to lies. I think if I so much as raised my voice in her Land of Lovely, she'd have a stroke. 'Oh, I see.'

'She definitely bought a dress in here though?'

'Oh yes, she bought one of the most expensive dresses we have. From the de Havilland range. She showed me a picture that a child had done, a cousin.'

I feel like Chief Brody in *Jaws* when the camera zooms in. 'Foy?' I say.

'Yes! Oh, are you Foy?'

I try not to start blubbing because I know I won't stop. I'd hated Ellis, momentarily, for lying about losing a baby. But in a heartbeat, I love her all over again.

'She said you and she designed your wedding dresses when you were little. You said if either of you got married, you had to wear dresses that looked like that. Lace, feathers, long sleeves. She bought the size sixteen. Four thousand pounds worth.'

Cathy shows me the picture in the catalogue. The dress is stunning and it truly was a living, breathing version of the one we drew as kids. A fantasy wedding dress. Why was she still living in this fantasy world we created as children? The answer fell on me like ice water – because that was when she last felt safe.

'She definitely took it with her? She didn't have to have it altered or anything?'

'No, it fit her wonderfully.'

'It's not at her flat.'

'Oh. Well, I don't know. She definitely took it away the day she tried it on, I remember distinctly. I have the receipt somewhere—'

'No, I believe you, don't worry.' The dress was definitely not in Ellis's flat; Neil and I had searched every inch of it. And then two tiny comets collided in my mind – the figure with the bin bag on the CCTV. The *heavy* bin bag. And the foam on the rocks. White foam. White dress? Is it too much of a long shot to pull the trigger on?

But why buy a £4,000 dress only to throw it in the sea? Why would she do that? Unless she *didn't*. Unless somebody else did. The one person who knew where she was – the last person to see her. I couldn't connect the dots quick enough.

'Okay, I have to go now,' I tell Cathy, unable to concentrate any further and returning my half-finished cup of tea to the glass table.

Cathy seems sad. 'Right, yes, well if we can be of any further assistance, Fleur.'

'Foy,' I say. 'You've been really helpful, thank you. Sorry to take up your time.'

'I hope you find her,' she says as I'm in the doorway, and she smiles so genuinely I feel bad for thinking she was an idiot.

*

I make my way down the slippery algae-strewn steps to the beach, scanning the sands for any signs of the dress or a large black bin bag that the sea has rejected. There are logs and dark clumps of seaweed and tyres and the odd plastic cup and mound of sea foam, but no black bin bags. I walk towards the sand and make my way over to the bigger rocks forming an isthmus out into the sea and separating the beach in two. There's white foam all over them. It's worth a look.

And it is just foam and bits of discarded polystyrene and plastic ice cream tubs. Everything white is not the dress. It was too long a shot. But I don't give up. I keep looking. I *know* that dress was in that bag. I *know* it went over that wall.

And then I spy a large expanse of foam on the ridge of big rocks. And I climb the rocks to get a closer look at it. It's not foam. My heart pounds, but logic kicks in. A sail perhaps, from a boat, brought in from the storm? A bedsheet, could be a bedsheet. But it's smaller than a bedsheet.

It has arms.

It's a dress. It's *the* dress.

'Oh my god! I don't believe it!'

I run closer to it, pumping my exhausted arms and legs until I've climbed the rest of the rocks. I reach out for it, slipping on the algae but grabbing it in time and pulling it down with me. I've got it. I climb down to the sand again, dragging the dress with me. It's got sea weed trails all over it, oil, sand, black dust and a couple of baby crabs have taken up residence in an armpit. The skirt is all raggedy and has lost most of its feathers but it's the dress from the catalogue Cathy showed me alright.

And then I see it, on the back of the dress, all up the silk and over the tiny buttons rising to the neck – a spray of pink. A spray of washed-out pink.

Pink that used to be red. There's no *pink* hair dye at the flat. No pink paint.

But there is blood.

*

I run all the way back to The Lalique, right at the other end of the seafront, the sodden wedding dress draped over my arm and soaking my jumper. By the time I get back to Neil's room, I can't decipher one breath from the next. When he lets me in, he has a towel wrapped around his bare waist and his blond hair is dark and damp.

'Where have you been?'

'Out,' I pant, hurrying inside the room. 'I left a note.'

'What's that you've got?' he asks, closing the door behind me.

'Dress,' I pant. 'Wedding dress.'

'Catch your breath,' he says. 'I'll get changed and then you can tell me about it. I've got something I need to talk to you about, too.'

I'm so confused. There are so many different emotions pinballing around my body. I'm upset from the different people I've met this morning who've called Ellis a freak or a weirdo or looked at me funny. I'm upset by the fact that she still seems to be living in an elongated version of our childhood and pretending to be the women on the gravestones we used to sit on in Carew, all those years ago. But most disturbingly of all, the day she disappeared, she bought a wedding dress. A wedding dress that was dumped over the sea wall that night, sprayed in blood.

When the bathroom door unclicks, a mere two minutes later, Neil appears, fully dressed in black jeans, socks and a navy jumper. His hair's still wet and he smells like Luc used to smell. Fahrenheit. Unmistakeable.

'Okay,' he says, sitting on the end of his unmade bed. 'What's with the dress?' I'm at the desk, still clutching the thing. 'Christ you're shaking.' He gets up and prises it from my arms. 'It's soaked. *You're* soaked.'

'It had washed ashore. It was on the rocks.'

'You found it on the beach?'

'It belonged to Ellis. I went to speak to Vanya or whoever she is, her line manager here. She said Ellis brought in a wedding dress to show it off, the day she vanished. I went to the only wedding dress shop in town and the lady showed me a picture of the one she bought. I remembered seeing something on the rocks when we were watching the coastguard yesterday. And I went down there and found it.'

'Why the hell did she buy a wedding dress?'

'Show of bravado, maybe? A couple of her colleagues seem like utter bitches so it wouldn't surprise me if she bought it just to stick it up their arse. It cost thousands.'

'She spent most of her wages on the cats and random stuff off the internet, but whenever she had a bit left over she'd save up.'

'So she was saving up for *this*?'

'I don't know. She was saving up for something. Her credit card's maxed out.'

I shake my head. 'I spoke to the handyman here – Trevor. He's done time for burglary. Did you know that? Did you know she was working with a criminal?' Neil shakes his head, less certainly than me. 'He's a burglar but maybe you should check him out, I don't know. It has blood on it.'

I look at him and it's all I can do not to have a full panic attack.

'The dress, I mean. There's blood.'

Neil lies the dress out on the carpet, and smooths the arms out. Turning it over, he squints his eyes at the faint pink spatters. 'Shit.'

'I think it might have been in the bin bag that we saw on CCTV. You know?'

'Yeah. You could be right. I need to call this in.'

'Will they take it seriously now?'

'They're already taking it seriously. They're out looking for her, aren't they?'

'But this is… this is something else now, isn't it?' I'm too afraid to hear his answer. But I need to hear him say it. He will tell me the truth.

'Yeah,' he says. 'This isn't good.'

'Neil? Did you know a woman was murdered in this hotel last week?'

He nods, slowly, expecting me to say something else. But I wait for him. 'Tessa Sharpe. She was strangled.'

'That janitor bloke said Ellis seemed too interested in her death. Like the killer was going to come for one of them next. Maybe her?'

'She thought the woman looked like her. She was paranoid that he got the wrong person.' He stands up and removes his phone from the charger on the desk.

'Who are you phoning?'

'Assistant Chief Constable's office. They have national portfolio responsibility for protected persons. They've been assisting on Ellis's case. I won't be a mo.'

He goes outside into the corridor to make his call. I don't earwig. I don't want to hear it. I'm left to pace the floor around the splayed-out wedding dress. Outside it starts to rain again, battering wind and rain which churns and angers the sea. I sit on the end of the bed and Google Tessa Sharpe. All the news items carry the same photo – a young woman, twenty-eight, fire-red hair, bright blue eyes, kind smile. Her hands were bound with cable ties. An ongoing investigation. Still no arrests.

It's usually Isaac who has to give me the pep talk when I start catastrophising, my mind going into full-tilt overdrive, imagining some man breaking into Ellis's flat and murdering her in her bed, stabbing her so hard the blood sprays all up the wedding dress that was hanging up on the wardrobe door. A body is going to wash in on that next tide, isn't it? Naked. Cold. I can't bear it. I can't *bear* this.

I need to breathe. I need to focus. I need to calm down. I need Neil to come back in and hold both my hands like Paddy does sometimes.

I grab the pillow on my bed and I release a scream into it. There's no consequence to that, except a slightly wet pillow. Neil doesn't come rushing in. Nothing happens at all. Nobody's there. I can't even hear him outside the door now. I grab my phone and scroll my contacts. I locate Paddy and connect.

'Hey-lo?' comes his cheery greeting. I swallow a bubble of emotion.

'Pads, it's me.'

'Hiya, how you doing? Is everything okay? Did you find Ellis?'

'No, not yet. Everything's fine though, don't worry.'

'Everything's fine or everything's *fine*?' he asks.

'It's fine, really,' I reply. I don't want him to share this agonising pain splitting my chest into two. I want him to keep that bouncy little note in his voice. 'No news.'

'Isaac mentioned some miserable detective bloke's on the case, is he?'

'Yeah, he's not really a detective. He works with the police in witness protection. He's not so bad. How are things there?'

'Yeah, good. Well, we had a bad storm the night before last and lost a couple of the tall trees along the drive.'

'Oh.'

'We're waiting for the tree surgeon to come out and take off some of the branches. Should give us a load of firewood for the store though.'

'That's good.'

'Yeah. Me and Isaac have made a start on the rendering in the downstairs loo and we've got some students from the local college in and they're doing the nettles and ivy down by the pond, digging all that out. Lysette's friend's husband's coming out tomorrow to look at those old lead water pipes in the stable. He knows a scrapyard, too. Might make a bit of money out of them, you never know.'

'Okay.'

'Oh and the pond's got a leak, that's the biggest news.

Joe noticed the water level was dropping a bit when he was out with the dog yesterday. And you were right about that plasterwork on the stairs. It's all got to come off.'

'Great,' I say, closing my eyes.

'Great? Haven't you been listening to me, Foy? It's all a massive head-fuck.'

'No, it's perfect.'

'You're not missing us by any chance, are you?'

'Bit.'

'When do you think you'll be back?'

'I don't know. Soon. I hope.'

'You sure you're not getting your hopes too high, sis?'

'Quite sure.'

I want to say, *I'll come home as soon as I have Ellis with me*, but I can't. Because I don't know that I will anymore. I feel tears coming.

And somehow, my brother being my brother, knows.

'Keep your chin up, Foy. You'll find her.'

I know he's bullshitting me. Because he knows I need it. I manage to squeak out a 'Bye' and hang up, throwing the phone to the end of the bed. I go to the window, panicking. I place my palms on the cool glass. I'm trying to think of a poem but I'm panicking too much. Need to breathe. Find the breath. Deep in for seven, out for ten. Still none come to mind, only that war one about the mad soldier in the ambulance counting his cabbages. Then one line emerges:

Now I am six, I'm as clever as clever. So I think I'll be six now forever and ever.

Now I am six, I'm as clever as clever. So I think I'll be six now forever and ever.

Now I am six, I'm as clever as clever. So I think I'll be six now forever and ever.

A.A. Milne wrote it. That's all I remember from it, that one line, like a stuck record. I'm still panicking.

Far across the bay on the jetty the coastguard's boat is coming in. It's only 1 p.m. I can feel bad news in the air. Ready to land on the next strong breeze.

Neil comes back in moments later, and my chest clenches tight.

'Why is the rescue boat coming back in? It's only lunchtime.'

'They've called off the search,' says Neil. 'That's what I wanted to tell you earlier. They're not treating it as a search and rescue anymore.'

'What?'

'It's been four days, Foy.'

I sit back down on the bed. 'You mean they're not looking for a living person anymore. They're looking for a body.'

Neil throws his phone on the bed too and bends down to pick up the wedding dress. 'I need to bag this up. Could you grab the suit bag from the wardrobe please?'

I don't move. I'm frozen. 'When did you know they were calling off the search?'

'This morning. I got a call from the police liaison guy who was here the other day.' He grabs the suit bag himself and bundles the dress inside, zipping it up the front.

'Can't we go out there? Charter a boat or—'

'No, we can't do that.'

'Why not?'

'It's too dangerous. Look at it.' The wind and rain in the bay have whipped up into a storm. Rain pelts the windows and it feels like the whole building will at any moment uproot and whirl off into the sky. 'The people who go out there and search are volunteers. It's not fair to send them out in a hurricane.'

'What can we do then?' I don't bother wiping my tears away.

He pulls the armchair forwards so it's next to me and sits down. 'I need to tell you something. But you've got to keep your temper in check, okay?'

I stare at him hard.

'I just spoke to Rani, my colleague back in Bristol. She's been following up a few leads on the database. Do you want to go and change out of that first?' He was staring down at my soaked top and jeans. I only realise it then, but I am very cold.

'No.' I fold my arms, readying myself. Like I did that day at the hospital when we got the news about Dad. When I got the news Paddy would need amputations. When the paramedic told me about Luc. When the sonographer told me there was no heartbeat. Twice. Folded arms is my default setting.

'There's a broken arrow in the investigation, one I haven't been aware of until now. In police terms it means someone fairly dangerous has gone off the radar. And in this instance, one of the cartel – a sometime member, not from the original cohort convicted – has gone off grid.'

'Which means?'

'Which means any witnesses that didn't get the message the first time, could be in danger. You didn't tell anyone Ellis's real name this morning, did you?'

Yeah, everyone. But I don't tell *him* that. 'No. Why?'

'Because Rani told me that our particular broken arrow has been in these parts in the last month. And he has fairly strong links to the Bristol cartel. They put a trace on his car which was found dumped in woodland about seven miles from here.'

'Who is he and why wasn't he in the original bunch who went to prison?'

'He was already *in* prison when Ellis and her dad were attacked. An unrelated crime. But he was very good friends with the blokes who got sent down for it.'

'Not the man who was the sex offender?' I say, my blood chilling at the thought. Neil says nothing. That says everything. 'Oh, Jesus. He is, isn't he?'

'When he got out, he joined up with the remaining members of the Bristol cartel and carried on operating in Bristol North East, for a time. Did a five-year stretch for a sexual assault on a woman leaving a nightclub. He was released in June.'

'And Ellis moved here—'

'—August.'

'You SAID she was safe here! You SAID she wasn't being followed! That it was all in her mind, that she was being paranoid!'

'This guy was not on our watch list. We didn't know about him until now.'

'So he's been living here the past few months, watching her?'

'We don't know yet. Rani's still running checks.'

'Was he staying here? Where she worked? Where that woman was murdered? What's his name? Is it Sean? Is it Kaden Cotterill?' I don't know who to believe anymore. 'That Trevor guy, the porter, Vanda said he'd done time.'

'Sean's nothing to do with it, and Rani's run checks on Cotterill and the Chinese guy at the supermarket Ellis visits and her landlord, they're clean as a whistle. This guy's name is Knapp. John Knapp. I've got my laptop here. I'll run my own trace on him.'

'Did Ellis know anyone called John Knapp? Can you think of anyone at all with that name? John? Johnny?'

Neil shakes his head. 'No. Off the top of my head, I can't.'

24

With the wedding dress safely sequestered in a suit bag inside Neil's wardrobe, we go back to the flats, only to find Ellis's landlord, Sandy Balls, has got there before us. The guy is tall and wide, with a mop of curly brown hair flecked with sawdust. He's brandishing a long screwdriver when we meet outside the flat.

'Hey, what are you doing?' says Neil.

'Changing the locks, what does it look like? And who are you?'

'We're... police.' I throw him a look but his stare is fixed and unwavering. 'You can't change the locks. She hasn't moved out.'

'Yeah, well I got Christmas presents to buy for my grand-children so I need this space filled. I got people lining up for this one. Top floor's already filled as of yesterday and I got the bailiffs coming tomorrow to kick them druggies out in between.'

'You can wait a bit longer, surely,' says Neil.

'Listen,' says Balls, pointing the screwdriver at Neil's solar plexus. 'I've been on the phone half the morning to your lot, asking me all sorts of questions about her, and I want her out of the place now, I don't want any more hassle.' He looks me up and down. 'She's not dressed like police.'

'She's helping with the investigation,' says Neil.

'I don't reckon *you're* police either.'

'You can't sign away this flat yet, sir. This could be a crime scene,' says Neil, but Balls scoffs and carries on unscrewing the Chubb. 'How much?'

'What?'

Neil parks his laptop underneath his arm and gets out his wallet. 'How much to rent it for another week?'

'I can only take six weeks' money at a time.'

'How much for six weeks then?'

'You ain't got £650 on yer,' Balls laughs. 'Knew you two weren't cops. She's done a bunk, hasn't she?'

'I've got three hundred. Keep the place empty for now, alright?'

Balls laughs, his neck wobbling like a turkey's. 'That ain't enough, is it?'

'This is a police investigation, Mr Balls,' says Neil, his grey eyes flashing like he's rearing up for a fight. 'I could have this place commandeered and cordoned off within the hour and then you'd get nothing.'

Balls laughs again. 'No you couldn't. Police said they weren't going to do that. They reckon she's gone over the sea wall. Nothing suspicious, they said.'

Neil rears up like a stag and for a second I think he's going to deck the man, so I dig into my rucksack for my purse and hand Neil £200 on top of his £300, leaving me just under £50 until I can get to an ATM. The Good Cop approach. 'Please, sir. She's coming back. We just don't know when.'

I feel Neil look at me, but this time *my* gaze is fixed and unwavering.

'Fine,' Balls says, snatching the money from both of us and shuffling the wad of notes into the back pocket of his shorts. 'I'll cancel the cleaners tomorrow. But I want that window mended, that carpet in the bedroom cleaned and that floor in the kitchen put right. And I'll be coming to inspect it first thing in January.'

'We'll see to all of it,' I say as Neil stands there, still fuming as Balls huffily puts the screws back in, clicks shut his toolbox and lumbers down the steps towards his van – *Sandy Balls Does It All. General Builder.*

'Twat,' says Neil under his breath as we watch the van bomb along the seafront, belching out fumes from a dangling exhaust. He checks his phone.

'Come on, let's go and see what state he's left the place in.'

Inside the flat, Balls has bagged up all Ellis's belongings into bin bags and placed them in the centre of the lounge, the same type of bin bags the wedding dress was in when it went over the sea wall. The damp smell is stronger now and all Ellis's trinkets and toys have been cleared away. The doll's feet stick out of one of the bags, along with several other cuddly toys and books. Her bed's been stripped and the sheets sit in an untidy clump in the corner. The bath's been emptied too. The contents of the cupboards sit in a cardboard box on the breakfast bar.

Neil sits on the edge of the sofa and opens the lid of his laptop, logging in to the trace he was running back at the hotel.

'Do you want a tea?' I offer, with no real intention of making one anyway as I can't immediately see a kettle or any teabags.

'No thanks,' he says. The clock on the microwave ticks over to 3.22 p.m. 'Think I'm getting somewhere here.'

'You are?' I say, returning to the lounge and sitting down next to him.

'Yeah. Knapp's record makes for sinister reading. Seems the coffin catalogue was one of his calling cards, back in the day. Along with silent phone calls. He did it to check his victims were suitably disturbed before he struck.'

'Oh Christ.'

'He was of no fixed abode,' he says. 'There's no paper trail for him at all. No social media. Oh, wait a minute... a garage lock-up. He was renting it in his own name.'

'A lock-up?' I repeat after him, my chest constricting. 'Where?'

'Not sure yet.'

A lock-up garage means nothing, I tell myself. It's just a lock-up where you keep an old car or tools. 'Why would he be renting a lock-up but not a flat?'

It's Neil's face that tips me over into full panic mode. He slams the lid of the laptop, grabs his coat and is out the door before I'm even on my feet. 'It's near here. Half a mile away.' He looks at me then tucks his laptop under his arm and makes to leave. I follow him.

*

The management company Knapp rents his lock-up from are called Frazer & Lloyd and they have an office at the top of the high street, above a hairdresser's. They're surveyors, in the main, but they also bought the plot of land and began renting out the garages twenty years ago. It's a blink-and-you-miss-it kind of place with a small plain board where the frosted glass should be out the front, visible from street level.

We're greeted on the second floor by a rather-too-brown office, an aged monkey puzzle, a smell of turps, and a short cross-eyed woman called Mandy whose shoes don't fit her properly. Neil dispenses with the pleasantries and asks her straight out about the lock-up in John Knapp's name.

'Oh, yes, certainly,' says Mandy, a sweet-natured Scouser who seems so in awe of Neil he could ask her to get undressed and I think she'd oblige. She doesn't ask for my ID, which is good because I don't have any on me. Strictly speaking, we shouldn't be doing this. The police have told Neil it's all in hand, but they haven't made the John Knapp connection yet and Neil has, so it's his collar. He hasn't said as much, but that's the impression I get. He's more animated than I've seen him before. And I don't think he's had a drink today. He's focused. Finally as hungry for answers as I am.

Mandy plods over to a large dark brown and taupe filing cabinet in the corner and pulls out the second drawer down, sifting out a file halfway along. 'Seventeen B, Larkwood Trading Estate. It's not far from here actually. Go up the high street and turn left at Clarks Shoes, and keep going along until you reach St Bartholomew's Road. It's halfway along there, down a little alleyway.'

'Do you remember the guy who's leasing it? Have you met him?' asks Neil.

'Yeah, vaguely,' says Mandy. 'Tall, quite stocky, rough-looking. Said he wanted the garage for his van I think.'

'What sort of van? Bedford? Camper?'

'Doughnuts.'

'Doughnuts?' I say, homing in on Neil's face. He's caught the same drift. He knows what I'm thinking: the doughnut van on the CCTV the night Ellis went missing. It was there, more or less opposite her flat. And it hasn't been there since. 'Oh god.'

'What's he done?' says Mandy, sitting at her desk and holding her coffee with two hands like she's preparing for a juicy bit of gossip.

'Is there a spare key for the garage?' asks Neil.

'No, the leaseholders put on their own padlocks I'm afraid. Once someone leases it, it's up to them how they secure it.'

'Okay, no bother. Many thanks for your help.'

'What's he done, though?' she's still asking as we're walking out the door. Neil doesn't say one word to me down the entire staircase. He doesn't say one word until we're on St Bartholomew's Road, breathing out cold air, scanning turnings for the Larkwood Trading Estate. And even then it's me who speaks first.

'That van hasn't been on that seafront for the past four days.'

'Doesn't necessarily mean anything,' he says.

'It means everything,' I say. 'What if she's in there?'

'Then we'll find her,' he says, and at that moment I want him to hold my hand so much but he doesn't. He slips his hands into his coat pockets and retrieves a pair of leather gloves. He pulls them on.

We turn into the trading estate down the narrow, puddle-strewn alley Mandy mentioned, and it opens out onto a wide expanse of gravelled land, flanked on both sides by garage blocks. They all have corrugated metal doors with their numbers scrawled on them in white paint. Neil keeps walking, so I keep walking. I can't remember the last time I took a full breath.

We walk quickly until we reach 15a then we slow down – 15b, 16a, 16b, 17a.

17b.

I look around to see if anyone's coming. Not a soul. For a garage right in the middle of town, it's surprisingly lonely. The distant main road thrums and I clasp the back of Neil's arm as he starts unpicking the lock with some implement on a Swiss Army Knife he's fished from his back pocket.

'What if *he's* in there?' I whisper.

Neil stands back and bangs on the door so loudly my chest ache radiates outwards, along my arms, sizzling into my hands. The whole estate echoes but no sound comes from within. I can't stop thinking about *The Silence of the Lambs*.

Neil continues to pick the lock and finally, with a satisfying *clunk* sound, the padlock releases and falls to the gravel, landing in a puddle with a resounding *splash*. He pulls back one of the doors and then reaches inside to release the chain bolt that's holding the other door in place.

And there it is – the doughnut van.

There are posters on its outer walls for *Extra Large Slushie's £2! Hot dog's and slider's! Candy Floss, from only £1.50 per bag! Five hot doughnut's for £1! Free can of drink when you buy ten churro's! We serve hot drinks to!* Everything comes with a side order of exclamation marks and misplaced punctuation. I'm trying not to focus on how much those extra apostrophes irritate me, trying to keep my brain focussed on the present. The van is the only thing in the garage, we can see that now. There's nothing and nobody else. Neil bangs on the side.

'Ellis? Ellis, you in there? It's Scants.' We wait. No answer.

He breaks the lock on the van door and slowly pulls it open, holding me back with his other hand. The pervading stench of burnt sugar and cooked onions wafts out, but there's still no sign of life. Just a small pile of boxes labelled Ribena and Sausages. Stacks of paper cups in plastic wrapping. Catering-size bottles of red and brown sauce with crusty spouts. Small and large plastic buckets of candy floss, blue and pink, lined up along the high shelves. Neil goes in.

'Anything?' My heart's beating like I've been running.

He's rifling through the two under-counter cupboards. He pulls out a black sports bag and settles it in the middle of the van floor. He unzips it, starts looking through. Clothes. Shaving foam. Disposable razors.

'What is that? What's in there?' I say, folding my arms.

'He's been sleeping in here, by the looks,' he says, pulling out a sleeping bag and a thin, stained pillow from the same compartment. He zips the bag back up again quickly, before I can fully see what he's found in there but I see enough. Unwashed clothes. Razors and shaving cream. Two kitchen knives. A roll of duct tape. A packet of reusable cable ties. Ripped open.

Neil pushes it back inside the cupboard. 'It doesn't mean he's got her. The good thing is it's still here.'

'The good thing?' I cry. 'What if he's used it already and put it all back here?'

'Don't think about that, Foy.'

'How can I *not* think about that?'

I utterly lose it outside the garage block. It's all Neil can do to calm me down. He locks up and somehow manages to get me back to Ellis's flat with only two passers-by asking me if I need any assistance.

Once inside, he settles me down on the armchair. I don't know when he did it but at some point between the garages and here, he's wrapped his coat around me.

'Maybe I should go back to the garages,' he says. 'See if anyone turns up.'

'Don't leave me,' I say. I don't want to be here, let alone by myself, surrounded by stark, oppressive lighting and the pervading smell of rotten cabbages and mould. Balls has even removed the lightshade from the one bulb.

Neil sits on the coffee table before me and rubs my arms up both sides. 'You're still shaking.'

'What do we do now?' He stands up. 'Where are you going?'

'Nowhere,' he replies. 'I'm just gonna have a look around.' He stands up and disappears into Ellis's bedroom. Seagulls squawk outside the patio window – someone's dropped a whole box of chips on the pavement. When Neil comes back in, he stands in the doorway, a quizzical frown on his face.

'Can I run something past you? Something that's been tossing around my head since we were here earlier.'

'Yeah,' I sniff, trying to hold my hand still.

'There was a picture hanging on her bedroom wall last time I was here, right? Frida Kahlo.'

'Who?'

'Doesn't matter, self-portrait. Anyway it's missing. When

I arrived here four days ago I found a few scraps of broken glass. Tiny scraps. Some in the bedroom, some in the lounge.'

'Right, so what?'

'The picture was in a glass frame, so let's imagine for a second that the picture fell and broke at some point the day she went missing.'

'Okay.'

'Her bedroom window has a crack in it. Now, I can't remember if it had a crack in it four days ago but the landlord seems to think it's a new development so let's assume that crack is fresh as well, right?'

'Which suggests…?'

'A forced entry.'

'Through the bedroom window?'

'Yeah. Window's hidden from the road under the fire escape. The lock's not working on it and the handle spins right round. Suggests a forced entry, doesn't it?'

'So you're thinking Knapp forced his way into the bedroom and knocked the picture off the wall?'

He shakes his head. 'Not quite. You said her bed was damp, yeah?'

'Yeah, it was. You said it was cos the whole place is damp.'

'Well, what if I was wrong and he got in there, expecting her to be in bed but she wasn't in bed. She was in the *bath* at the time.'

'Okay.'

I don't know where he's going with this but I'm still shaking so much I can barely focus on his face. He's moving about the flat from one room to another, like he's retracing the steps, his long coat sweeping out behind him.

'He comes into the bathroom, surprises her. She's in the bath, or maybe she's just got out of it. She goes to scream but he grabs her by the neck. That's why nobody heard anything. They struggle.'

I don't want to think about this but he's forcing the images into my mind.

'She manages to get away, runs into the bedroom and tries to shut the door but something's hanging on it, a coat.' He points up to the bedroom doorframe where there's a chunk of wood gouged out. 'Consistent with a hanger, yeah?'

'Yeah. But that could have been done any time.'

Undeterred, he continues. 'Knapp bursts in to the bedroom. Grabs her again. More struggling, maybe against the wall, the picture falls to the floor and breaks.'

'Maybe she cuts her foot on the glass because she's barefoot,' I suggest. 'And that's where the blood comes from?'

'Maybe, yeah. Then he forces her down onto the bed. That's why the bed was damp. Because *she* was still wet from the bath.'

'Oh please, Neil, I don't want to hear anymore.'

He stops talking. Next thing I know he's kneeling down in front of me, looking into my eyes. 'I need you to go back to The Lalique and wait for me.'

'No. Why?'

'I think whatever happened to Ellis happened right here. I don't think he took her anywhere. Do you remember the landlord saying he wanted three things put back right by January?'

'Yeah, the broken window, he wanted the carpet cleaned and— ' We both look into the kitchen at the same time. 'Something about the floor.'

Neil walks over to the kitchen and stands in the middle of the rug. 'There was white lino down here last time I visited Ellis. I know that because I had a go at her about it. It was looking grubby. She said the landlord was going to fit it properly, it was only a cut off. But it's not there anymore. Now there's just this rug.'

'What do you mean?'

He kicks up one corner of the thin, ugly looking rug. 'It wasn't bare floorboards before.'

'Maybe Sandy Balls took up the lino himself when he tidied?' I suggest, watching him pull back the whole rug into a long roll. Neil walks around on the bare floorboards. A couple of them wobble. They're loose. And there's bloody fingerprints on one of them. Neil's looking at me but I can't take my eyes off the boards.

And it's then that the smell registers – a smell that brings bile into my mouth. The smell that's been in the room all along, but was masked by the damp and the aromas of thousands of cooked meals permeating the wallpaper. A smell that now becomes stronger with the revealing of the bare boards.

My hands go to my mouth and I want to be sick. All I can do is shake my head. Neil comes back to me, holding me firmly by both knees. 'Go back to the hotel. I'll come as soon as I can.'

I shake my head again, tears falling down over my fingers.

'I don't want you seeing this.'

'Don't make me go. I need to stay here. If she's here, I need to be here.'

He stands. 'Go into the bedroom then. Don't come into the kitchen, alright?'

Again, I ignore him and walk behind him into the kitchen. He kicks back the rug in its entirety.

He grabs his Swiss Army Knife from his back pocket and bends down to inspect the boards more closely. Two of them wobble under his touch. I pull my jumper cuff over my mouth and nose. I don't know if it's in my mind or if it's in the room but the smell is even stronger now.

25

We visited the little shop two days before Bonfire Night that last year Ellis was staying with us – the last November I ever saw her – and Old Beattie who worked in there had a surprise for us. Books, books and more books.

'I'm moving to Australia,' she says, 'to live with my son. And I'm getting rid of all my books. You two are my best customers so you get first pick.'

And so we were shown through the back of the shop, the magical place we never dreamed existed, into a rather ramshackle stairwell and up the little steps into a small flat. In one room was a huge bookcase that filled the wall and it was stacked with books by every author we'd ever heard of. Dickens, Shakespeare, Wilde, Austen, the Brontës, and loads and loads of children's books too.

'They were my son's,' Beattie says proudly, leaning on her cane. 'You take what you like, girls. Any that don't go, there's a van coming to collect them for charity.'

Beattie's already asked Mum if we would like some books, but Mum says we can only have three each. We 'have enough books as it is' apparently. And choosing the three I want is terribly hard. Ellis doesn't have any problem at all – she chooses a Beatrix Potter compendium which is cheating really because there's loads of books in there, a picture book called

The Reluctant Giant and a pop up *Hansel and Gretel*. I pick a Roald Dahl treasury, which is cheating really too because it's lots of books in one but if Ellis can do it then so can I, a book about horses and a treasury of children's verse.

That's where the poetry book came from. Beattie's house.

I still repeat some of the poems to myself every now and again at odd moments in my life – before exams, job interviews, smear tests. 'Wynken, Blinken and Nod', *Kookaburra Sits in the Old Gum Tree,* 'Matilda, Who Told Lies, and was Burned to Death', *There Was an Old Woman Who Swallowed a Fly, Never Smile at a Crocodile*. They sort of calm me.

I'm internally repeating the Old Woman one now, as I process this latest awful discovery. There is a body under our feet. And it could be my best friend.

'He must have watched her for weeks,' says Neil, trying to prise up the first of the two wobbly floorboards with the slotted screwdriver on his Swiss Army Knife. I stand over him, holding the pink Snow White and the Seven Dwarves torch he's found in one of the bin bags. 'Right opposite her flat. Right under her nose.'

'She swallowed the goat to catch the dog, She swallowed the dog to catch the cat, She swallowed the cat to catch the bird—'

The smell makes me gag, as the first board comes up. I stuff my jumper cuff into my mouth and try to concentrate on the smell of washing powder but the stench still gets through – rotten meat and a sickly sweet perfume. It's making water leak into my mouth. Neil keeps asking if I need to go but I stay and hold the torch, still wrapped in his coat. I can't feel my own fingernails as they dig into my arms.

'She swallowed the bird to catch the spider, That wriggled

and jiggled and tickled inside her. She swallowed the spider to catch the fly, I don't know why she swallowed a fly – Perhaps she'll die.'

One floorboard is out. Then, with some effort, he pulls up the other one. I can't look inside the hole. I just look at Neil.

'Torch?' he says, holding out his hand for it. I pass it to him. His forehead is sweaty and his cheeks all red from bending over. He's opened up a large gap in the boards and ducks his head down inside, angling the torch to illuminate the void. When he comes up, he breathes out long and hard. His face gives nothing away.

I can't remember any more of the rhyme. It's stuck in a groove *Perhaps she'll die. Perhaps she'll die. Perhaps she'll die.* It doesn't matter anyway – it hasn't helped. I'm bursting at the seams, ready to lose myself completely to a meltdown. I'm a dam holding in a raging tide. All I can do is pray. 'Please God, please God, please—'

Neil can't lie to me. But he can't tell me the truth either. I start unravelling.

'Is it?' I ask, steeling myself. 'Is it her?' He still says nothing. 'Neil, is it her? Please tell me. Is it Ellis?'

'I can't see it clearly. It's wrapped up in the lino,' he says. He bends over and roots around for a little longer. The waiting is agony.

'Get her out of there, get her out, get her out! Please, please, please—'

I don't think my heart can take anymore and I can't remember taking a complete breath in minutes. When he comes up, he just looks at me.

'WHAT?'

'It's not her. It's not Ellis,' he pants. 'The face is wrapped up but I'm sure from the clothes it's *him*. He's got a big piece of glass in his neck.'

The air leaves my body and I slump against the kitchen cupboards.

'She's killed him? John Knapp? She's killed him?' I gasp.

Neil turns to me, blinking. He can barely process it either. 'Yeah, she has.'

26

There's a poem by Hillaire Belloc I keep thinking of from the book. It reminds me of Ellis.

Matilda told such dreadful lies, it made one gasp and stretch one's eyes... that night a fire did break out, you should have heard Matilda shout. For every time she shouted Fire, They only answered Little Liar. And therefore when her aunt returned, Matilda and the house were burned.

It goes round and round my head – an earworm eating all my other thoughts until the other thoughts rise up and bite back. Neither me or Neil could have prepared for this. I had been preparing to find Ellis's body, not Ellis's *victim*. Neil had been preparing to find nothing. All we could do was breathe, and even that was difficult through our jumper cuffs as the smell was almost intolerable.

Matilda told such dreadful lies...

But Ellis didn't tell lies, did she? She really *was* being followed – by the detective *I* hired. And by this guy. She *did* have silent phone calls. She *was* sent a catalogue full of funeral accessories. Someone *did* kill Tessa Sharpe thinking it was her. And it was this guy who did it all. Whether Neil was ready to admit that or not.

Halfway through helping Neil remove two more kitchen boards to give us better access to the body, he stops altogether and wipes his gloved hand over his face.

'Stop stop stop, we can't. I need to call this in now.'

'Call it in? But if you call it in—'

'It'll be a murder investigation, yeah, I know. But that's what we're dealing with now, isn't it? She's killed a man.' He stands up, rubbing his knees and flexing his feet.

'No, we can't report this to the police. They'll be looking for her.'

'I thought you wanted the authorities to look for her.'

'But they'll arrest her,' I say. 'She'll do time for this.'

'I've got to call this in,' he repeats, wearily, removing his phone from his jeans. 'And if you want another reason other than doing the right thing, then Tessa Sharpe. If this bastard killed her before he tried to kill Ellis, then the police need to know.'

'Why do they?' I ask, standing up to face him. 'Tessa Sharpe's dead.'

'Yes, and her family need to know why.'

'No,' I say, reaching across and holding his hand over the phone. 'Don't.'

...it made one gasp and stretch one's eyes.

His grey eyes stare at me. 'She's killed him. He's been dead for days.'

'Yeah, I know, I can smell him,' I say, barely stifling my own nausea. 'But you can't have Ellis arrested for this.'

'Foy, you're not suggesting—'

'You *can't* have her arrested for this, Neil. If what you said is true, she did this in self-defence. Right?'

287

'Well, yeah, but—' He rubs his mouth and nose. 'I don't have a choice. Look what she's done.'

'I don't *care* what she's done. As far as I'm concerned she's killed a murderer and a rapist. She's done the world a favour. She's done Tessa Sharpe a favour too.'

'The woman's dead! What does it matter to her now?! And even if this *was* self-defence, Ellis needs to face up to what she's done.'

…that night a fire did break out…

'Don't you think she's been through enough? So she goes on remand for weeks on end, then she goes through a trial, then she has to relive this whole nightmare in court. She *knows* it was wrong, that's why she's run away. She's scared, and this is what she's scared of. And she knows now that this is really serious, and there are consequences.'

'We've got to hand this over, Foy.'

'No,' I say. 'She'll go to prison. She won't survive in there. You know what she's like. She can't cope with the outside world, let alone an adult prison.'

…you should have heard Matilda shout.

'Well what do you want me to do? Huh? Take the rap for her? Hide this back under the floorboards and hope nobody notices the stink?'

'You can deal with this,' I tell him. 'You know ways of dealing with this. People who can deal with this.'

'What, because I work with the police? They're not all bent. It's not like *Luther*.'

'You can make this go away. If you really wanted to.'

'Foy, for Christ's sake, no I can't. I'm not in the police, I can't bend the rules.'

'Yeah, you can. You must know someone. Or some*where*.'

He stares at me. He looks down at the body. Down at the scattered floorboards. The rug. He looks back at me. 'You can't be suggesting that.'

'He's off the grid, you said. Nobody's looking for him, he's a lone wolf. God knows what he did to Ellis before she stabbed him. I'd say justice has already been served. You can't expect her to pay for this. She's not like you and me. She's… a child.'

'Foy, please don't ask me to do this.'

'I'm not asking you,' I say, shaking my head. 'I'm not asking you.'

Neil rubs his mouth for the longest time and stands back by the breakfast bar. 'You can't be here.'

'It's alright. I think I know where to find her.'

'You do?'

I shrug out of his coat and place it on the back of one of the stools. 'I need to go to her. You do what you need to do. I've said my piece.' I rummage about in my rucksack for my North Face coat and pull it out, smoothing through the creases. 'I want to be the first one to find her. I *have* to be.'

'It's getting late. You can't go now.'

'Tomorrow it'll be five days since she went missing. She can't wait for me much longer. I'm going.'

And therefore when her aunt returned, Matilda and the house were burned.

I use the toilet before I leave, grabbing my things and heading for the front door. John Knapp's body lies still wrapped in the lino in the centre of the kitchen floor, a mummy in its tomb. Neil closes the door of Ellis's flat carefully and sees me out. I turn to him on the doorstep and for a second I think he's going to close the door on me but at the last moment he leans in and we kiss. Solid and hungry, desperate and warm. And after the kiss, we become a hug. Tight and safe.

'I'll sort it, okay?' he whispers. 'Don't worry. I'll be with you as soon as I can.'

I don't want to let him go. As we release he rests his forehead against mine.

'I hope I'm not too late.'

*

I buy a pack of cigarettes and a lighter at Frankly Services. I haven't smoked for years but tonight I'm drawn to them like the Little Mermaid being beckoned into Ursula's underwater cave. They promise me freedom from the chronic anxiety marauding through my body, and I weaken under their heady influence. Anyone would.

One of the loneliest places on earth is a service station in the middle of the night. At first sight it's inviting and warm and everything glows neon and stinks of fresh coffee. But times like these it just reminds you of how big and commercial and fake the world is. And how alone you really are.

There are tired families milling about, reading magazines, hand-dryers echoing around the shop units from the bathrooms, a hen party hollering and flashing their tits at a stag party in the arcades. I get a double espresso and a toastie from Costa, use the loos and, after topping up my petrol, I'm on my way again, out into the freezing night in my rental car. The weather report by the time I reach Preston warns of snow flurries in the South West but it's not too bad until I reach Bristol. Another hour or so to go, traffic-willing. I *will* make it before it hits too heavy. I will get to her.

I only mean to have one cigarette, to take the edge off, but I end up going through the pack. Adrenalin kicks in around Clevedon at 5 a.m. and by the time I get into Taunton, I'm out of fags, patience and my petrol light is flashing for the second time. It is snowing hard now, and I have the wipers on full-pelt. The radio is warning of two inches of snowfall. I will walk the rest of the way if I have to. I have good boots. I have my coat. I need to get to her.

Maybe our knights will save us, Foy.

No, we'll save us this time, Ellis. We can use our own swords.

My phone rings as I reach the large roundabout near the retail park. It's Neil. I can't get to it in time as it cuts out but within a minute it *bing*s a voicemail message.

'Foy? It's Neil. I've been to the bus station. Asked to see their CCTV of the night she went. She took a bus to Bristol very late. So it looks like you're on the right track anyway. The other problem… is sorted. Let me know if there's any news. Bye.'

He says nothing more. No more clues about Knapp, or if he had the body in his car when he went to the bus station, nothing. I get the feeling I'm not going to find out either. I wonder if he went over the sea wall. I wonder if the furious tide opened its hungry jaws and ate him up.

It's six fifteen in the morning when I finally turn the car into the long, barren white stretch of Long Lane. Dread pumps through me like poison. In my head, so many times, I had imagined myself back here. I open the window and a freezing crisp breeze pumps in as I round the perilously icy corners into Carew St Nicholas.

None of the buildings have changed, all still standing at different heights with their roofs of thatch, tile and slate. There's still the same sign on the road, half-hidden by brambles and thorns – *Welcome to Carew St Nicholas – a Thankful Village. Please drive carefully.* But the little wooden sign that had stood on the green for years – *Slow Down, Ducks Crossing* – has gone. So have all the ducks.

The church of St Nicholas perches on its hill above the churchyard. The war memorial. The Old Cider House. They're all still standing too. I round the bend into the main street and I expect to see the shop and the post office but they've both gone – no metal pavement signs advertising Cornettos swinging in the wind. They're terraced houses now, with hatchbacks parked on gravel hard standings.

The pub is still there and I'm filled with the sight of it as I turn into the car park through the open gates. The Besom Inn. I don't want to be here. It's a time warp of happy memories and sad losses and it doesn't feel right to be standing here anymore. The new owners have painted the exterior walls of the pub duck egg blue – it was white when we had it – and it doesn't suit it at all. The sign's still there which I'm both happy and sad to see – my dad hand-painted it. I park up beside a building I don't recognise. It used to be the skittle alley. Now it's four mini chalets for B&B guests called *Besom B&B*. Over the back wall is the churchyard.

I didn't want to look at the headstones but my head automatically turned that way and I spot them instantly – Mum and Dad, next to one another, between Mary Brokenshire and the village witch, Bridget Wiltshire, all of them topped with thick drifts of snow. The sight doesn't upset me as much as I thought it would.

Across the car park, the beer garden is smaller than I remember – they've moved the fence to make the back garden larger, and there's some building where half the garden used to be. A shed or storage unit. Ugly and modern. It's tables and chairs now. It's like we were never here at all. The handprints in the cement at the bottom of the climbing frame have long since been dug up and grassed over. Our initials in the fence post, made with compasses after school one day – no sign of them. All of the play equipment – the climbing frame, the swings, the see-saw – have vanished. Dad's bonfire patch, grassed over. All the trees cut back to stumps.

And with an enormous ache I realise – the treehouse has gone too. Our castle. That's where I'd convinced myself all the way here that Ellis would be hiding.

Desperation kicks in then. I can't think of anywhere else to go. Do I call Neil? Do I get back in the car? Was there somewhere else we went as children she may have run to? Panic jumps in and every other rational thought splashes out. There's no poem I can call on either. Everything's silent and white and the snow's still drifting down silently. There's no cars troubling the new blanket of snow on the road. No dog walkers. No people at all. It's like I'm stuck in a silent nightmare except everything's real. The one thing that kept me going during the night was the thought that she would be here, waiting for me. But she's not.

'ELLIS!' I shout, void of all other options. 'ELLIS!' Our voices used to echo here, our laughter would ring out all around the village, but there's so many new houses on the hilly climbs surrounding the village now, nothing comes back. Long gone are the views and the centuries-old trees. It's all rendered brick and uPVC windows now. But it doesn't matter to me. All that matters is her.

'ELLIS!' My voice doesn't carry. Nobody comes.

I trudge round to the front of the pub and rap on the door. After an age and a lot more knocking, a light goes on upstairs in the room that used to be Paddy's. Next to the lounge. Next to the back stairs where me and Ellis used to steal crisps.

There's a small rectangular sign above the pub door. *Roger and Miriam Bartram, Licenced to sell Beers, Wines and Spirits to be Consumed on these premises.* It used to read Michelle and Stuart Keeton. I swallow a gulp of tears.

'What's going on? Who's there?' comes a groggy growl above me.

I stand back and look up, the snow falling heavily now onto my face. I can barely see him. For a split second once my eyes have adjusted, I think it's my dad leaning out – he's the right age – but it dawns on me too quickly that it's the current landlord, his eyes all thin and puffy.

'I'm sorry to wake you up but I'm looking for somebody.'

'Who?' he barks.

'A girl, a woman. She's about my age, and she's got red – black hair down to here, brown eyes, she's about my height, I think—'

'Do you know what time it is?' he grunts.

'Yes I do, and I've driven through the night from up near

Blackpool to get here. Have you seen a woman with black hair and brown eyes, my height and age? That's all I want to know. Then you can get back to bloody sleep.'

'No, I ain't,' he barks and slams the window. I stand there for moments, looking out across the road at the silent rows of cottages, at the curtain twitching in one of them. I'm about to start calling for Ellis again when there's another noise above me. I'm expecting a bucket of piss to come pouring out on me this time but it's a woman in her dressing gown, a fluffy pink one, like Mum used to wear.

'Is everything alright, love?'

I look up at her. 'Please,' I say. 'My cousin is missing and I think she might be round here somewhere. Have you seen a woman with black hair, brown eyes, about my height in the last few days? Please can you think for a minute? It is urgent. She's missing. She could be dead by now, I don't know.'

'Sorry, love, I don't think so. Oh,' she stops.

'No, what?'

'Actually, we did have a girl here a few days ago, but she didn't have black hair, she was blonde. And she seemed a bit odd.' My heart sinks. She can't mean Ellis. Until she says, 'I think it was a wig though. It didn't look right on her.'

'Really?'

'Yeah. She did have blue eyes though. She came in, ordered a basket of chips and chicken nuggets and asked to have it out in the beer garden which I thought was strange because it was so cold. She said she wanted to see the treehouse.'

'Oh my god, that was her, yes! That would be her!'

The woman frowns. 'Course, she was very disappointed when I said it wasn't there anymore – said she used to come here as a kid. What's the big deal with it anyway? We gave it to the school for their playground.'

But I don't hear anymore, my legs are going and I turn and go with them, in the direction of Parsonage Lane towards our old primary school. The snow is thick underfoot – no way would I get the car up here – and the cold creeps in through some crack in my boots into my socks. I keep running, keep heaving myself through for two miles, though it feels like five.

I reach the school driveway, boiling hot in my coat, my eyes watering with the whiteness of the snow. The school gates are closed. I run around the back via the little alleyway and am relieved to see the hole in the chicken wire fence is still there, though I can barely get through it now. Once inside, I look around and head straight for the playground. And I see it – the treehouse. In the corner underneath the trees. On the ground. Health and safety. No window boxes anymore. Not blue as it used to be but black and drawn all over in colourful chalk.

There's something inside it. At the back. Or is it my eyes? A bundle of clothes. A sleeping bag. Someone's in there! *Please be her*, I think as I race towards it. I can barely see in the heavy snowfall but it has to be her, I think. There's nowhere else she'd go. Please. *Please.*

'Ellis?' I call out. 'ELLIS?' I cry.

I drag myself heavily and breathlessly through the snow like a butterfly in glue. Heart pounding. Legs like jelly. Tears freezing on my cheeks.

'Ellis?' I shout as I ease my way inside the treehouse.

The bundle doesn't move. I tear at it, searching for a face or an arm or anything inside it. And then I find her, right at the bottom, underneath all the clothes she's brought with her and wrapped up in a sleeping bag. It's her. My Ellis.

'Ellis!' I grab her arms and shake her. Her face is cold to the touch. I shake her again. 'Ellis! You wake up now, you wake up now. Ellis! I'm here, I'm here now. It's Foy!'

Her eyes open a sliver. And she sees me. 'Chelle?' she croaks. 'Auntie?'

'No, Ellis, it's me. It's Foy.' My tears fall on her face but she doesn't flinch. She's so cold she can't feel them. Her lips are so dry.

'Foy?' she mutters.

I wipe my cheeks. 'Yeah.'

'I think I'm dying, Foy.'

'Ellis? Ellis!?' She slips back into unconsciousness and doesn't answer me again.

I hold her close to me, as though some of my life will go into her. Something crinkles – a large piece of paper, tucked into the front of her coat. I pull it out – it's a note, written on the back of a painting of some woman with weird eyebrows. A confession. Everything she did, everything she lied about. It's addressed to Neil.

'Ellis, please wake up. Please.' I throw down the note and tear off my coat, wrapping that around her as well, even though she's already well insulated. But she's still so freezing to the touch. She's been out here for so long. Five whole days. But I'm not too late. I'm here now. She's alive now, she's talking to me.

But she's so cold. I find her hands and I put my own gloves on them but her fingers are frozen. I hold one of them. 'Squeeze my hand, Ellis.'

I feel a slight squeeze but it's like I can't reach her. She's there, beside me, but she's slipping away. I can barely dial 999 because my fingertips are frozen too.

'Please hurry,' I cry to the operator. 'Please *please* hurry. I can't lose her again.'

27

The doctor who keeps popping in is called Dr Shelley Buhari, which is somewhat comforting as I sit beside Ellis's bed, falling in and out of consciousness myself. Even though she spells her name differently to how Mum did, I feel like in some way Mum is here with us. She has the same skin colour, the same curly hair. I've asked her three times now if Ellis will be alright but she keeps saying variants of the same thing:

We will have to see. We will let you know if there is any change in her condition.

We are keeping a close eye on her but it's a waiting game.

She is responding well to her treatment and her heart rate has returned to normal but only time will tell.

It's all vague bon mots and pleasantries and the nurses keep popping in to check Ellis's drip and empty the piss bag by the bed but I get no new information. She's breathing via a thick blue tube and her machines are bleeping at least. I just have to wait now.

So I do. I hold her hand and I talk to her and I wait. Even with the heat pads they've placed on her limbs, her skin's still so cold. I watch TV and I stroke the top of her hand and her cheek and her dyed black hair and I wait. I read the paper,

I go to the vending machine and I sleep and I eat and I read and I watch TV and I wait.

I haven't long since returned from the vending machine with a Crunchie and a bag of crisps when I step through the door of her room and there's all this movement and noise – two nurses stand over her, removing her tubing. She's blinking wildly, coughing, taking big slurps of breath.

'Oh my god, what's happening?' I say, dropping my sweets to the floor.

'It's alright,' says one of the nurses. 'She's awake.'

Never were two words more welcome or cherished: she's awake. I've waited hours for this moment. Ellis is lying there, still coughing and breathing big breaths when the nurses settle her down, her eyes watering with the ferocity of her coughs. Her cheeks are rosy. She starts looking around. She sees me. She frowns.

Her voice is husky. 'Auntie Chelle?'

I grab her hand. She feels warmer.

'No, it's me. It's Foy.'

'You're Auntie Chelle.'

I shake my head. 'No, it's me. I promise. I just look like her.'

Her face crumples but I get to her before any of her tears can fall and we hold each other. She's shaking, like I was shaking. But now I am strong. I am strong for her. I pull back and wipe my eyes.

She won't let go of my hand. 'You grew up.'

'Yeah. Sorry about that.'

'You found me.'

'Can you remember what happened?'

'Yeah,' she croaks. And then she looks at me, guilt in her eyes. 'I did a bad thing, Foy. I did a really bad thing.'

'I know. It's okay. It's all going to be fine.'

'Is it?'

'Yes. I promise.'

'But… I killed him. Frida Kahlo knows.'

'Who's Frida Kahlo?'

'On my picture, where is it?'

My thoughts go to the note I found on her in the treehouse, written on the back of the scary eyebrows woman. The one I burned with my lighter at the back of the school and stamped into the snow while waiting for the ambulance. 'Don't worry about that now.'

'Where am I, Foy? Is this Heaven?'

'You're at Musgrove in Taunton. They brought you in with hypothermia. You've had to have a couple of toes off, Elle. You had frostbite.'

Her lips are all dry as she talks. 'They moved the tree-house.'

'I know, I know.'

'I thought you'd all be there. At the pub. But you'd gone.'

'We left the pub years ago.'

'Isaac and Paddy,' she smiles, closing her eyes. 'Are they here too?'

'No, they're back at home. They both send their love. We live in France.'

'Do you live with them?'

'Yes. We all live together. Isaac's husband Joe lives there too, and their little boy Jonah, and Paddy's wife Lysette and their two girls.'

'And Auntie Chelle and Uncle Stu?'

I so want to tell her good news and keep her smiling but it's impossible because she already sees it in my eyes. I can't lie to her, ironically. I shake my head.

'No. They're not there.' But she seems to know. She reaches up for me again and we hug and cry together.

'Both of them?' she whispers. I nod. 'It's okay. It's okay,' she says, and then it's *her* comforting *me*.

'Mum always wanted me to find you,' I tell her, pulling back. 'She said we needed to know. It was like a hole running right through her.'

'She was the only mum I had. We're sisters really, aren't we, you and me?'

'I wish we were.'

'Foy – I was going to kill myself. I took some pills—'

'It's okay, I know.'

'I didn't take all of them. Only two, I think. I didn't want to do it. I couldn't.'

'It's okay, it's okay.'

'Most of them fell into the bath when that man—' She stops. Closes off.

'There's plenty of time to talk about everything, don't worry.' I kiss her forehead. 'God, I can't believe you're here. I feel like I'm going to wake up.'

'How did you find me?'

I sit down on the bed beside her, still holding her hand within my own. 'You remember Kaden? The man who lived in the flat above you?'

'He works at the gym. He went weird on me. Did you know him?'

'He was working for me, Ellis. He was a private detective I hired to find you.'

She frowns. 'No, he works at the gym. He taught me self-defence. That saved my life, Foy.'

'He was only working part-time at the gym. That was his cover. He was working for me. I wasn't interfering. I just wanted to know you were happy.'

'I wasn't happy, was I?' I shake my head. 'Is he here? Is Kaden here?'

'No. He went back to London. Pretty much as soon as *you* disappeared, so did *he*. Cheap git. I'm not paying him for half a job.'

'There were pictures of me on his phone.'

'Yeah. I asked him to take them for me. I'm sorry if that was wrong.'

'I looked for you too.'

'Did you?'

'They wouldn't let me send you any letters.'

'It doesn't matter now,' I say, stroking her face. 'It really doesn't. I was worried about you. Neil thought you'd faked your own death.'

'Neil?'

'I think you call him Scants?'

'How do you know Scants? Why does *he* care?'

'He was at your flat before I was. We've been spending a lot of time together, trying to find out where you were. He worked it all out.'

'And you found me.' She grips my hand. 'Does he hate me? I bet he does.'

'No, he doesn't hate you. He was very worried about you.'

'I thought he didn't want anything more to do with me.'

'He made a mistake. He didn't know what to think. You've told lots of lies.'

'I know.'

'Why?'

'To make myself feel better. But it didn't.' And then she looks at me, and a smile appears. And I know what that smile means. I know exactly what she's going to say. 'You're blushing. You fancy him, don't you?'

I can't stop the grin tearing into my face. 'That doesn't matter now.'

'It does,' she smiles. 'Urgh, he's really old. And he's miserable. And he drinks.'

'I know all that. I've got to know him quite well over the past week.'

'Have you... done naughties yet?'

'We were a little preoccupied trying to find you, actually. He messaged me earlier. He's on his way down.'

'Did he put a kiss on the message?'

'Three.'

Ellis smiles and tries to squeal in excitement but coughs at the same time. When she's finished and sure she's not going to cough again, she asks, 'Am I going to go to prison, Foy?'

'No.'

'No?'

'No. Neil has dealt with it.'

'The doughnut man?' she whispers. 'How?'

'You know Scants, Ellis. He keeps his cards close to his chest, doesn't he?'

'You called me Ellis.'

'That's alright, isn't it?' I say. 'Would you rather I called you something else? How about Mary? Or Charlotte? Or Genevieve? Ruth? Joanne?'

'No,' she says. 'I like you calling me Ellis.'

'Then I'll call you Ellis. I want you to come and live with us. With all of us.'

'You do? In France?'

'Yeah, in France.'

'Do you have enough room?'

'Uh, yeah, you could say that.' I smile and remove my phone from the little side table where it's charging in a power socket. I rip out the wire and unlock it, going into Photos. I scroll through and find the right album before handing it to her. She fumbles with it, like she's forgotten how to use her fingers, then flips the phone on its side to see the pictures better. 'We've got sixty-four rooms, actually.'

She frowns, scrolling through. 'You can't live here. It's a palace.'

'It's a castle, actually,' I grin. 'A chateau. We bought it cheap between us and we've been doing it up. The ground floor's almost finished.'

'It's a castle, Foy. You bought a *real* castle?!'

'Yes we did. Chateau Eleanora. It's got sixty-four rooms, a wine cellar, a pool, an orchard, a forest and five outbuildings. It's in what the French call a *Zone Loisir Constructible* which means we can get planning permission easily for things like a campsite or some chalets. We're going to focus on that next year. The boys are going to have two of the outbuildings eventually as self-contained chalets – Paddy wants an art studio and Isaac wants a gym, but that's our way-in-the-future plans.'

'Oh, wow!'

'You can have your own room, en suite.'

'Can I?'

'Of course, eventually. We'll have to get it ship-shape first though. Most of the rooms above the first floor are derelict at the moment. And then there's the mice.'

'Mice?'

'Yeah. We have to share it with them, which isn't ideal. But we manage. And we're together.'

'Any unicorns?' she smiles.

'No, not yet. I'm keeping an eye on eBay for a T-Rex though.'

'It sounds perfect,' Ellis laughs, a tear trickling down her cheek as she scrolls slowly through the pictures. 'It's the most magical place I've ever seen. Where is it?'

'About fifteen minutes from Bergerac airport. Four hours from the Eurostar. It is a bit remote but—'

'I love it.'

'So you'll come? Really?'

'Try and stop me! I used to have cats. They could have dealt with your mice.'

'Oh that reminds me,' I say. 'We found The Duchess.'

'You did? Where was she?'

'In your airing cupboard. And she wasn't alone. She'd had six kittens.'

'Oh, wow! I didn't know she was having babies! Is she alright?'

'Yeah, they're all fine. Sean the RSPCA man came and collected them, and took them back to his place. He was worried about you when we told him you were missing.'

'Oh, was he?'

'Yeah, he was. You don't fancy him by any chance, do you?' I say, nudging her and then it's her turn to go red in both cheeks.

'Bit,' she replies, smiling so wide her dry lips begin to crack and bleed.

'I left a message for him earlier. He wanted to know you were alright.'

'That's nice of him.' She grips my hand tighter, two tears escaping both eyes and dribbling down to the pillow beneath her head. I remove Thread Bear from my bag and her face lights up as his paw strokes the water away.

'I keep thinking you're going to disappear,' she says, gripping my hand – a good strong grip now. 'I don't want to let go of you.'

'Then don't,' I tell her. 'Don't ever.'

DECEMBER 23RD
ONE YEAR LATER

Selfridges,
Oxford Street, London

28

ELLIS

'So what are your plans for Christmas?' asks the make-up lady as she applies my second coat of lip tint – Rosy Blush. I picked it out specially.

'Well I live in France now – my cousin has a chateau and we all live there. Me, my cousin Foy and her fiancé Neil, and her two brothers Paddy and Isaac and their partners and kids, so we're going to have a nice big family Christmas at home.'

'A chateau?' She gives me the eyebrow. 'Wow. Sounds like a fairy tale.'

'No, it's real,' I say. 'It really is a chateau. I can't believe it myself sometimes but look.' I show her my screensaver, the picture we took on the Easter egg hunt this year, all of us together stood outside with our baskets.

'Aww, what a lovely picture. You've got a right houseful there, haven't you?'

'Yeah, we have. It's wonderful.'

'How come you're back in London then?'

'To do our Christmas shopping. My boyfriend still lives over here but he's hoping to join us next year. He's going to live with us as well.' I scroll through my photos to show her one of many pictures I have of him.

'Blimey, even more of a houseful!'

'Yep, there's sixty-four rooms.'

'You're having me on.'

'No, honestly. My cousins bought it with their inheritance money from their parents who died a few years ago. Now they're doing it up. We're turning the old pigeonry into a gym at the moment, and the pump house is going to be an artist's studio. My cousin Paddy is going to do workshops over there. It's going to be terrific. Me and Sean are going to look after all the animals.'

'Close your eyes for me a second.' She dusts my lids with peach shimmer. I can't see how shimmery it is of course but I'm not worried at the moment. 'This colour goes perfectly with your beautiful red hair. Really shows it off.'

'Great,' I smile. 'Sean booked this appointment for me cos it's my birthday.'

'Ahh, that was sweet of him. Happy birthday.'

'Thanks!'

'Dare I ask?'

'I'm twenty-nine today,' I say proudly. 'He took me out for a meal at lunchtime too. A lush Chinese restaurant in Soho. And he got me some DVDs. And a framed photo of us with our dogs. We've got three dogs now and seven cats. All rescues.'

'*Seven* cats?'

'Yeah. My cat The Duchess had six kittens and I didn't want to get rid of any of them so we kept them all. There's plenty of room for them at the chateau and they keep the mice problem down. Foy's got horses, too, a whole field of them.

She's hoping to set up a riding school in the new year when she's had her baby.'

'Proper family affair over there then, isn't it?'

'Yeah it is. Most of the rooms aren't finished yet so we're all living in the one wing, all ten of us, including the baby. It's due in May. I count the baby as one extra already though. I've bought so many cute things for it. It's going to be a little girl.'

'Ahhh, bet you'll spoil her rotten.'

'Oh, definitely. I'm her fairy godmother.'

'Have you got any kids of your own?'

'No,' I say, opening my eyes and looking at her straight on, even though she's waiting to apply more shimmer to my lids. 'No, I can't have children.'

'Oh,' she says, straightening up.

'It's okay. I have more than I ever dreamed. I have my family back. And I have Paddy and Isaac's kids to play with. And I teach at a primary school in the next village. I'm surrounded by kids.'

'Do you know, I think you've got the best of both worlds there. You get all the fun stuff then you can give them back at the end of the day.' She affords me a conciliatory nod then a smudge of my cheekbones, holding up the mirror to show me her artwork. 'Would you like me to add any more to your eyebrows? Any strobing?'

'Yeah, why not?' I say.

'No problem.'

She feels sorry for me, cos of the no kids thing, I can tell by the amount of freebies I get in my bag, but I don't think I've laid it on too thick, unlike her with my rosy blush lipstick. It's supposed to be a tint – looks more like a paste. I buy the concealer, the most basic item I use in daily life, but she bungs in a whole host of extra goodies – samples of a brand new volumising eyebrow gel, two sachets of foundation, a lip gloss sampler, two discontinued eye shadows and a Horse Kind make-up brush.

'Well, have a fantastic Christmas, Ellis,' she says, upon handing me the little bag and my receipt. And I know she means that with every fibre of that make-up brush.

'Thank you so much,' I say, and I mean that too. And I try not to skip out of there, full of the joys of a brand new face.

Sean's waiting for me by the escalators. 'Hiya. How did you get on?'

'Good thanks,' I say, fluttering my eyelashes as he plants a kiss on my lips, then licks his own lips and frowns. 'Mmm, Turkish Delight.'

We hold hands as we start walking towards the exit. 'She put too much on really. What do you think? Is it me?'

'Maybe?'

'Maybe? She spent forty-five minutes doing this.'

'Yeah, I know, but you look gorgeous with or without make-up to me.'

'Oh, you liar.'

'I'm not lying!' he laughs. 'I fell in love with you when you had badly dyed black hair and mud all up your leggings and you walked into the RSPCA crying with that broken duck in your arms.'

'Aww, yeah, you did. Did you get the book for Paddy?'

'Yeah, and I got Isaac a really nice scarf. Armani.' He checks his watch. 'I'm getting a bit worried about time. When's the latest we have to be back at St Pancras?'

'Half three.'

'I think we should get cracking, babe. What floor are the luggage lockers on?'

*

A man called Horace meets us at Gare du Nord with a sign saying Kemp-Lowland on an A4 placard which makes us giggle, even though we haven't talked about marriage yet. Horace doesn't speak much English but my time in France talking to delivery guys and builders means I know more than the average expat, and I manage to make conversation in his air conditioned Mercedes throughout the three hour journey. I tell him all about our two weeks spent with Sean's parents in Surbiton. Our visit to Dad's grave in Scarborough. I don't think he understands but he nods politely like he does.

He offers us the odd mint from a small green tin and in between falling asleep and playing I-Spy, and talking about what Christmas presents we bought in London, me and Sean cuddle up and stare out the window at the beautiful French countryside streaming past as the sky darkens and the clouds disappear within it. Eventually Horace puts the radio on – French news. I pick out the odd phrase. A school bus accident in the Loire Valley. The presidential visit to Malta. Football results.

'Nous y sommes presque,' he eventually announces.

'Uh, pardon?' says Sean.

'Uh, we are... arriving in the soon?'

'Oh right, merci.'

The Mercedes swings right down the country lane, barely wide enough for a small car, let alone us. 'C'est trop difficile.'

'*Oui*,' I laugh, even though it's not remotely funny. And it's then that I see the shape in the distance.

'Where's the house then?' asks Sean.

'It's not a house,' I tell him. 'It's a chateau. Château Eleanora.'

Horace is concentrating hard on the road ahead, what little there is of it. And all of a sudden he stops outside a pair of tall black gates with a sign outside them, hanging from a little fence post. *Château Eleanora, entrée.*

'I'm sorry, this road *c'est... trop étroit.* You have to... with the feet?' He makes the gesture of fingers walking along his forearm.

'*That's* where she lives?' Sean cries. 'That massive place over there?' He points out the two peaks, just visible behind the hedge and lit by floodlights.

'Yeah. I told you it was big.'

'I take your bags for you,' says Horace.

'No, no it's fine. We can do it,' I tell him.

'*Non, madame, je devrais t'aider.*'

'We will be fine. *Merci beaucoup Monsieur.*' I get a €20 note out of my purse and hand it to him. 'It was a... great journey, Horace. *Un voyage magique!*'

This makes him laugh. 'Okay *Madame. Au revoir Monsieur.*'

'*Au revoir*,' says Sean as we stand on the grass verge with all our bags around us and watch as the car backs up along the road in the direction we have come.

'They've applied for planning permission to widen this part of the road,' I explain to him. 'Isaac's working on it with the French notary but it's proving to be a bit of a pain in the old *derriére*. Come on.'

Sean's staring through the gates with his mouth open. 'Wow.'

'Do you like it?'

'It's the most incredible place I've ever seen.' And then he laughs. 'It's like the Magic Kingdom.'

'I know! What's so funny?'

'I used to imagine playing in a castle like this when I was a kid. Me and my brother used to imagine being knights and riding little hobby horses around it. But in reality it was a large cardboard box.'

'Well this ain't no cardboard box,' I say, pressing the button on the gates. 'This is very real. Wanna come in?' He nods enthusiastically, like a little boy.

There's a click on the intercom. Paddy's voice. 'Yo.'

'Hey, Pads, it's me. We're here.'

The gates buzz open slowly to welcome us.

Watching his reaction, I knew that nothing could have prepared Sean for the sight beyond that first set of trees. I love looking at his face as it dawns on him. I see it all over again through his eyes as we round the bend with all our bags and the chateau appears to us at the end of the long grey gravel track. It's straight out of a fairy tale. Bordered by spindly trees and endless areas of short lawns. All around the main steps of the chateau are tiny lights, square-bottomed glass tumblers with stubby candles in them, embracing the castle in a fairy ring of natural light. No other words are needed. They would only have been clichéd exclamations of pure surprise anyway and the occasion doesn't need it. The lights in the tumblers are dancing for us just as adequately.

'I can't walk fast enough with these bags,' he laughs.

I stop walking, drop all the bags to the side of the drive and take his hand.

'Let's run then.'

He drops his bags too and grips my hand tighter and we run the rest of the way towards the building, lit by a distant crescent moon and the light of a thousand Christmas lights in the trees lining the route. We have to get closer to it, to touch it, to stand beneath it and feel as small as we are. As small as we have always been.

The double doors open at the top of the steps and everyone's there, backed by a yellow glow from within. Paddy wheels his chair down the ramp with his little girl Estelle on his lap, as her sister Helene follows close behind. The girls are already in their pyjamas. Everyone else comes down the steps – Isaac and his husband Joe, both in their Christmas knits, Joe holding their sleepy son Jonah in his Rudolph onesie, and Paddy's wife Lysette has tears in her eyes because she always has tears in her eyes at anything in the least bit sentimental. She's a Disney fan, like me, but it's not so bad watching the endings now – she cries more than I do. Arthur, Sean's dog, bolts out of the door and gallops up to Sean, jumping up into his arms. The Duchess sits in the Grand Salon window licking her paws, backlit by the Christmas tree lights.

The boys all greet Sean with a hand-grasp which turns into a hug, and Foy greets me as usual with a hug so vital and true, it's like medicine.

'You got even fatter since I left,' I laugh.

She yanks my plait. 'Oi, don't you start, I get enough of that with this lot.' She strokes her bump and hugs me again. 'I'm so glad you're back,' she says. 'I couldn't get into the Christmas spirit without you here, but now you are, it can begin. Hey, Sean, how are you?' And she envelops him in a hug as true as mine.

'I'm good thank you.' He's still a bit awestruck I think. 'It's like the Magic Kingdom!'

'Can you do our hair, Auntie Ellis?' Estelle asks me.

'Of course, go and grab our bags along the drive. Don't peep inside, will you?'

'Race you?' says her sister and she and Helene both sprint off into the darkness.

Scants appears behind everyone else, smiling broadly, which looks odd on him, but not exactly out of place. He's holding a glass of what looks like red wine.

'It's hot Ribena, don't worry,' he says, holding it out for me to sniff. And he folds me in a hug as well, kissing me on the forehead. 'How was your journey?'

'Great, thanks. Dad's got his headstone now. And Sean helped me plant some roses around it.' I show him the picture we took of it on my phone.

'Looks great.' He hugs me again. 'And so do you two. You look happy. I'm very proud of you, you know.'

'Yeah I'm proud of me too,' I say. 'It was a nice visit but it's good to be home.'

*

Maybe this is all too good to be true; that's what I keep thinking as I'm opening my presents that Christmas morning.

Maybe, I think, as I watch Scants smiling with his hand on Foy's belly, as she puts on her paper hat at the dinner table, I will wake up one day and all of them will have gone and I'll be rattling around in this place on my own.

Maybe, I think, as I sit with Sean and with his parents

playing board games with the little ones and plaiting the girls' hair before the afternoon film, it's all just a gorgeous dream.

Maybe the smells of Christmas puddings and logs burning on an open fire are wafting over to me from a nearby cottage in Carew and I'm still in the old treehouse, freezing to death as the snowflakes float down on me and Foy is dragging my body across the snow, screaming my name.

My name.

Maybe the images in my head are all false ones, flickering candles in a dying light. Visions in a Christmas bauble. Shadows in the snow.

Maybe I'm already dead and this is my Heaven. I don't know anymore, what's real and what's not. What are lies and what are truths. And I don't care. Because if this *is* my death, I can certainly live with it.

Author's note

It was my big sister, Penny Skuse, who first planted the seed of this idea in my brain. Penny came up with the concept of *The Alibi Clock* when she was at film school. In her graduate film of the same name, a woman is having her hair washed in a salon. She chats with the hairdresser and gradually reveals details about herself, her husband, children and the blissful security of her marriage. The next time we see her, she's in a different salon, wearing different clothes, spinning a different yarn. This time she talks about her life as a businesswoman, her independence and her ambivalence toward children. Another time, in another salon, she has yet another appearance and persona. Finally, we see her back at her sparsely furnished, dingy bedsit, sitting in the centre of the room in the only threadbare chair, staring into space. It has all been a pack of lies.

This was all there was of the story – a woman who lies about who she is and lives a very lonely life at odds with all her tales. We never find out her true identity. The title struck me as being something I could work with because the concept was so strong – a clock which tells one time, chimes another with neither one being the truthful time. I thought 'Who could this woman be? What is the truth and why is she running from it? What's happened to her to bring her to a life of compulsively telling lies? If there's such a thing as an Alibi Clock, then who is the Alibi Girl?'

And so a pendulum began to swing in my mind. And it is here where it finally stops.

C J Skuse, March 2019

Acknowledgements

This book was a pain in the arse to write, frankly, but it wouldn't exist at all without the help and inspiration of the following people:

My sister, Penny Skuse – thanks for letting me steal your concept and run off with it. And for being 'Mother Pen' and taking us on day trips. And for always being the voice in my head that says 'You're being a twat' whenever I'm being a twat. Which is a lot.

My auntie, Maggie Snead, for all the 'grist' for my mill – and no, Auntie Chelle isn't you, don't worry.

My cousin Emily Metcalf – thanks for putting me up in your mansion while mine was being decorated. And all the spins around the car park on our Lamborghinis. And the trips to the skittle alley supermarket for Jurassic Chum.

My cousin Matthew Snead – thanks for annoying us as kids. And introducing us to *Moonlighting* so we could be pretend detectives. And for the assault courses. And for letting us play with your *Star Wars* toys.

My agent Jenny Savill for your continued belief in me. You must be utterly insane.

My editor Clio Cornish for believing in this story and helping me to unpick it from that cowpat of a first draft.

Everyone at HQ/HarperCollins who works so hard for all my books all year round.

All the people who've taken the time to respond to my annoying little queries along the way, namely Kate Kaufman at the College of Policing, Lisa Cutts, Kate Bendelow, Neil Dickerson and Cassie Powney.

Did you enjoy The *Alibi Girl*? Keep reading for an extract from *Sweetpea*, another dark, twisty and shockingly funny thriller from C J Skuse – out now!

Sunday, 31 December

1. *Mrs Whittaker – neighbour, elderly, kleptomaniac*
2. *'Dillon' on the checkout in Lidl – acne, wallet chain, who bangs my apples and is NEVER happy to help*
3. *The suited man in the blue Qashqai who roars out of Sowerberry Road every morning – grey suit, aviator shades, Donald Trump tan*
4. *Everyone I work with at the* Gazette *apart from Jeff*
5. *Craig*

Well, my New Year has certainly gone off with a bang, I don't know about yours. I was in a foul mood to begin with, partly due to the usual Christmas-Is-Over-Shit-It's-Almost-Back-To-Work-Soon malaise and partly due to the discovery of a text on Craig's phone while he was in the shower that morning. The text said,

Hope you're thinking of me when ur soaping your cock – L.

Kiss. Kiss. Smiley face tongue emoji.

Oh, I thought. It's a fact then. He really *is* shagging her.

L. was Lana Rowntree – a kittenish 24-year-old sales rep in my office who wore tight skirts and chunky platforms and swished her hair like she was in a 24-hour L'Oréal advert. He'd met her at my works Christmas piss-up on 19 December – twelve days ago. The text confirmed the suspicions I'd had when I'd seen them together at the buffet: chatting, laughing, her fingering the serviette stack, him spooning out stuffing balls onto their plates, a hair swish here, a stubble scratch there. She was looking at him all night and he was just bathing in it.

Then came the increase in 'little jobs' he had to do in town: a paint job here, a hardwood floor there, a partition wall that 'proved trickier' than he'd estimated. Who has any of that done the week before Christmas? Then there were the out-of-character extended trips to the bathroom and two Christmas shopping trips (without me) that were just so damn productive he spent all afternoon maxing out his credit card. I've seen his statement – all my presents were purchased online.

So I'd been stewing about that all day and the last thing I needed that New Year's night was enforced fun with a bunch of gussied-up pissheads. Unfortunately, that's what I got.

My 'friends' or, more accurately, the 'PICSOs' – People I Can't Shake Off – had arranged to meet at the Cote de Sirène restaurant on the harbour-side, dressed in Next Sale finery. Our New Year's meal-slash-club-crawl had been planned for months – initially to include husbands and partners, but, one by one, they had all mysteriously dropped out as it became a New Year's meal-slash-*baby-shower*-slash-club crawl for Anni. Despite its snooty atmosphere, the restaurant is in the centre of town, so there's always yellow streaks up the outside walls and a sick puddle on the doormat come Sunday morning. The theme inside is black and silver with an added soupçon of French – strings of garlic, frescos of Parisian walkways and waiters who glare at you like you've murdered their mothers.

The problem is, I need them. I need friends. I don't want them; it's not like they're the Wilson to my skinny, toothless, homeward-bound Tom Hanks. But to keep up my façade of normality, they're just necessary. To function properly in society, you *have* to have people around you. It's annoying, like periods, but there is a point to it. Without friends, people start labelling you a 'Loner'. They check your Internet history or start smelling bomb-making chemicals in your garage.

But the PICSOs and I have little in common, this is true. I'm an editorial assistant at a local snooze paper, Imelda's an estate agent, Anaïs is a nurse (currently on maternity leave), Lucille works in a bank, her sister Cleo is a university-PE-teacher-cum-personal-trainer and Pidge is a secondary-school teacher. We don't even have the same interests. Well, me and Anni will message each other about the most recent episode of *Peaky Blinders* but I'd hardly call us bezzies.

And it may look like I'm the quiet cuckoo in a nest of rowdy crows but I do perform some function within the group. Originally, when I first met them all in Sixth Form, I was a bit of a commodity. I'd been a bit famous as a child so I'd done the whole celebrity thing: met Richard and Judy; Jeremy Kyle gave me a Wendy house; been interviewed on one of those *Countdown to Murder* programmes. Nowadays, I'm just the Thoughtful Friend or the Designated Driver. Lately, I'm Chief Listener – I know all their secrets. People will tell you anything if you listen to them for long enough and *pretend* you're interested.

Anni, our resident Preggo, is due to drop sometime in March. The Witches Four – Lucille, Cleo, Imelda and Pidge – had spared no expense on the nappy cake, cards, streamers, balloons and booties to decorate the table. I'd brought a fruit basket, filled with exotic fruits like lychees and mangoes, starfruit and ambarella, as a nod to Anni's Mauritian heritage. It had gone down like a whore on a Home Secretary. At least I wasn't driving, so I could quaff as much Prosecco as my liver could cope with and snuggle my brain into believing I was having a good time while they were all clucking on about the usual.

3

The PICSOs themselves like talking about five things above all others:

1. *Their partners (usually to slag them off)*
2. *Their kids (conversations I can't really join in with 'cos I don't have any, so, unless, it's cooing over school Nativity photos or laughing at Vines of them wiping poo up the walls, my contribution just isn't called for)*
3. *IKEA (usually because they've just been or are just going)*
4. *Dieting – what works/what doesn't, what's filling/what isn't, how many pounds they've lost/put on*
5. *Imelda's wedding – she only announced it in September but I can't actually remember a time when it wasn't on our conversation rota*

In my head I'm usually thinking about five things above all others...

1. *Sylvanian Families*
2. *My as-yet-unpublished novel,* The Alibi Clock
3. *My little dog, Tink*
4. *When I can go to the toilet and check my social-media feeds*
5. *Ways I can kill people I don't like... without getting caught*

Before too long a tray of drinks came over: Prosecco and a selection of slightly smudged glasses.

'What's this?' Imelda asked.

'Compliments of the gentlemen at the bar,' said the waiter, and we looked over to see two types leaning against the counter, evidently looking to score with the nearest friendly vagina. The one wearing gold-hoop earrings and too much gel raised his pint in our direction – his other arm was in a sling. His friend in the Wales rugby shirt, and sporting tattooed forearms, a cut on his left eyebrow and a protruding beer gut, was unashamedly salivating over Lucille's ridiculous breasts. She says she 'doesn't do it on purpose'. Yeah, and I don't bleed from my crease every month.

'How marvellous.' She smiled, swooping into the bread basket. We each took a glass and 'cheersed' the men, before continuing our conversational merry-go-round – babies, boyfs, IKEA, and how draining it was just generally having tits.

Anni opened her presents, all of which she thought were either 'amazing' or 'so cute'. Of all of them, I found Anni the least annoying of the PICSOs. She always had an anecdote to share about someone brought into A&E, with a Barbie doll shoved up their arse or a motorcyclist with his head hanging off. This was at least mildly entertaining. Of course her baby would come soon and then there would be nothing left for us to talk about other than Babies and What Fun They Are and How I Wish I Had One. That's how these things usually went.

We all ordered steaks, in various sizes with various sauces, despite the rainbow of diets we are all on. Mel's on the Dukan, or GI, I forget which one. Lucille's on the 5:2, but today was a five day so she had three rolls and twenty breadsticks before her meal hit the tablecloth. Cleo 'eats clean', but she's had Christmas and New Year off. I'm on the Eat Everything in Sight Until 1 January Then Starve Self to Death diet, so I ordered a 10oz sirloin in a béarnaise sauce with triple-cooked French fries – I asked for the meat to be so raw you didn't know whether to eat it or feed it a carrot. The taste was unreal. I didn't even care if the cow had suffered – his ass was delish.

'I thought you were going veggie?' said Lucille, tearing off another hunk of complimentary bread.

'No,' I said, 'not any more.' I couldn't believe she remembered me saying that about eighty-five years ago. It was actually my

GP who told me to give up red meat to help with my mood swings. But the supplements were doing their job so I didn't see the point of going full McCartney for the sake of a few bitch fits. Besides, I always find earwigs in broccoli and sprouts are the Devil's haemorrhoids.

'Did you get anything nice for Christmas?' Cleo asked me as the waiter brought out a selection of lethal-looking steak knives.

'Thank you,' I said to the guy. I always made a point to thank waiting staff – you never knew what they were stirring your sauce with. 'Some books, perfume, Netflix voucher, Waterstones voucher, Beyoncé tickets for Birmingham...' I left out Sylvanian stuff – the only people who understand how I feel about Sylvanians are Imelda's five-year-old twins.

'Ooh, we're seeing Beyoncé in London in April,' said Pidge. 'Oh, I know what it was I wanted to tell you guys...'

Pidge started this inexorably long speech about how she'd gone to six different pet stores before she found the right something for her house rabbits – Beyoncé and Solange. Pidge's conversation starters were always somewhere between Tedious and Prepare the Noose; almost as dull as Anni's midwife appointments or Lucille's Tales of the Killer Mortgage. I zoned out, mentally redesigning the furniture in my Sylvanians' dining room. I think they need more space to entertain.

Despite the ongoing gnawing fury in the centre of my chest, courtesy of Le Boyf, the meal was nice and I managed to keep it down. I noticed there were fake flowers in the vases on all the tables – which won't please the Tripadvisor fairy – but as restaurants go, I'm glad I went. It was almost worth the two hours I'd spent crowbarring myself out of the pyjamas I'd lived in since Christmas Eve and dolling myself up. Well, it was until the subject of Imelda's wedding came up. Lucille was the culprit.

'So, you got your hair sorted out yet for the Big Day?'

Now this was the rare occasion when Imelda *did* hear what Lucille said – because she had asked about Imelda or weddings or Imelda's actual wedding.

'No,' she whined. 'I want something up at the crown but not spiky. French plaits for the bridesmaids, keep it simple. Did I tell you about our photographers? We're having two. Jack found this guy from London and him and his partner – his work partner that is (cue chorus of unexplained laughs) – are coming down to see the church in May. He's going to be at the back so that he can take pictures of everyone's faces as I come down the aisle, and his mate's going to be at the altar.'

'No chance of anything being missed then?' I added.

'Exactly.' Imelda smiled, seemingly ecstatic that I was taking an interest.

'What you wearing for your night do? Did you decide?' asked Anni, returning from a third toilet break.

'Oh, the dress again, definitely.'

'You're going to have it on all day?' said Cleo.

'Yeah. It's got to be something striking. It *is* my day and everyone will be coming to check me out so... and that way, the people who didn't get invited to the day do will be able to see it then.'

'Yeah, wouldn't want *them* missing out on anything,' I mumbled, checking my phone. And again she smiled, like I was right on her wavelength.

Anni nodded, biting her lower lip. 'You'll be stunning, Mel. It's gonna be such a good bash. And I'll be able to drink again by then, too!'

I cleaned off my steak knife with my napkin. There was an abundance of veins in my left wrist. I could have ended it all right then if I'd had the balls.

'I won't be stunning,' said Imelda. 'I'll probably break both camera lenses!'

Lucille's turn: 'Babes, you're gorgeous. You'll be all princess-like and there'll be flowers everywhere and with that amazing church... it'll be like a proper fairy tale.'

'Yeah,' she scoffed. 'If I can't shift this bloody muffin top in the next six months it *will* be a fairy tale – *Shrek*!'

Cue the shrieks.

'And June's always sunny, so you're bound to have the best weather for it,' said Pidge, rubbing Imelda's arm. 'Don't worry, it'll be wonderful.'

Enough?

'Yeah, I suppose you're right.'

(Note: I have cribbed this endless ego massage here but please understand, Dear Diary, that Imelda's wedding takes up at least 90 per cent of every social occasion.)

Then she brought up the very thing I've been dreading since it was first mooted last September – the Weekend That Must Not Be Named.

'You're all coming to my hen weekend, aren't you? No buts. You've got six months' notice after all.'

Fuck it. In a fairly large bucket.

'Oh, yeah, what are we doing again?' asked Anni, swigging her orange juice.

'Not sure yet – possibly Bath for a spa day or Lego Windsor. But it's deffo Friday to Sunday.'

'Rawther!' Lucille giggled. She was matron of honour.

Then it was onto Man Bash Central – Woman Bash Central in Cleo's case – how Rashan/Alex/Jack/Tom/Amy had stayed out all night on a job/booze run to France/coach trip to Belgium/job/pub crawl/austerity protest. How Rashan/Alex/Jack/Tom/Amy had got so unadventurous in bed these days. How big Rashan/Alex/Jack's dicks were (Cleo and Pidge always carefully avoided this subject) and finally how Rashan/Alex/Jack/Tom/Amy had given them a Rolex/flowers/Hotel Chocolat salted-caramel puddles/a holiday/a hug just to say sorry after a row that Anni/Lucille/ Imelda/Pidge/Cleo had instigated.

The only thing Craig ever gave me that meant anything was bacterial vaginosis, but I kept that to myself.

'What's Craig up to these days, Rhiannon?' asked Anni. She always brought me into the conversation. Imelda sometimes did this when vying for the gold medal at the Passive Aggressive Olympics. She'd ask, '*Any news on your junior-reporter thing yet, Rhee?*' or '*Any sign of Baby Wilkins in that womb of yours yet, Rhee?*', when she knew full well I'd have mentioned it if I had news of huge job change (please, God) and/or womb invader (please, God, no).

'Uh, the same,' I said, sipping my fifth glass of Prosecco. 'He's fitting out that shop in the High Street that used to be a hairdresser's. It's going to be a charity shop.'

'Thought there might be something sparkly waiting under the Christmas tree this year,' said Imelda, loudly to the entire restaurant. 'What's it been now, three years?'

'Four,' I said, 'and, no, he's not *that* thoughtful.'

'Would you say yes if he *did* propose, Rhiannon?' said Pidge, her face full of wonder, like she was thinking about Hogwarts. (She and Tom were planning to get married at the Harry Potter Experience in Orlando soon – I shit you not.)

I hesitated, the gnawing in my chest biting down harder. Then I lied: 'Yeah, of course–' I was about to qualify that with an *If he could stop taking Lana Rowntree up her aisle for five minutes long enough to walk me down one*, but Lucille cut me off before I had a chance:

'Talking of charity shops, I bought this great vase in the one opposite Debenhams; such a bargain...' she began, launching into a new topic of conversation and leaving me behind on my Island of Unfinished Sentences.

Not that I *wanted* to talk about Craig or Craig's dull job.

Neither were interesting subjects to talk about. He built things, ate pasties, smoked the odd spliff, liked football, played video games and couldn't pass a pub without eating enough pork scratchings to fill Trafalgar Square. That was Craig – *Gordon Ramsay clap* – done.

So they were all wanging on about The Weekend That Must Not Be Named when a random bloke with bad neck zits appeared at our table, clutching a glass of lager.

'All right, girls?' said Random Bloke with Neck Zits. He produced a couple of red-wine bottles, emboldened by a six-strong gaggle of blokes with neck *and* chin zits at the bar. Surprisingly, the corks were still in the bottles so there was no danger of us being Rohipped and dragged to the nearest Premier Inn for a semi-conscious rape-fest. Yeah, I think of these things, another reason I'm a useful friend.

These weren't the same guys who'd bought us Prosecco, this was a different lot. Younger. Louder. Zittier.

'Mind if we join you?' Winks and knowing looks all round.

Cue giggles and shrieks.

I had intended to order the double chocolate brownie with clotted cream for pudding but we were at the part of the evening where we all had to hold our stomachs in so I resisted, wondering if I could get home for some leftover Christmas tiramisu ice cream before the bongs signalled the death knell of fun-eating habits.

Imelda, Lucille and Cleo made the usual ribald comments, clearly turned on by the attention. Pidge started joining in too, once a sufficient amount of wine had been imbibed. She was always too Christian to participate in either tittage or bants before alcohol allowed her to. I wasn't nearly pissed enough for either.

So the evening dragged on like a corpse tied to a donkey cart as the Seven Dorks squeezed onto our table and allowed their eggy breaths and chubby fingers to fog our air and tweak our knicker elastic. We had Grunty, Zitty, Shorty, Sleazy, Fatso, Gropey and Mute.

Guess which one I got stuck talking to. Or rather, at.

And, one by one, the PICSOs all left me. They each did the 'you're only young once' speech and hooked up with the Dorks to go on to a club for a New Year's foam party – can't remember which one as I had no intention of following them.

'You coming, Rhee?' asked Anni, weighed down with gifted baby detritus. 'Me and Pidge are just gonna shove this lot in the car and meet them there.'

I don't know why she was so excited to be tagging along to a nightclub. She was the size of a barge and was on orange juice and bi-hourly toilet breaks. Nightclubs weren't known for facilitating either.

'Yeah, I just need the loo,' I said, sinking my wine.

I was testing them now. Testing to see who would actually wait for me. Who was the true friend? But, as I expected, nobody waited. I paid my part of the bill, stood on the doormat of Cote de Sirène and watched them all waddling and cackling up the street with the Dorks circling them like sharks around chum. Not a second thought did I get.

So there I was, alone, in the centre of town, preparing to hike the two miles back to my flat, on New Year's Eve.

But this is where my fun began.

As it turned out, walking across town went without incident. I'm not counting the tramp with a tinsel halo, pissing in streams down both legs, using NatWest as a walking aide. Or the couple shagging behind the wheely bins at the back of Boots' car park. And I'm not counting the fight that broke out inside Pizza Express then spilled onto the pavement, during which a bald man in a striped shirt yelled, 'I'M GONNA RAPE YOUR FUCKING SKULL, MATE!'

None of that was particularly noteworthy.

Whereas, what happened down by the canal, was.

It must have been about 11.30 p.m. by the time I reached the playing fields and took the short cut along the cycle path and down to the canal towpath, a mere five hundred feet from our flat. It was here that I heard footsteps behind me. And my breath shortened. And my heart began to thump.

I shoved my hands into my duffle-coat pockets and turned around to see a guy I recognised. He was the one in the Wales rugby shirt with the tattooed forearms who'd bought us the first lot of Prosecco at the restaurant.

'Where you going then, baby?'

'Home.'

'Aww, can I come?'

'No.'

'Please? We can make each other happy tonight. Still got a bit of time before the bongs, ain't we? You look sad.'

He sidestepped in front of me. I stepped away. He stepped back. He laughed.

'You followed me, didn't you?' I said.

He leered, eyeing me from head to toe with a lingering look at my crotch area, which I'll admit did look inviting in my too-tight skirt. 'Just seeing where you were going, that's all. Don't be like that. I bought you a drink.'

'I said thank you at the time.' Like, of course *that* would be enough.

He put his hands on me.

'Could you take your hands off me, please?'

'Come on. You were giving me the eye.'

'Don't think I was. Get off.' I wasn't raising my voice. I didn't need to. His molestation attempts were pathetic. A hand on my boob. A motion to his belt buckle.

'How about you get your laughing gear round my old boy then? Just for "Auld Lang Syne", eh?'

He was strong; a prop four or something. As well as the cut on his left eyebrow, he had the beginnings of a cauliflower ear. He slathered all over my face and I let him. Nobody else was around. Even if I screamed, the nearest people over in the Manette Court complex would take five minutes to get to me. And that's if they even bothered. He'd have come in me and gone by then and I'd be another statistic, getting vaginal swabs and drinking tepid tea in some police waiting room.

No. That might be my sister but that would not be me.

'Come in here,' he gasped in my ear, taking my freezing hand inside his hot clammy one and pulling me towards the bush. An upended Lidl shopping trolley lay on its back.

I stayed rooted. 'There's no room in there.'

'Yeah, there is.' He tugged harder on my hand.

'Pull your jeans down,' I said.

He smirked like his ship had just come in – a ship with a massive hard-on. 'Oh, yes, baby girl. I knew I could thaw you out.'

Unsteady on his feet, he fumbled at his belt. Then his zip. His over-washed jeans collapsed in a heap at his ankles. So did his boxers. There were little Homer Simpsons all over them. His cock sprung out like a small Samurai, ready to do battle.

Ba-doing!

It had a bend in it. I wasn't sure whether he was pleased to see me or giving me directions to the bus station.

He stroked it upwards. Well, upwards and towards the bus station. 'All yours,' he said.

'Mmm,' I said, 'lucky old me.'

The temptation to laugh was so strong but I choked it down and made it look as though I was starting to wriggle out of my knickers under my skirt. All keen.

'Can you get on all fours?' he panted.

13

'Like a dog?'

'Yeah.'

'Why?'

''Cos I wanna fuck you like a dog.'

I grew breathless. 'But the ground's hard.'

'So's my dick. Get down. Go on, don't tease.'

'I'll suck you off but no more,' I said.

'That's a start,' he said, eyes lighting up. I crouched down and took his little warm Samurai in my grip.

'Shall I finger myself as I'm sucking it?' I asked, heart in my throat.

'Fuck, yeah! Dirty bitch!' he chuckled, growing harder and more veiny.

He waited for it – for my lips on his bell-end. I pulled on his dick as though about to milk it.

'Knew you were a dirty bitch.'

I saw Craig's face on his as I held the cock steady and, reaching into my pocket, I closed my fingers around the handle of the steak knife. Bringing it out slowly while stroking him into full submission, I waited until his eyes had closed and his chin tilted to the sky in ecstasy before I hacked down hard on it and started carving through the gristly meat. He screamed and swore and beat at my head with his fists but my grip was tight and I sawed at it through slipping, bloody fingers until I had yanked his penis from its roots and pushed him backwards into the murky green water. His forlorn manhood dropped to the cold canal towpath with a bloody slap.

The splash was loud and he was still screaming but, despite all the hullaballoo, no one was coming to either of our rescues.

'Aaaaaaarrrgghhh! Aaaaarrrrrrgghh!' he went, splashing around like a child at its first swimming class.

A little curl of steam rose up from the penis, lying dejectedly on the towpath. I found a spare dog poo bag in my coat and picked the severed member up, then ran towards the footbridge, my heart still banging like a bastard on a jail-cell wall. I lost my breath completely as I reached the top and looked down over the water.

'Fucking... sick... bitch!' he gargled, flopping about.

He kept splashing, sinking under the murky water, then bobbing up again and spluttering. The last thing he must have seen in this world was my face, on the bridge, smiling in the moonlight.

Thanks to my cruel improvisation, I was feeling something I hadn't felt for a long time. That same feeling you get when you're a kid and you spy an adventure playground. Or when you poke your foot out of the bed on Christmas morning and feel your full stocking hanging there. It radiates out from a deeply exciting inner squiggle until your whole body feels electric all over. The best feeling in the world. It's an exquisite privilege to watch someone die, knowing you caused it. Almost worth getting dolled up for.

ONE PLACE. MANY STORIES

Bold, innovative and
empowering publishing.

FOLLOW US ON:

@HQStories